Billowing clouds
rose from the run...

Ronni closed the bathroom door behind her, then leaned against it. Logan's naked silhouette was visible through the tinted glass of the shower door. Ronni stood there staring. And absorbing. And anticipating. She started to peel off her clothes....

With a trembling excitement, she crossed the short distance to the shower. Heart hammering, she slid open the glass door and was greeted by a rush of steam. "What the ..." Logan swung around, and Ronni's breath caught in her throat.

Soap suds were coasting down his sleek tanned flesh like icing on a cake. Wet, his hair appeared almost black, but it was his expression that did her in. After an initial look of surprise, his face had darkened with emotion. And then his eyes were making a thorough assessment of every inch of her naked body....

"Aren't you going to come in, sweetheart?" he murmured.

ABOUT THE AUTHOR

Multitalented author Pamela Bauer has obviously struck a chord with readers. For the second year in a row, she's received an award for her writing. Readers of a popular magazine voted *Walking on Sunshine* one of the best romance novels of 1988. Her book *His and Hers* was the previous winner. Pam lives in Minnesota with her husband and their two children. Fans should watch for her next book, which is about a high-school reunion and an unsolved mystery.

Books by Pamela Bauer

HARLEQUIN SUPERROMANCE
236–HALFWAY TO HEAVEN
288–HIS AND HERS
330–WALKING ON SUNSHINE

Don't miss any of our special offers. Write to us at the following address for information on our newest releases.

Harlequin Reader Service
901 Fuhrmann Blvd., P.O. Box 1397, Buffalo, NY 14240
Canadian address: P.O. Box 603,
Fort Erie, Ont. L2A 5X3

The Honey Trap

PAMELA BAUER

Harlequin Books

TORONTO • NEW YORK • LONDON
AMSTERDAM • PARIS • SYDNEY • HAMBURG
STOCKHOLM • ATHENS • TOKYO • MILAN

Published November 1989

First printing September 1989

ISBN 0-373-70378-3

For Birgit Davis-Todd,
with gratitude.

PROLOGUE

Vienna, Austria

"It would seem your wife did not board the plane in New York."

To the untrained ear, the man's English was flawless. But American Peter Lang, a linguist whose area of concentration was the Slavic languages, detected the slightest trace of a Russian accent in the softly spoken words.

"Not on the plane...no messages...." The lifting of broad shoulders was accompanied by a dubious shake of his head.

"I know she's coming," Peter insisted, trying to keep the anxiety from his voice. "Her connecting flight to New York was probably delayed. Airplanes in the United States are seldom on schedule." At this point he didn't dare think that his wife had chosen not to join him in Vienna.

"Wouldn't she have left a message for you had that been the case?" The man frowned as if puzzled, then began edging away from the waiting area.

"We aren't going to leave without her, are we?" Peter didn't want to beg, but he knew he would if it was necessary.

"We have no choice. We cannot delay your departure without putting the entire operation at risk. By this time tomorrow, the whole world, including your wife, will know where you have gone."

"But I was assured she could go with me," Peter protested.

"Had your wife cooperated, yes. But I don't think I need to tell you the danger you will place yourself in if you remain here. Even in a country like the United States, where convicted murderers are allowed back on the streets after a short incarceration, espionage is still a crime punishable by life imprisonment. No woman is worth that."

"It isn't my wife I want with me. It's my daughter. I'm afraid that if I leave now I may never see her again."

"If you end up in prison, you will be no good to your daughter...or your son. Or have you forgotten about your son?" The man gave a twisted smile.

"It's because of my son that I'm here, as you well know," Peter reminded him. "I've waited a long time to see him again."

"First we must get you safely out of Vienna and to your destination. There you will be reunited with your son and our agents will do all they can to see that your daughter joins you, as well. In the Soviet Union you will be a hero, receiving great respect from those who will be your pupils. You will have a position of great honor. Your son will have a father, and who knows..." He paused, giving Peter another twisted smile. "Maybe Svetlana will be assigned to Little America, too."

"Just let me check to see if my wife is on the next flight." Peter started toward the reservation counter, but an arm of steel stopped him.

"*If* she is still coming," the man began in a tone that matched the hardness of his grip, "someone will be here to escort her and your daughter to the Ukraine."

"I prefer to wait for them myself," Peter said, squaring his shoulders defensively.

"That would be foolish," the other man warned. "It would be to your advantage to continue to cooperate until our mission is complete. You have been successful in securing all the necessary information, and now it is imperative that we return with that information as quickly as possible." Subtly he turned and nudged Peter toward the exit.

"What possible harm could a couple of hours make?" Peter backed away from the subtle pressure and laughed nervously as panic began to swell inside him.

This time there was no twisted smile, only an icy glare. "We have our orders."

Peter wanted to tell him he could shove his orders. The mission wasn't complete and wouldn't be until he had his daughter. Before he could utter another word, however, he felt a piercing sting in his left arm. Within seconds he was surrounded by several men, all dressed in identical dark suits.

With incredible difficulty, he tried to resist sinking into arms ready to support him as his legs buckled and a great cloud of haziness descended upon him. He could feel himself slipping from the haziness into the darkness, yet he was powerless to stop the slide. Before the world was gone entirely, he heard his own voice, as though it were coming from a great distance.

"I need Steffie," he mumbled, then fell unconscious.

CHAPTER ONE

Melbourne, Florida

"Is Steffie all right?" Clara Summers hesitated in the doorway of the hospital room, her face as pale as the stark white sheet draped over the small child asleep in the crib.

"She's fine, Mom." Ronni Lang rose from the vinyl-covered sofa to greet her mother with a reassuring hug, then gently led her over to the crib. She understood her mother's anxiety; just the sight of her daughter lying perfectly still in the hospital bed was enough to send a chill down her own spine. "Really, Mom...she's fine. She's just sleeping."

"You don't sound so sure of that," Clara whispered, her eyes taking in every inch of her granddaughter. She lifted the sheet and with loving fingers caressed the little arms poking out of the hospital gown. "When I heard your voice on my answering machine, telling me Steffie had taken an overdose of cough syrup, I had these horrible visions of—" She broke off with a shudder.

"I know, Mom." Ronni placed her hand on her mother's shoulder. "I'm sorry you had to hear about it that way. But honestly, she's going to be fine."

"Are you sure? Her cheeks look flushed." With tender fingers, Clara smoothed the delicate curls that hung like tiny red corkscrews on Steffie's forehead, then pressed her fingertips against the rosy cheeks.

"Her cheeks are always flushed when she sleeps. And you don't need to whisper. The doctor said she probably won't wake up until morning...the cough syrup made her more than a little drowsy."

Clara murmured a few words of endearment over the sleeping child, then kissed Steffie's fingers before tucking them back under the sheet. With a sigh, she stepped back from the crib and faced Ronni, her hands on her hips. "I don't understand how this could have happened. How did Steffie manage to get into cough syrup? I thought you kept all your medicines in a locked cabinet."

Ronni, too, had moved away from the crib and was standing next to the window, where the lingering rays of the setting sun cast striped shadows across her face.

"It didn't happen at my house," she explained with a gentle toss of her head. "I wasn't even with Steffie when it happened. Lisa was watching her so I could finish packing."

"Oh, Veronica, you didn't leave her in Lisa Bergstrom's care," her mother admonished. Ronni recognized the tone as the same one Clara used whenever she felt her daughter wasn't giving her granddaughter the attention she deserved. "Didn't I tell you that sooner or later something like this would happen?"

Normally Ronni would have defended her next-door neighbor, as she had often done in the past whenever her mother had questioned her friendship with the artist. But guilt was already fluttering inside her like a trapped butterfly. Her mother wasn't saying anything Ronni hadn't already said to herself. Right now, however, what she didn't need was to be defending herself to her own mother.

"Mom, you always do this to me. If Steffie gets an upset stomach, it's something I've fed her. If she's got a cold, I didn't dress her properly." She turned to stare out at the city she had lived in nearly all of her life, both arms wrapped tightly across her chest. "That's my daughter lying in that crib. Don't you think I know that Steffie wouldn't be here if I hadn't left her at Lisa's?"

After a few moments of uncomfortable silence, Ronni felt her mother's hand on her elbow. "I wasn't blaming you, Veronica."

The words sounded stiff to Ronni, but considering how difficult it was for her mother to express her feelings, they were enough to cause Ronni to give her mother's hand an understanding squeeze. "I know you weren't, Mom. You're just worried about Steffie...the same as I am."

"You seem to forget, Veronica, that she's not like other children," Clara reminded her, glancing back at the sleeping child. "She's so delicate."

"Mom, she's a typical fifteen-month-old baby," Ronni insisted. It never ceased to amaze her how one small child could turn her normally reserved mother into such a softie. Even thirty years after her discharge from the army, Clara still looked a bit like a drill sergeant, with her gray hair pulled back into a French roll. Ever since Ronni could remember, her mother had never been demonstrative. Gestures of affection were usually initiated by Ronni, who often attributed her mother's cool reserve to her military background. Yet with Steffie she was a doting grandmother.

"You still haven't told me what happened," Clara said, lowering her slightly overweight frame onto the vinyl sofa.

Ronni leaned back against the window ledge and began to explain. "Remember how I told you Lisa's little girl, Angela, had that same flu virus Steffie had last week?" Seeing her mother's nod, she continued. "Well, it was Angela who gave Steffie the cough syrup. Lisa's always commenting on how Angela likes to play mommy to Steffie. Apparently Steffie was coughing so Angela decided to be a good mommy and give her some cough medicine."

"And where was Lisa when all this was happening?"

"She'd gotten a long distance phone call and took it in her studio. She said she was only out of the room a few minutes."

"But long enough for a five-year-old to feed cough syrup to a toddler." Clara shook her head disapprovingly. "Any mother can tell you it takes only a few minutes for something to happen with children. That medicine shouldn't have been anywhere near Angela's reach."

Ronni exhaled a long sigh. "No, it shouldn't have, and I'm sure Lisa's learned a lesson from this. I know she feels terrible about what happened."

"I suppose we should be thankful it wasn't anything worse than cough syrup that Steffie swallowed. When will you be able to take her home?" Clara asked, glancing once more at the crib.

"The doctor wants to keep her overnight as a precaution. I'm going to sleep here just in case she should wake up."

"Would you like me to keep you company?"

"Thanks, Mom, but if you're going to leave for your cruise tomorrow morning, you need to get a good night's sleep."

"Oh, I'm not going to go...not until I make sure Steffie's recovered completely." Clara waved her hand in a dismissive manner.

"Mom, she's fine," Ronni insisted. "In fact, the doctor told me there's no reason Steffie and I can't leave for Vienna tomorrow."

"You're not still going to see Peter, are you?" Her face had a look of near horror.

Ronni ignored her mother's shocked expression and reached for her purse. "That reminds me. This all happened so fast I haven't been able to call Peter." She rummaged through the leather shoulder bag until she found a small business card, which she passed to Clara. "Would you see if you can reach him? He's probably worried sick about us."

"If he is, it'll be the first time," Clara muttered.

No one knew better than Ronni just how true her mother's words were, yet she couldn't help but say, "Mom, even though Peter will soon be my ex-husband, he's always going to be Steffie's father."

"She doesn't need a father like that," Clara stated brusquely.

"I think we'd better end this discussion right now. It's obvious you and I have different opinions about the importance of a father in a girl's life." This time it was Ronni's tone that was stiff.

"Obviously we do. I happen to believe a father should love his daughter and take care of her. So far, Peter Lang hasn't shown me he's capable of doing either one."

"That may be true, but I think Steffie should have the opportunity to know her father if she chooses." She paused before adding quietly, "I never had that choice."

"You sound as though you blame me for that," Clara retorted, the stiffening of her back revealing even more than the tone of her voice.

"Blame you? Mom, I never expected you to get married again just so I'd have a father." Ronni studied her mother. "Why do you always get so defensive when I bring up the subject of fathers?"

"I'm not defensive," Clara said huffily. "It's just that I did my best to bring you up properly after your father died, and now, ever since you've been separated from Peter, you seem to want to blame everything that goes wrong on the fact that you don't have a father."

Ronni could see she had upset her mother, and immediately felt contrite. "Mom, as a single parent you were the best, and I'll always be grateful. But that doesn't mean I don't often wonder what it would have been like if Dad hadn't died." Her voice softened. "All I have is a couple of photographs. I never had the chance to get to know him. It would help if you would just talk to me about him."

But as usual, Clara had no inclination to talk about William Summers. "He's been gone twenty-five years, Veronica."

"But you must have memories."

"I've already told you about him—dozens of times. I don't really know what else there is to say." There was an edge to her voice, and her white-knuckled grip on her purse echoed her agitation.

Ronni could see from the set of her mother's jaw that even if there had been anything else, she wasn't going to say it. She had her drill-sergeant look firmly in place, and after twenty-eight years, Ronni knew better than to ask any more questions.

She wasn't surprised by her mother's unwillingness to talk about William Summers. As a child, Ronni had always been afraid to mention her father's name, for it would invariably put her mother in a sullen mood. Initially Ronni had believed it was because Clara had loved him so deeply and couldn't bear the pain she felt at the memories. As time went by, however, Ronni began to wonder if her mother's reticence was truly due to grief. The older Ronni became, the more she began to suspect that her mother and father's marriage had been a troubled one, despite her mother's contention that William Summers would always be her one and only true love. Of course, Clara would never discuss such personal feelings with her daughter, and dispiritedly Ronni gave up trying to find the answers.

"I guess you really can't compare the two situations. My father's dead. Steffie's is alive. The courts will determine whether she'll have a father," Ronni finally said. "At least this will be the last time we'll have to visit Peter. To be honest with you, Mom, I feel much better about us visiting him rather than him visiting us. I don't want him here in Florida," she stated firmly.

"Well, I for one will be happy when you're both back home safe and sound." There was a hint of relief in Clara's response.

"Does that mean you'll call him for me?"

"I guess I can tolerate speaking to the man for five minutes," she reluctantly agreed as she stood up.

"Thanks." Ronni reached for her mother's hand and squeezed it gratefully. "Tell him I'll phone as soon as I've arranged another flight."

Clara nodded and stepped back over to the crib. "I don't care what you say, she looks delicate to me." She lifted Steffie's hand and surveyed the little wrist. "Is that a rash on her arm?"

"Mmm-hmm. She must be allergic to the metal in her Medic-Alert bracelet. She probably inherited the allergy from me. You know I can't wear anything but sterling silver."

"Can't you get this one in sterling?"

Ronni nodded. "I've ordered one for her. I had hoped it would come before we left for Vienna."

"The poor little dear," Clara crooned affectionately, then brushed a butterfly kiss across Steffie's forehead. "She's had her share of problems. First she was born premature. Then there was that bout with pneumonia. Now this." She shook her head regretfully. "Is it any wonder I worry?"

Absently Ronni ran a hand across the crib railing. "No, I guess not. Mom, you will call Peter as soon as you get home, won't you?"

"Yes, although I'm sure that by now he's checked with the airlines and learned you never boarded the plane. Don't you think it would be a good idea to wait a day or two before you reschedule your flight?"

"I'll think about it, all right?" She steered her mother toward the door. "Now I want you to go home, finish your packing and think about all the fun you'll have on your vacation. By the time you return from your cruise, Steffie and I will be back from Vienna, and we'll have dozens of stories to share."

When Clara would have left with only a wave of her hand, Ronni reached for her mother and gave her a hug. "Thanks for coming."

Clara mumbled a good-night and made Ronni promise to call her first thing in the morning.

After she'd gone, Ronni considered her mother's suggestion carefully. Maybe she shouldn't be in such a hurry to leave for Vienna. The thought of calling Peter and telling him Steffie was too sick to travel danced tantalizingly before her. Each time she'd seen her husband in the past two years it had taken her weeks to get over the emotional upheaval their meetings always created. Yet the sooner she confronted him about the divorce, the sooner she would be able to get on with her life.

She studied her daughter as she slept so peacefully. Steffie was such a beautiful child; it hardly seemed fair that she should have two parents who could barely utter a civil word to each other. Or that she hadn't been conceived out of love, but a futile attempt to salvage a hopeless marriage. It was because of Steffie that Ronni would go face Peter. She only hoped that his feelings for his daughter weren't as fleeting as the light summer rain that evaporated before it ever reached the ground.

THE HEAT WAS RELENTLESS. Scorching. Suffocating. It sucked every inch of air out of Logan McNeil's body until his lungs felt like two raisins. His clothes clung to him, damp from the moisture that seemed to pour from his skin, while the heat robbed him of his strength, his determination, his sanity. Yet he knew he had no choice but to sit in the car and wait for the signal. Just when he thought he could no longer bear another minute of waiting, he saw the woman in the black-and-white polka dot dress getting a drink at the water fountain.

Logan climbed out of the car and headed for the opposite end of the park where several wooden barricades surrounded a newly erected bronze sculpture. Ignoring the sign that warned the area was closed to the public, he climbed over the wooden barrier and headed to the right of the massive sculpture. As soon as he spotted the wooden bench, he saw the drop—a package wrapped in what looked like old newspapers. But before he could reach the bench, a shiny red ball went rolling past him, followed by a little girl with long blond curls and the most angelic face Logan had ever seen.

"What are you doing?" he asked when she fell to her knees beside the bench.

"I have to get my ball," she answered breathlessly, smiling up at him.

"Wait," Logan called out. "I'll get it for you. My package is under there, too."

"It's all right. I can reach it," she said, and crawled under the bench.

Before Logan could say another word, an explosion sent a rocket of fire mushrooming around him. Pain engulfed him, blinding him to everything but the furnace of heat threatening to drag him into its abyss. He reached for the screaming child, but she eluded his grasp, and he cried out in frustration. With a feeling of desperation he frantically grasped at thin air, until the pounding in his head reached such a tempo he thought he'd die. In a natural reflex he closed his eyes, only to discover when he opened them again that the world around him was in total darkness.

"I can't see! I can't see!" he repeated, panic-stricken.

Logan awoke from his nightmare with a start. He heaved a long shuddering sigh of relief at the sight that greeted him. The old iron bed with the faded pink chenille bedspread, the aging chest of drawers with its brass knobs, the still life on the wall of a bowl of fruit. He wasn't in southern France, but southern Florida. Automatically he reached for the dark patch that covered his right eye. His peripheral vision was gone, but he wasn't blind. He knew, however, that the tormenting nightmare would continue to haunt him, because even though he wasn't blind, the little blond girl had been killed in the explosion.

The room was stifling and close, and Logan could only guess that his air conditioner had gone on the blink again, as it had a habit of doing with greater frequency now that it was July and the humidity rose higher than the temperature. Logan wondered if there wasn't a fault in the electrical circuit, as the large ceiling fan had ceased to whirl, as well. Suddenly he realized that the pounding he had heard in his head was actually someone knocking on his front door.

With only a pair of khaki shorts covering his lean frame, he rolled off the bed and stumbled out to the kitchen, where he splashed cold water in his face and swiped at the slick sheen of perspiration glistening his torso. Grabbing a bottle of imported beer from the refrigerator, he opened it on the side of the counter, then took a long swallow, welcoming the cool relief with a satisfied sigh. When the knocking persisted, he reluctantly started toward the sound, but changed his mind in midstride. There was only one person who knew his whereabouts.... The thought brought a frown to his face.

Slipping out the back door, he crept around the side of the house until he was close enough to the porch to snatch a glimpse of his visitor. To his surprise, a feeling of homesickness washed over him at the sight of the heavyset man banging impatiently on the front door. Quietly Logan stepped up onto the wooden veranda, then drawled softly, "You look like a man who could use a cold beer."

Startled, the gray-haired man turned around. "It's good to see you again, Logan," he said sincerely. He thrust his hands into the pockets of his pants, as though unsure whether he should embrace the younger man.

Logan had no such qualms. He set the bottle of beer down on the porch railing and wrapped his arms around the slightly rounded shoulders. Watching the other man's eyes dart nervously about their surroundings, he said, "It's true what Hemingway said, Doc." Logan looked off in the near distance, where sun lovers littered a beach strewn with seaweed. "People don't stare in Key West. I doubt if anyone down here would even care that a United States senator was talking to a beach bum."

Doc glanced around self-consciously. "Maybe we ought to get a megaphone so you can announce it to the world," he said dryly, propping one leg up against the porch railing.

"You're looking well, Doc," Logan remarked, taking in the older man's familiar face, a face he remembered better than his own father's. But, then, Doc was more like a father to him than his own dad had been. As a youth he'd spent most of his free time in the campaign office of Senator Potter rather than on the farmstead of Lawrence McNeil.

"I'm still thirty pounds overweight and I smoke too much." As if to confirm his statement, Doc unbuttoned his light blue suit jacket and extracted a cigarette from his shirt pocket. "How do you stand this heat?" he asked, wiping his brow with the palm of his hand.

"This is nothing compared to what I've been in over in the Middle East. You want a beer? It's about the only thing that's going to cool you down here. My air-conditioning's on the blink."

"Is that all you've got?" He gestured with his cigarette toward Logan's bottle of imported brown beer.

Logan nodded. "At least I drink it cold." He smiled, remembering how Doc used to chastise him for not drinking the beverage warm. "Wait here and I'll get you one."

When Logan returned, Doc had removed his suit jacket and was fanning himself with an old newspaper Logan had left lying on the porch. "How did you find me?" Logan wanted to know, handing his friend the bottle dripping with moisture, then added, "or shouldn't I ask?"

"You certainly didn't make it very easy for me." He expelled a steady stream of smoke as he talked. "You don't need to worry. No one knows I'm here—not even Smithson."

"You actually came without the Senate's number one congressional aide?" Logan arched one eyebrow and raised his bottle in a mock salute.

"Smithson's loyal and discreet, but that doesn't mean he needs to know my every move. Besides, he's visiting his mother in Cocoa Beach." Doc raised his beer bottle in acknowledgment, then after taking a swallow said, "You're looking much better than the last time I saw you."

"Yeah . . . well, hospital patients seldom look good, do they?" Logan's lip curled cynically at the memory.

"I thought maybe the bandage would be off by now."

Doc had a habit of looking him squarely in the face, which annoyed Logan now that he was forced to wear the black eye patch. The loss of sight in his right eye had been an emotional as well as physical adjustment, leaving him reluctant to be around people. He wasn't sure which bothered him more—the way people would stare at him curiously or the way they would deliberately look away at the sight of the patch. When he responded now, his voice carried his annoyance. "It doesn't matter much. I can't see with or without the patch."

"Wounds take time to heal, Logan," Doc reminded him.

"Well, that's one thing I've got plenty of, isn't it?" He was peeling the silver label off the bottle with his fingernail.

"You're still seeing a specialist, aren't you?"

"There's one in Miami I see."

"And?" Doc prodded.

"He says exactly what all the others have said. It's a fifty-fifty shot. The eye might work again, and again it might not."

"What about the rest of you?"

"Fit as a fiddle." Logan avoided looking at Doc as he spoke, but stared out at the Gulf of Mexico, where the sun, in its daily descent, was bathing the shrimp fleet in a golden serenity. Even though Doc was like a father to him, Logan felt uncomfortable with his concern. "Doc, you didn't come all the way down here to inquire about my health."

The senator smiled without revealing any teeth. "Logan, I need to ask a personal favor of you. I need your help with something."

Logan's immediate response was a humorless laugh. "A man in your position doesn't need an old broken-down case officer."

Doc chose to ignore the sarcasm. "Oh, yes, I do. I need you to help me find someone."

"In case you hadn't noticed, Doc, I don't see so well anymore." Defiantly he snapped the elastic band holding the black patch in place, then took another long swallow of beer. "Have you forgotten that the Company retired me? I don't look for people anymore...only fish."

"Fish?" Doc made a disgruntled sound. "Then it's true? You really are spending your time taking tourists out to look at a bunch of fish swimming around in the ocean?"

"The coral reef is more than 'a bunch of fish swimming around in the ocean,'" Logan gently chided. "There's another whole fascinating world out there in the reef. You know, I think if I had to do it all over again, I would have studied marine biology in college," he said thoughtfully.

"And the United States would have missed out on one heck of an agent. You're the best I've ever seen in intelligence work."

Seeing the intensity in the older man's face, Logan said, "I *was* the best. I think you're forgetting about what happened in France. I lost the big one, and I'm not just talking about the sight in my right eye, Doc. I don't have what it takes anymore."

"That's rubbish, and you know it," Doc exclaimed. "What happened wasn't your fault. You were betrayed."

"I was careless." With the admission came a sigh of remorse. "Look, if you're trying to recruit me back into service, you're wasting your time. I like being a conch here in Key West."

"You don't look very happy to me," Doc remarked, grinding his heel on the remainder of his cigarette.

"I'm as happy as I deserve to be." Bitterness laced his words.

"I've never known self-pity to be one of your faults, Logan." The older man shook his graying head. "What happened to that patriotic kid from Kansas and his strong sense of justice?"

"He finally admitted to himself that he couldn't right every wrong in the world."

Doc gave him a shrewd look. "Are you sure you don't mean it's easier not to try?"

Logan could see the disappointment in his mentor's eyes, and it still had the power to disturb him. Why was pleasing the senator so important to him? "Doc, I wouldn't be any good to you. I've lost it—that ruthless, cunning drive that makes the ends always justify the means."

"Aren't you even a little bit curious about why I've come?" Doc tempted him.

Logan could feel his interest growing, but he didn't want to let the senator know that. Instead he chose sarcasm. "You've got more children I can lead to the slaughter?"

Doc tightened his fists and shook his head disapprovingly. "I've got a child you can save from the slaughter," he told him with more than a hint of reproach in his tone. He pulled a snapshot from inside his shirt pocket and handed it to Logan, who gave it a cursory glance.

Clutching a striped beach ball was a wide-eyed baby with a toothless grin and a dusting of red fuzz on its head. But it was the woman kneeling on the patterned blanket beside the baby who drew Logan's attention. She was wearing a one-piece swimsuit of jade green that left little to the imagination, although it generated quite a bit of activity in Logan's imagination. Her features weren't as stunning as her figure, but there was something rather appealing about the almost gamine face framed by blond curls. It was a happy face, as though its owner possessed a zest for life.

"I didn't realize the Senate Intelligence Committee was involved in child protection services." Logan's attempt at irony couldn't disguise his curiosity.

"It isn't, and you know that."

"Then why show me the picture of the baby? Just who is it you want me to find? The baby or the woman?" As much as he hated to admit it, Logan was intrigued.

"Both. They're mother and daughter. Veronica and Stefanie Lang." Doc extracted another cigarette from his shirt pocket. "Actually, I know where they are. What I need is information."

As Doc lit the cigarette, Logan noticed his hand was shaking. It was so out of character for the senator to be nervous about anything, Logan found himself asking, "What kind of information?"

When the senator hesitated before answering, Logan prodded, "Are you in some kind of trouble because of this woman?"

Doc shook his head. "Not in the way you're thinking." He took another swig of beer. "Andrew left a few things at the house the last time he visited. That picture was one of them."

Suddenly Logan understood the reason for the senator's concern. "If this is Andrew's girlfriend and you want her investigated, I'll give you the name of a private investigator in the Melbourne area."

"It's not as simple as that," Doc cut in impatiently, pulling a second photo from his pocket and handing it to Logan.

It was a wedding photo, and Logan quickly recognized the bride as a younger version of the woman in the picture with the baby. "Andrew's girlfriend is married to someone else?"

"That's not the worst of it." He exhaled a narrow stream of smoke. "I think the child may be Andrew's. There's a very good possibility that Stefanie Lang could be my granddaughter."

Logan could see how disturbing the whole idea was to the senator. "I know it's probably not easy for you to accept that your son is involved with a married woman, Doc, especially if there's an illegitimate child involved. But if you're worried about your political career, I don't think the public would hold you accountable for your son's personal relationships. I mean nowadays, the idea of a senator's son having an affair with a married lady is probably not even newsworthy."

"It would be if that lady's husband was under investigation by the Senate Intelligence Committee. Smithson found that photo in one of the case files that came through the office last week—the one concerning certain defense secrets that have been ending up in enemy agents' hands."

Logan whistled through his teeth. "Andrew's lady is married to a spy?"

"An alleged spy. His name's Peter Lang. That's why I need to know what her relationship to Andrew is, and whether Stefanie could be my granddaughter."

Logan was silent for a few moments, as though deliberating whether he should say what was on his mind. When he did speak, all traces of sarcasm were gone. "Do you have any reason to suspect that Andrew has any connection whatsoever to this Peter Lang?"

"That's what I need to find out. I need you to prove he doesn't." The words were almost a whisper, a plea filled with pain. "You know as well as I do that when it comes to electronic technology, Bartron has had a distinctive edge in the marketplace, which is why they've been awarded some of the largest government contracts for the space program. Peter Lang was working for Bartron when Andrew was hired. Although they weren't in the same department, they did work together in the same plant." His voice faltered. "I can't believe my only son could be a traitor to his country, Logan."

Logan's immediate reaction was the same as Doc's. He felt stunned by the implication. Although he and Andrew had been at odds throughout most of their lives, he knew him well enough to feel relatively certain that he wouldn't betray his country.

Logan glanced at Doc, hardly believing they could be having this conversation. Then his espionage mentality asserted itself, and he knew it was possible that Andrew could be a spy. He had seen firsthand what money, desire for revenge and thirst for intrigue could make people do. Andrew had always lived in the shadow of the senator, never quite measuring up to his father's expectations. But was that shadow dark enough to turn him into a traitor?

"I need you to find out what you can before the authorities get dragged into this. Because sooner or later they'll make the connection between Andrew and the Langs," Doc explained anxiously.

Logan looked again at the picture of Veronica and Stefanie Lang. "What do you know about this woman?"

"Smithson's done a little investigating for me and uncovered a few things. She's a schoolteacher, been married to Peter Lang for eight years, which means she married him when she was only twenty. The only reason she was mentioned in the Agency's report was that she's still legally married to her husband, although they've lived apart for several years. Actually, Smithson had trouble finding any information on her at all."

"Can I have this?" Logan flicked the photo in his hand.

"Does that mean you'll help me?" Doc asked carefully.

For the first time, Logan noticed the shadows beneath the senator's eyes. "This is really troubling you, isn't it?"

The wooden railing creaked as Doc rested the bulk of his weight against it. "I knew Andrew was seriously involved with someone a couple of years ago. He became very secretive about his private life, and I guessed that it was because the woman was married. He knows I'm old-fashioned when it comes to that sort of thing. Smithson checked it out and discovered it was her— Veronica Lang."

"So you think the baby is Andy's?" Logan was studying the picture again, trying to pinpoint any similarities between the baby and Andrew.

"Yes. Just look at her hair—it's the same shade of red as Andrew's. And he's crazy about her. He says it's because she's his godchild, but I'm convinced she's his daughter. Veronica lived with him for a while around the time Stefanie would have been conceived. The thought that I might have a granddaughter innocently caught in such a mess..." Doc's voice trailed off. "Logan, you're the only one I can trust with this. I'm not asking for myself but for the child."

Cautiously Logan said, "If I agree to help you, I'm going to have to talk to Andy."

"Do you think that's wise? I mean, knowing the way he feels about you?" Andrew Potter had made no secret of his feelings for Logan. In his eyes, Logan had usurped his role as son and was everything his father had hoped he would be. Their friendship had been a stormy one, and in recent years, the few occasions they'd been together there had always been friction between them.

"You want the truth, don't you, Doc?" When the older man agreed, Logan added, "No one will have any reason to suspect me. As far as the rest of the world is concerned, I'm out of intelligence work. You said no one knows you're here, right?"

"Smithson thinks I'm in Washington." Doc reached over and withdrew a legal-size envelope from inside his suit jacket pocket and handed it to Logan. "All the information I have on Veronica Lang is in here."

"What about the baby's birth certificate?"

"It's in there, too. It shows Peter Lang as the father."

"Where's this Lang now?"

"Employed as a linguist for an American firm in Vienna. During his tenure at Bartron, he never worked in any of the departments requiring security clearance. He translated technical manuals into foreign languages, but of course it's probable that he had contacts in all the right places. You can read about it in there." He pointed to the envelope fat with papers, which Logan was absently tapping against his palm.

"Are you going back to Washington tonight?"

Doc nodded. "I've got a cab waiting around the corner to take me to the airport."

"Does that mean you won't join me for some supper at Bubbles?" Logan knew of the senator's weakness for pasta.

"It wouldn't be wise, Logan." Doc's smile was filled with regret. "When will you leave for Melbourne?"

"As soon as I've cleaned up, although if I went looking like this, Andrew would simply believe the rumors floating around that I've lost my mind." He rubbed his fingers along his unshaven jaw.

"You do look a bit like a drunken pirate. By the way, I have a new secure telephone...courtesy of the government." Doc rattled off a string of digits. "Got it?"

Logan nodded. "I'll contact you as soon as I've talked with Andrew."

"I appreciate this more than I can tell you, Logan." This time he didn't hesitate to embrace his friend. "It's not hard to see why Andy fell for someone like her. She's easy on the eyes," he said, indicating the photo.

Logan gave a sardonic chuckle. "She looks like she should be singing in the church choir, not married to a spy."

"I figured if she could charm Andrew, she could charm anyone. Maybe I should tell you to be careful. We don't have much information on her, which is rather odd."

"You don't need to worry about me, Doc. I can take care of myself—even when it comes to pretty little blondes." He poured the last few drops of beer onto the parched lawn.

But long after Doc had disappeared out of sight, Logan found himself staring at Veronica Lang's picture and wondering how a guy like Andy could have attracted such a beautiful woman.

CHAPTER TWO

"VERONICA, I can't find Peter."

"What do you mean, you can't find him?" Ronni asked her mother, propping the telephone receiver between her ear and her shoulder so she could fold the hospital blanket she had used during the night. "Did you try his office?"

"I have been calling all over Vienna looking for that man," Clara declared a bit indignantly. "His home phone has been disconnected and his secretary at his office told me she hasn't seen him in two days."

Ronni would have sworn she could feel the hairs rise on the back of her neck. "Something's not right, Mom. Why would his phone be disconnected? That's the number he gave me to call in case of an emergency."

Clara made a derisive sound. "As if you could ever turn to him in an emergency."

Ronni let her mother's comment pass. "There must be some logical explanation. Are you sure his secretary understood what you were asking her?"

"Yes. I'm telling you, she didn't know where he was. She seemed a little perturbed with me—as though I were responsible for his failure to show up for work."

"I wonder where he could be? It's not like him to miss work. Despite all his faults, he's always been very conscientious when it comes to his job." She gnawed unconsciously on her lower lip. "Now what am I supposed to do?" she pondered aloud.

"You'll have to wait for him to contact you. I left a message for him at his office, as well as at the airport in Vienna. He should be calling you sometime today... if he's going to call you." It was obvious from Clara's tone that she didn't think he would.

"I guess that means we won't be leaving for Vienna today," Ronni concluded.

"I really think it's better if you don't," Clara agreed. "Listen, Veronica, I'm just getting ready to call the taxi to take me to the airport, but I'm still not comfortable about leaving you like this. Has the doctor been in to see Steffie yet?"

"Yes, and he's given her a clean bill of health. She's sitting up in the crib, stacking plastic rings on a peg."

"Oooh...let me say goodbye to her," Clara pleaded.

Ronni held the receiver next to Steffie's little ear and watched her daughter reach for the spiral cord. While she fought the battle to keep Steffie from pulling the cord from the phone, Ronni could hear her mother cooing endearments. Finally Steffie gurgled a garbled sound and Ronni snatched the receiver away.

"There, Mom. She says she loves you, too." Ronni looked at the cherubic face, which was starting to wrinkle in displeasure at having the telephone yanked out of her grasp. "We'd better say goodbye. I think I hear the breakfast cart out in the hall."

As soon as she had hung up, Ronni dressed Steffie in a one-piece terry-cloth romper, then set her in the high chair the nurse's aide had wheeled into her room as soon as dawn had broken. Whereas Steffie was bright eyed and full of energy, Ronni felt stiff and headachey. Unlike her daughter, she hadn't slept well, having tossed and turned on the lumpy couch, waking each time the nurse entered the room to check Steffie's vital signs.

Now, without a shower and change of clothes, Ronni was feeling distinctly out of sorts. Actually she was feeling downright irritable. She longed for the comfort of her small, but homey two-bedroom rambler with its peeling paint and missing roof tiles. If she didn't go to Vienna she could cash in her ticket and hire someone to paint the house and repair the roof. In her present frame of mind, she could have easily made the decision without a second thought.

"I must really be tired," she told her daughter, who was trying to force the plastic rings onto the peg in the wrong order. "Your mama always gets silly when she's tired." Ronni gently eased the red plastic ring from Steffie's hand and gave her the yellow one, instead. Steffie immediately shoved the yellow ring into her mouth, as though she could tell by its taste whether it was supposed to be the next one on the peg. After a couple of chomps on the plastic, she managed to slip it onto the stack of colored rings with a squeal of delight.

"Way to go, Steffie!" Ronni clapped her hands, then, seeing Steffie's breakfast being carried into the room, slipped the final red ring in place before whisking it off her tray. "Time for breakfast," she announced, tying a large plastic bib around her neck.

While Ronni spooned creamed cereal into Steffie's mouth, her thoughts drifted to Peter. Deciding to visit him in Vienna had been a difficult decision, one she didn't want to have to reconsider. Now faced with the opportunity to change her mind, she felt unsettled, and just as nervous as when she had originally made the decision to go. The fact that her mother hadn't been able to reach him only added to her uneasiness. Why had his phone been disconnected? Now she would have to go home and wait for him to call her. Once again, Peter had her waiting for him, as so often had been the pattern in their relationship.

Steffie's little fingers had discovered the oatmeal and, as usual, were tracing patterns across the high chair with it. By the time she had finished her breakfast, oatmeal graced her red curls, her ears and Ronni's elbow.

"Steffie, my darling, I do believe we're making progress," Ronni proclaimed as she wiped away the cereal with a wet cloth. "None on your nose!" She accentuated each word with a tap of her forefinger on the tip of Steffie's tiny nose.

Her daughter's response was to grab the washcloth and suck on it.

"Here. Chew on this for a few minutes while I get our stuff ready, and then we'll go home." Ronni gently eased the washcloth from Steffie's mouth and handed her a teething biscuit, which she proceeded to gnaw on, humming contentedly to herself.

As she did every day, Ronni turned on the local morning program on TV to catch the latest news and weather updates. Dividing her attention between Steffie and the movie review being given, she gathered up the few toys Steffie had been playing with in her crib and began stuffing them back in the diaper bag. One of the plastic rings had rolled under the crib, and Ronni had to scoot down on her hands and knees to retrieve it. It was only as she stood back up that she happened to glance once more at the overhead television.

Expecting to see the face of the movie critic, Ronni gasped at the image staring back at her from the television. For an instant she couldn't talk or even breathe, for the photo on the screen was of Peter.

"Oh, my God!" she exclaimed, her hand flying to her gaping mouth. Why was Peter on the national news? Her immediate thought was that he must have been killed in an accident, but then she saw the filmed footage that followed, and she quickly reached for the TV's remote control to turn up the volume.

"U.S. officials caution that it is too soon to speculate on the impact the thirty-nine-year-old linguist's defection will have on U.S. intelligence. Lang was employed by Bartron for seven years, but it is not known whether he had access to top secret defense information or was merely the liaison in a network of spies. Unofficially we've received word that Lang will be holding a press conference later this morning concerning his defection to the Soviet Union."

"Defection to the Soviet Union!" Ronni repeated, sinking down onto the couch. Peter a *spy*? No, it couldn't be. She shook her head in disbelief. There had to be some mistake. He was proud to be an American. Hanging on the wall in his parents' home was a picture of him with the president of the United States, taken the day he was one of fifty high school students honored for writing essays on the topic "What it means to me to be a citizen of the United States."

Peter would never give up that citizenship! When Ronni had suggested they get rid of his old navy uniform, he had protested indignantly, telling her it represented not only his time spent in the service, but freedom itself. He would never willingly leave it all behind. How could he? She jabbed at the button on the remote control to switch channels, hoping to catch another news report that would repudiate what she had just heard. But after a rapid succession of images on the screen, she knew there would be no such report.

Suddenly the disconnected phone number made sense. As did the Swiss bank account she had stumbled across when she had cleaned out an old chest he had hidden in the attic. And the many business trips he had always been so secretive about. At the time she had thought he was seeing another woman, that he was betraying her. But he wasn't just betraying *her*, he was betraying his country, and the thought filled her with revulsion.

She was married to a stranger. A dangerous stranger. A spy. The notion was both revolting and alarming. But it was only as she looked at Steffie, happily munching on her teething biscuit, that she realized how angry she was with that stranger. What would the consequences of Peter's actions be for her and Steffie? A chill ran down her spine.

She reached for the phone and immediately dialed her mother's number, letting it ring at least a dozen times before accepting that her mother had already left for her vacation. Who could she turn to? Certainly not Lisa—not after yesterday. She started to dial her mother-in-law's phone number, but stopped after the third digit. Evelyn and Marshall Lang hadn't spoken to her since her separation from Peter, and by now they were probably in their own state of shock.

Names of several of her friends flashed through her mind, but there really was only one person she knew she could count on to help her through this mess. She quickly dialed his number, silently praying he'd be home. When she heard his voice, she practically cried in relief.

"Andrew, it's Ronni."

"Ronni! Oh, thank God you didn't go with him! Where are you? I've been trying to reach you since yesterday morning."

"Andrew, is it true about Peter? I just saw the news and I—" She broke off, choked with emotion.

"Ronni, listen to me. It's important that I talk to you before..." He changed thoughts in midstream. "Where are you?"

"I'm at the hospital. Steffie accidentally swallowed some cough syrup and she had to stay overnight. That's why we missed the plane."

"You missed the plane," he repeated.

There was a queer emotion in his voice that Ronni was unable to identify.

"How's Steffie?" he went on. "She's all right, isn't she?"

"She's fine, Andrew, but I don't understand why Peter did this—"

"Listen to me," he cut in. "I want you to bring Steffie over here as soon as she's released from the hospital. Will you do that? Will you come directly to my house?"

Ronni had never heard Andrew sound so distraught.

"Of course I will, but you have to tell me what you know about all this. Did you have any idea that Peter was—"

Again he interrupted her. "I really don't think we should be talking about this on the phone. For all we know, they could already have a bug on my line."

Ronni automatically pulled the receiver away from her ear and gave it a cursory glance. "They? Who's 'they'?" A frown wrinkled her brow.

"The government's going to be questioning anyone who's had any connection whatsoever with Peter. I did work at Bartron when Peter was there," he reminded her. "What time do you expect Steffie to be released?"

"The doctor's already been in. I'm just waiting for the nurse to bring me the forms."

"Have you talked to anyone else about this?"

"No. I just saw it on the television. I tried calling my mother but she'd already left for her vacation." Ronni massaged her temple where a dull ache was rapidly becoming a throbbing pain. "My God, Andrew! This is all so horrible. I don't know what I'm going to do!"

"Ronni, you're going to have to trust me on this. It's important that you come directly to my house and not talk to anyone, all right? At this point we don't know who we can trust. Do you understand what I'm saying?"

"No, I don't understand any of this!" she exclaimed, raising her hand in a helpless gesture of frustration. "Yesterday I was supposed to meet my husband in Vienna. Today I learn he's a Soviet spy and you tell me I shouldn't trust anyone. Next I suppose you're going to tell me I'm in danger."

There was a prolonged silence and Ronni gasped. "Oh, my God—we're not in danger, are we?" She glanced anxiously at Steffie.

"No, of course not," he denied. "I'll just feel a lot better when you and Steffie are here with me and I know you're safe. Peter was hanging around people with few scruples . . . people who'd stop at nothing to get what they want."

"But Steffie and I don't have anything they want!" she protested.

"I know, I know," he said soothingly.

But she was not calmed. When a nurse slipped quietly into the room, Ronni lowered her voice. "Look, Andrew, I've got to go. Steffie's nurse is here."

"All right. Remember what I said . . . and please, be careful."

"We'll be there soon." As she hung up the phone and turned her attention to the nurse, Ronni tried to shake off the sense of foreboding that had descended upon her. Like a thick fog, it pervaded her emotions as well as her logic, and she couldn't help but worry that Peter's actions had jeopardized their safety. By the time she was ready to leave the hospital, the apprehension was close to becoming panic, and she was surprised that her wobbly legs were able to carry her and Steffie out to her car in the parking lot.

All the way to Andrew's, she tried to make sense out of what she had heard on the television, but there seemed to be no explanation for Peter's behavior. If he had been planning his defection all along, why had he arranged for her to come to Vienna? Unless— She nearly ran a stoplight at the realization. *He thought that she would consider going with him!* It was almost too bizarre to consider, yet what other explanation could there possibly be?

More than anything, what she needed right now was a friend. Thank goodness Andrew was there for her, just as he had been more times than she could remember. He had helped her through the most painful period of her life. She knew she could trust Andrew. With her mother away, he was the only person she could really turn to.

She only hoped Andrew would have some answers to her questions. It wasn't like him to sound so worried. Images of James Bond spy scenes came to mind, and automatically her eyes moved to the rearview mirror, as though expecting to find someone tailing her. But none of the drivers behind her looked like anything except impatient motorists disgusted with traffic. She heaved a sigh of relief, but still found herself glancing into the rearview mirror from time to time.

Not a single car followed her off the freeway exit to Andrew's, which led her to believe she was letting her imagination run wild. She was glad Steffie had fallen asleep in her car seat, for she didn't need her daughter to witness her paranoia. If Steffie sensed her mother's tension, she'd be fussing, and whining, as well.

Ronni smiled at the sight of the little head that dipped to one side of the car seat. Steffie looked so peaceful, so totally unaware of all the craziness going on around her. If only she would never have to know the horrible truth about her father.

Ronni made the final turn onto Andrew's street and her smile vanished. In front of his home were a police car and an ambulance, both with their red emergency lights flashing. She pulled into the driveway and parked next to the house. Without waking Steffie, she slipped out of the car, leaving the door wide open as she rushed toward the house.

"What's happened?" Ronni asked a police officer who was filling out a form on a clipboard.

"Are you a relative of Mr. Potter's?"

She shook her head. "No, but I spoke to Andrew not more than an hour ago and he asked me to come right over . . . he's expecting me."

"From what I can see, your friend has had a heart attack. The paramedics are with him right now," the officer told her, his face grim.

"A heart attack? But he's only thirty-three," Ronni squeaked.

The policeman could only lift his shoulders regretfully.

She hurried toward the front door, but was met by two uniformed men carrying a stretcher bearing Andrew. His face was ashen white, his eyes closed, and an oxygen mask rested over his mouth. Ronni was shocked by his appearance. Only two days ago they had had dinner together and he'd been the picture of health. Now he looked like the shadow of death.

"Andrew, are you all right?" she asked. "It's me . . . Ronni."

Andrew's eyes fluttered open, then widened in recognition, and Ronni took his hand in hers. "He's trying to tell me something," she said to the paramedics as she trailed alongside the stretcher with Andrew's hand clinging to hers. She bent closer to him.

"Steffie?" he mumbled through the oxygen mask, his eyes searching about frantically.

"Steffie's fine," she assured him. "She's in the car. Don't try to talk now. Save your strength."

The hand that wasn't clutching Ronni's reached up and pulled the oxygen mask away from his face. "You've got to be careful. Don't trust—" Suddenly his face took on a deathly green pallor, and his eyes bulged. He was no longer looking at Ronni, but at the man who had just stepped into view.

"What are you doing here?" Andrew managed to croak, just seconds before the paramedics forced the oxygen mask back into place despite his reluctance to have it hampering his ability to speak.

Ronni's eyes flew to the man who had caused her friend such distress and she nearly gasped. Standing across from her was a suspicious looking dark-haired stranger. At first she thought it was the eye patch that gave him a menacing appearance, but his jaw was hard, and there was something somber about the planes of his face. He was either hiding secrets or sorrow. In any case, Ronni didn't want to know which.

"I'm a family friend. What's happened?" He was speaking to the paramedics, but staring at Ronni.

"Coronary. We've got to get him to the hospital right away," one of the attendants stated.

Andrew continued to mumble inaudible words, waving his hands wildly in Logan's direction. Maybe the paramedics didn't notice his obvious distress at seeing this so-called family friend, but Ronni knew that Andrew was definitely upset at the man's presence. And with good reason, she thought. The stranger was watching her with an intensity that was at odds with the concern he'd voiced for Andrew. He had a height advantage of at least six inches over her, and next to Andrew's pale figure he looked rugged and strong.

"Is he going to be all right?" she asked the paramedic as Andrew was lifted into the ambulance.

The man shrugged. "We're going to do everything we can to assure he is. Are you a relative?"

Again Ronni shook her head. "Only a close friend."

"Then I'd call before you make the trip to the hospital. Only immediate family members are permitted in the coronary care unit."

Ronni nodded, a bit dazed by the speed at which everything was happening. Within seconds the ambulance doors were being shut and the vehicle was moving away from her, taking out of sight the one person she could trust. If it wasn't for Steffie asleep in the car, she would have climbed inside along Andrew and gone to the hospital with him. Now all she could do was watch the flashing lights disappear around the corner until she was left standing alone with a man dressed in a Hawaiian print shirt, navy blue shorts and wearing an eye patch.

Ronni cast a suspicious look in his direction. Who was he and where had he come from? Andrew's reaction was enough to convince her he wasn't a friend. She wanted nothing to do with the man and would have walked away without another word to him, but he was determined to speak to her.

"You must be Veronica Lang."

The fact that he knew her name rooted her to the spot. Seeing her surprise, he added, "Andy told me about you...and your daughter, Stefanie. I'm Logan McNeil, an old friend of the family's."

Ronni detected a hint of a challenge in the way he stared at her, and she realized he was deliberately trying to intimidate her into looking away from him.

Logan McNeil. The name didn't sound familiar to Ronni. She thought about offering her hand—in fact, wiggled it nervously at her side—but settled on nodding in acknowledgment. One dark eye scrutinized her and she was the first one to break eye contact, looking in the direction of her car. "I think I'm going to go to the hospital...just in case."

"You won't be able to see him. You heard what that guy said—immediate family only." This time the tone was more icy than polite.

"That may be the case, but I'd still like to be there." Her ash-blond hair was tied back with a green ribbon, but the wind had loosened several strands and they were skipping across her face. She brushed them away with shaky fingers.

"I'm going to have to call his father," Logan stated soberly.

"You know Senator Potter?" The tilt of her head challenged him.

"Yes. I said I was an old friend of the family's," he returned, meeting her challenge with a chilling glare.

Her answer was a look that said she was skeptical of everything he said.

"I grew up on the farm that bordered the senator's back in Kansas. Andy and I used to play tag in the cornfields," he explained evenly.

Ronni regarded him carefully. The few times Andrew had confided in her about his family, there had always been a bitterness in his tone. He hadn't wanted to talk about his childhood, except he'd told her that his best friend had grown up to be Mr. Perfect—the kind of man his father had expected him to be. Somehow she couldn't see Andrew aspiring to be like this man, who looked as if he should be playing guitar with the Beach Boys.

"Were you here when it happened?" he asked her when she remained silent.

"No, I only arrived a few minutes before you did." She tried not to stare at him, but there was something compelling about the expression in his eye. She thought she detected a flicker of admiration, and for just an instant, she experienced a feeling of déjà vu, as though they had stood staring at each other some other time, some other place. It was an odd sensation, one that sent goose bumps along her flesh and at the same time brought a flush to her cheeks. Suddenly a child's cry carried on the summer air, breaking the silence.

"That's Steffie." Ronni turned and walked toward her car, followed by Logan. When she saw him ap-

praising Steffie through the window, her initial apprehension returned and Andrew's warning echoed in her
mind. *Don't trust anyone.*

"You'll have to excuse me." Ronni climbed in the car
and started up the engine, her thoughts on getting away
as fast as she could. As she backed out of the driveway,
she saw Logan walk over to the policeman, say a few
words, then proceed to enter Andrew's house.

Ronni wondered what he had said to the cop. That he
wanted to use the phone? Who was he really, and what
was he doing at Andrew's? And why had Andrew re-
acted so strongly to his presence? Maybe it was better if
she didn't know. Right now she was so confused that all
she wanted was to take Steffie and run far, far away
from all this madness.

All the way home, her mind held vivid images of Logan McNeil digging through Andrew's desk drawers,
searching through his personal belongings with that
one, dark brown eye that had seemed able to gaze right
into her soul. She could still hear the rich deep timbre
of his voice, and the way her name had rolled off his lips
in an almost familiar manner. The memory was enough
to cause her to shiver, and then to wonder. If he knew
her name, did he also know her address?

CHAPTER THREE

WHEN RONNI ARRIVED HOME, she found a white van with the blue-and-red call letters of a local television station painted on its side parked out front. Standing on her doorstep was a reporter with microphone in hand and a cameraman at his side. It was obvious that they were filming, and Ronni wondered of what possible interest her modest home could be to anyone.

As soon as she drove her Honda Civic into the driveway, the reporter came rushing across the yard with the cameraman in tow. Ronni was undoing the strap on Steffie's car seat when her door was flung open and a microphone thrust under her nose.

"Mrs. Lang. What can you tell us about your husband's defection? Isn't it true you had arranged to go with him, but your daughter's illness prevented you from joining him?"

Ronni shrank from the microphone and shook her head distastefully at the appearance of the television camera over her shoulder.

"I don't know anything!" she insisted, trying to shield Steffie from the camera's probing eye. "Please, leave us alone." She clutched Steffie against her chest and with head down got out of the car and made her way over to the front door, ignoring the camera and the questions that were being fired at her in an almost hostile fashion.

She fumbled with the lock as Steffie wiggled impatiently in her arms, eager to be set down. Through the metal door she could hear the telephone ringing. With her purse and the diaper bag slung over one arm, and the baby close to her hip, squirming like a worm, Ronni had to lean against the door and give it a shove with her shoulder to get it open. As a cool blast of air greeted her, she quickly slipped inside, then shoved the door shut with her rear end. Before she answered the telephone, she deposited Steffie on the living room floor, dropping her purse and the diaper bag beside her.

"Hello." She was slightly out of breath by the time she reached for the phone.

"Mrs. Lang, this is Bill Mason from the *Times*. I want to ask you—"

"I'm sorry, I can't talk right now," Ronni interrupted, in no mood to face another reporter. She replaced the receiver with more force than was necessary, only to have the phone ring again. She took several calls in succession, each of them from reporters wanting to ask her about Peter. And she told every one of them the same thing—that she had no comment. Only, with each successive call she became more annoyed by the questions, until finally she left the receiver off the hook.

Steffie had found Ronni's yellow plastic laundry basket that doubled as a home for her stuffed animals and was happily tossing the furry creatures around the living room. When the doorbell rang, Ronni was tempted to ignore it, thinking that it was probably the television reporter persistently pursuing a story. Reluctantly she went to see who it was, and was relieved to find Lisa and Angela Bergstrom on her doorstep, looking concerned.

"Hi. We wanted to see how Steffie was doing," Lisa greeted her. "I tried calling, but your line's been busy."

"I know. Come on in," she answered, stepping aside for the two of them.

"Here." Lisa handed Ronni a small stack of envelopes and a tiny package as she walked past. "I grabbed your mail. I wasn't sure if you still wanted me to take it in for you."

"Thanks." Ronni casually glanced at the return address on the slim package and said, "This must be Steffie's new Medic-Alert bracelet."

"How is she?" Lisa asked nervously.

As if she knew she was being talked about, Steffie came toddling out into the hallway, a big smile erupting at the sight of Angela.

"As you can see, she's fine." Ronni scooped her into her arms and smoothed the red curls back from her face. "Why don't we go into the kitchen, and I'll get us some iced tea and the girls can play?" She set Steffie back down and watched the two little girls make a bee-line for the toys in the living room.

"Ronni, I think you ought to know that a television reporter was at my house, asking all sorts of questions about you and Peter," Lisa told her as she followed her into the kitchen. "Of course I didn't tell him anything," she quickly added.

Ronni paused with her hand on the refrigerator door. "A reporter was at your house?"

"Yes, and I know he's been here, too, because I saw him in the yard. Ronni, what's going on?"

"You haven't heard?"

Lisa shook her head.

"Peter's done something horrible. It was on the news this morning. I thought the whole world would know by now." Ronni filled two glasses with cold water, then briskly stirred in the instant tea.

"How horrible is horrible?"

"It's worse than anything I could ever have guessed."

"Does this mean you're not going to Vienna and getting the divorce?"

"Peter's not in Vienna, Lisa." She handed her one of the glasses.

"Did he come back here?"

"No. According to the news, he's not coming back—ever."

"And that's bad news for you?" Lisa questioned, lifting one eyebrow.

Ronni considered not telling her friend the whole story, but she knew it would only be a matter of time before she learned what had happened. She didn't realize, however, how difficult it would be to admit what Peter had done. She took a deep breath to steady herself, then said, "Lisa, the reason he's not coming back is that he's decided he wants to live in the Soviet Union. Peter has defected."

"Defected? Why would he defect unless he's a..." Her voice trailed off in disbelief. "Ronni, you don't mean he's a...a..." She couldn't seem to speak the word aloud.

"Spy," Ronni completed soberly.

"A spy!" Lisa finally said, a distasteful fascination in her tone. "You're kidding, aren't you?"

Ronni took a sip of her tea. "I still can't believe it myself, but it's true."

"And all this time you never had any idea what he was doing?" There was a flicker of incredulity, then amazement on Lisa's face.

"Of course not!" Ronni denied emphatically.

"No wonder the television cameras have been prowling the neighborhood," Lisa said, slowly shaking her head. "This is incredible!"

"I've had to take the phone off the hook. Reporters keep calling, asking all sorts of awful questions. Then there was that guy waiting for me when I got here." She raised her arms in helpless supplication. "Look at me. I've slept in my clothes, my hair's all greasy and I don't have a stitch of makeup on. This is how I looked while they were filming me."

"You don't look that bad," Lisa sympathized, setting her glass on the counter. "You probably feel worse than you look." She moved over to the window, where she lifted the lace edge of the curtain.

"What are you doing?" Ronni asked.

"I wonder if they've got the house under surveillance."

"Surveillance? Who would have us under surveillance?"

"The government, Ronni." Her neighbor was looking at her rather oddly, almost suspiciously. "The FBI's probably going to be involved. Spying is pretty serious stuff. I mean, it's not like committing a misdemeanor."

"Peter hasn't lived with me in almost three years," Ronni shot back defensively.

"That doesn't matter. You are still legally married to the guy."

Lisa was moving from window to window, lifting curtains and shades carefully, as though she expected someone to be watching her. Ronni followed her from room to room until they came to her bedroom.

"I don't see anything that seems out of the ordinary, but there is a guy out there in a pickup who looks a little odd, although he doesn't exactly look like an FBI agent.'' Lisa's voice was barely a whisper.

Ronni pushed her aside and stole a peek out the window. ''Where? I don't see anything.''

''Look around the corner—behind that overgrown bougainvillea Mr. Klemmons refuses to trim.''

''Oh, no!'' Ronni moaned as her eyes spotted the orange pickup with Logan McNeil sitting inside. ''What's he doing out there?''

''You know him?'' Lisa narrowed her eyes again suspiciously.

''Not really.'' Ronni let the curtain slip back into place, then went back into the living room, where Steffie and Angela were playing.

''Well, who is he?'' Lisa asked, trailing after her.

''He says he's a friend of Andrew's.'' Ronni chewed on her lower lip.

''You mean Andrew's in on this whole mess?'' This time Lisa's eyes widened.

''No! Of course not,'' Ronni vehemently denied. ''Andrew's had a heart attack. He's in the hospital.''

''A heart attack? When did that happen?''

''Just this morning.'' Suddenly Ronni was feeling distinctly uncomfortable with the way Lisa seemed to be absorbing every bit of information. It was as though she had a morbid curiosity about her friend's predicament, and Ronni was beginning to regret telling the woman anything at all. ''Look, Lisa, if you don't mind, I'm really tired and I'd like to take a shower and get cleaned up. I also want to call the hospital and check on Andrew's condition.''

''Oh, sure, I understand,'' Lisa replied, although Ronni detected a coolness in her tone. ''Steffie can stay with me if you want to go visit Andrew,'' she offered.

Ronni knew she couldn't accept, not after what had happened. Diplomatically she said, "I don't think it would do me any good to go. If he's in the coronary care unit, they won't let anyone but family in."

Lisa moved toward the door, pausing on her way out to say, "I'm really sorry about Peter. If I can help in any way, let me know." She looked anxiously at Ronni, who assured her she would, then thanked her for the offer.

Unlike Ronni, who was relieved to see Lisa and Angela leave, Steffie was unhappy with the loss of her playmate. Still suffering from the effects of the cough syrup, she was rubbing tightly balled fists across her eyes and fussing. Usually Ronni read her a story and rocked her in the big wooden rocking chair before putting her down for her nap, but in her present state of mind, she found Steffie's whining to be just another source of irritation. With a brisk movement she swept the little girl up into her arms and carried her into the nursery.

"Steffie, you need a nap."

But Steffie didn't appreciate her mother dumping her in the crib. While Ronni pulled the shades and wound up the clown music box, she stood against the side rails, screaming in protest.

"Steffie, go to sleep," Ronni ordered before closing the door on the red-faced child. As she moved around the living room picking up Steffie's scattered toys, the muffled sounds of her daughter's crying penetrated the hard barrier her frazzled nerves had built around her heart. She reached for the book of Mother Goose nursery rhymes and returned to the bedroom.

"Come on, pumpkin," she said, giving Steffie a kiss as she lifted her from the crib. "Just because the rest of the world has gone crazy doesn't mean we have to join them, does it?'' she said softly, settling into the wooden rocker. With Steffie sagging against her bosom, Ronni read several rhymes, gently rocking the chair, until after only a few minutes, the tiny red lashes were fanned out across plump cheeks and Steffie was asleep.

Ronni had just deposited her back in the crib, when the doorbell rang. A quick look out the living room window told her it was two men dressed in dark blue suits and stark white shirts. Leaving the chain lock in place, she slipped the door open just far enough to speak to them.

''Mrs. Veronica Lang?'' one of the men asked as the door partially opened. Before Ronni could either confirm or deny his assumption, a badge was shoved into the crack in the door. ''I'm Doug Mahoney and this is Stan Wicklund. We're from the Federal Bureau of Investigation and we'd like to ask you a few questions.''

Ronni released the safety chain and stepped aside, allowing the two men to enter. She led them into the living room, where they chose to sit side by side on the peach-and-blue camelback sofa. Ronni took the wing chair across from them.

''Mrs. Lang,'' the man who had identified himself as Doug Mahoney began, ''I'm sure you must know why we're here.''

''I'm assuming it's about Peter,'' she returned steadily, clasping her hands in her lap.

''When was the last time you saw your husband?''

''I'd appreciate it if you'd refer to Peter as my ex-husband,'' Ronni insisted. ''We're in the process of getting divorced. We haven't lived together in over two years.''

''Are you saying you haven't seen him in two years?''

"No, I saw him at Christmastime. We have a daughter and he came to visit her."

"And you haven't spoken to him since then?" While Doug Mahoney asked the questions, Stan Wicklund wrote furiously in a small notebook.

"Not in person. He's called on the telephone, but I haven't seen him. He travels a lot and recently he's been living in Vienna," she explained.

"Weren't you yourself planning on joining him in Vienna yesterday?"

"Yes, I had planned a trip to Vienna," Ronni answered candidly. "I was supposed to take our daughter over for a visit and our divorce was going to be finalized."

"So why didn't you go?"

"My daughter, Steffie, had an accident and we had to spend the night in the hospital. As a result, we missed our flight."

"Then had your daughter not been taken ill, would you have met him in Vienna and gone with him to the Soviet Union?"

"No! Of course not!" she protested, straightening in her chair.

"You just told me the only reason you didn't join him was that your daughter was ill," Doug Mahoney reminded her.

"That was because I didn't know what he was planning!" she exclaimed. "There's no way I would have gone to Vienna if I'd had even the slightest hint he was a spy."

"Then he is a spy?"

"He must be if he's defected, mustn't he?" She was getting flustered by the way he wanted to put words in her mouth. "Why are you asking me? You're the ones

who are supposed to know about this kind of stuff."
Ronni realized he wasn't simply asking questions but
interrogating her, and it was obvious from his tone of
voice that he was suspicious of her.

"So you're saying that until today you had no
knowledge he had any connections to the Soviet
Union?"

"No," she replied firmly. "I told you. We've lived
apart for nearly three years."

"I thought you told me it was two years?"

"It's been two years since we tried a reconciliation,
but we've been legally separated for three years."

"Yet you were married and living together when he
worked as a translator for Bartron?"

"Yes."

Mahoney withdrew several black-and-white photos
from his coat pocket and set them out on the coffee table in front of her. "Do you recognize any of these
people?"

Ronni thought the pictures looked like mug shots.
She studied them carefully, but didn't recognize any of
the faces. When she looked up at the agents, she noticed that while she had been studying the photos, they
had been studying her reaction. "Why are you looking
at me like that? Should I recognize these people?"

"You're the one to be answering that question, Mrs.
Lang."

His suspicious attitude angered her, and it was in-
creasingly difficult to keep that anger in check. "Look,
I don't know what you came here hoping to hear, but I
can assure you it was probably a greater shock for me
to learn about my husband's activities than it was for
you."

"If that's the case, Mrs. Lang, you won't mind if we ask your cooperation in not leaving town until we've concluded our investigation."

"Leave town? I've got no reason to leave town." She saw both men glance toward the suitcases that still sat packed and ready to go in the hallway, then exchange guarded looks, which had Ronni wondering if anything she said would make them think any differently. Apparently she was guilty by association.

"Good." Both men stood at the same time. "Then you won't mind if we put a tap on your phone. It's for your own protection, Mrs. Lang."

"Protection?" Ronni rose from her chair. "Why would I need protection?" she asked, her voice rising slightly.

This time it was Stan Wicklund who spoke. "Your husband was only a small part of a spy ring—a ring that's still operating here in Florida. Until we identify who your husband's contacts are, it's in your best interest to have our protection." He snapped the cap of his pen in place and tucked his notepad into his breast pocket. "Keep in mind one thing, Mrs. Lang. There are two sides to this game. We're the side you can trust."

Ronni looked at his beady little eyes and never felt more dubious in her entire life. The one person she would have given her trust to implicitly was lying in a hospital bed, fighting for his life. These men were strangers—as Peter was to her right now. The thought brought a chill to her skin.

Doug Mahoney reached inside his pocket and produced a business card. "Here's the number I want you to call should you receive any information that might help us, or—" he paused dramatically "—if you need our help."

Ronni accepted the card. "I don't see how I could possibly help you. I've already told you everything I know."

"For your sake, I hope that's true."

Again she resented the implication that she wasn't being honest with them. "What possible reason could you have to think otherwise?" she asked.

Doug Mahoney's answer was another warning. "Your husband was trading secrets with devious people, Mrs. Lang. People who would stop at nothing to get what they want."

"And I told you I don't know what my husband was doing," she said adamantly. "I do know that I don't have anything that could be of interest to anyone."

"I hope you're right." He glanced around until he spotted the telephone on the desk, then walked over and turned it upside down.

"What are you doing?" Ronni asked.

He paused to look at her. "You said you didn't mind if we monitored your calls."

"I don't, but are you sure it's necessary? The only people who have been calling are pesky reporters."

"Oh, it's necessary, Mrs. Lang," Doug Mahoney assured her as he fished a small round disk from his pocket and placed it on the underside of the telephone. Signaling Wicklund, he moved toward the door. "We'll be in touch." Again he paused. "A word of advice. I'd be careful who you trust. As I already said, your best bet is to call us."

FROM HIS SPOT behind the overgrown bougainvillea, Logan watched the feds leave Veronica Lang's house. Judging by the expression on her face as she showed them out, she hadn't found their visit reassuring.

Wicklund and Mahoney were not the smoothest when it came to interrogation, and he was a bit surprised the Bureau had assigned them to this particular case. Judging by the expressions on their faces, they weren't overjoyed with their assignment, either. But, then, he couldn't really blame them. It simply wasn't a case for the likes of Wicklund and Mahoney.

But, then, it wasn't a case for him, either. He was no longer with the Agency, and even if he was, this case would be under the jurisdiction of the FBI, not the CIA. Even Doc had suggested they let the feds handle it from now on, since Peter Lang had gone and put all of his cards on the table.

Logan knew he should start up his engine and drive away. There were other ways of learning about the paternity of that baby without getting involved with this case. All he had to do was drive away and forget he had ever met Veronica Lang.

But that's where he was having a problem. He *had* met her. And during that brief meeting, something had happened that wouldn't let him forget. There was something about her and that baby that was calling him to take an interest—besides the fact that she had a beautiful face with perfect white skin and gentle blue-gray eyes. The photo Doc had given him hadn't nearly done her justice. The kinky blond curls were now smooth, chic tresses, and although her shapely legs were hidden by the long skirt of her sundress, she had a graceful way of moving no photograph could capture. After the murky world of espionage, she was like a breath of fresh air and sunshine.

From the information Doc had given him, things weren't adding up. He couldn't figure out why she would have married a slimeball like Lang in the first place, let alone be a partner to what he had done. Nor could he believe she had been Andy's mistress. Both ideas were equally repulsive, and it was because he wanted to prove Doc wrong that he decided he wouldn't drive away.

He would pay her a short visit. Just long enough to find out the answers to a couple of questions that were bothering him. Unofficially he wanted to learn the truth about Andy before the feds did—for Doc's sake. At least, that's what he told himself was the reason for walking up to Veronica's house and ringing the doorbell.

Just as she had with the feds, she kept the chain lock in place, only opening the door a crack.

He could see the fear in her face and wondered if it was him or the feds who had done a pretty good job of scaring her.

"How did you know my address?" she asked through the narrow opening in the door.

Logan was beginning to suspect it was him and he didn't like the feeling one bit. "I found it in Andy's desk," he lied.

She gave him a look that left little doubt about what she thought of his riffling through Andrew's desk.

"Why have you been watching my house?"

She caught him off guard with that one. "What makes you think I have?"

For an answer she slammed the door shut on his face. Logan rapped on the door with his knuckles. "I'm sorry, Veronica. Please open the door. I need to talk to you about Andy and I have something to show you." He knocked again, a knock accompanied by another plea, and was just about to leave, when the door opened once more.

"What is it you need to tell me about Andrew?" she asked.

He could tell by her tone of voice that he had found a vulnerable spot. "Do you think maybe you could let me in? I'm not crazy about carrying on a conversation through a crack in the door, and it is rather hot out here."

"I'm not in the habit of letting strangers in, Mr. McNeil."

"What did you call those two suits who just left?"

"They at least had identification." She flung the words back at him. "I don't even know who you are."

"I told you. I'm a friend of Andy's."

"He's never mentioned your name to me," she said skeptically.

"Andy doesn't call me 'Logan.' Ever since we were kids I've been called 'Mick.' It's short for McNeil," he explained.

The door closed again, but this time he heard the chain slide open and the next thing he knew she was gesturing for him to step inside. As he walked past her, he said, "Then you do know who I am? Andy has spoken of me?"

"Yes, but I'm not sure he'd approve of your being here," she told him, indicating he should follow her into the living room.

"Aha." He bobbed his head knowingly. "I guess you know that we're not exactly best friends anymore."

"I guess I do," she returned dryly. "You've got five minutes to convince me differently."

CHAPTER FOUR

"I DON'T SUPPOSE I could get a nice cold glass of water," Logan said, giving the suitcases in the hallway an interested glance as he followed her into the living room. He moved casually, looking very relaxed as he gazed around.

"Wait here and I'll be right back," she told him, noticing how he was taking in the contents of the room with a sweeping glance. When she returned with a bottle of spring water, he was nosing around her desk, but didn't look the least bit guilty at having been caught doing so.

"Make yourself at home," Ronni said wryly, handing him the bottle of water.

He transferred the newspaper he had been holding in his hands to under his arm. "Thanks, but tap water would have been fine." He held the bottle up in a gesture of gratitude, then twisted off the cap and took a long swallow before setting the bottle down on her desk.

Ronni quickly slipped a coaster under it.

"Oh, sorry." Logan shrugged, then turned his attention to the telephone.

"What are you doing?" she asked when he found the small metal disk Doug Mahoney had attached to her phone.

"The suits left a calling card."

"I know. It's a phone tap."

He gave her a look that said, "Are you for real?" then shook his head. "It's a bug. As in microphone." He held the disk up between his fingers. "This little thing will pick up whispers from a distance of twenty-five feet."

"You mean they can hear everything we're saying?"

A hint of a smile creased his cheeks. "Not anymore." He toyed with the device briefly before slipping it into his pocket. Then he picked up the bottle of water and the coaster and moved to the sofa, where he sank down, setting the water on the coffee table—this time with the coaster beneath it. Unlike the FBI men, who had looked very uncomfortable sitting on her sofa, Logan appeared completely at ease.

She tried not to let his presence affect her, but her eyes were drawn to his strong, tanned legs, so she lowered her gaze to his feet, bare except for a pair of worn huaraches. "Maybe you ought to tell me why you're here, Mr. McNeil." Instead of sitting, as she had done with the FBI men, she remained standing with both hands on the back of the chair.

"The name's Logan." He lifted the bottle to his lips and took another long drink. "And as I told you, I came because of Andy. I was hoping you could answer a few questions for me. It was quite a shock to arrive at his house and find him being taken away in an ambulance."

"I think the shock effect was mutual. It was also rather obvious that your being there was upsetting Andrew. Why is that, Logan?" She said his name for the first time, and found that she liked the way it sounded.

"You have to understand that Andy and I didn't exactly part on friendly terms the last time we saw each other. Have you ever met Andy's father?"

Ronni shook her head. "Andrew's not very close to him."

"No, he's not, and unfortunately I may be partly to blame for the distance between them. You see, the senator's been like a father to me, which hasn't always made it easy for Andy and me to be friends."

Ronni suspected that what he said was probably true. She knew that Andrew's estrangement from his father was due in part to his own feelings of inadequacy as a son. He had often told her that he hadn't been able to measure up to the standards of his father. If Logan McNeil was the man he had to compete with for his father's affection, it wasn't so hard to understand why. Despite the fact that he was dressed more for the beach than a boardroom, there was something commanding about him, an inner strength that would refuse to be subdued by anyone. Ronni's eyes roved over muscular legs dusted with wispy dark hairs and her heartbeat quickened. Yes, next to Logan, Andrew would definitely look wimpy.

"The reason I went to see Andy this morning was to try to patch things up between him and the senator." Logan sighed. "I only hope it's not too late."

"Too late?" Her eyebrows drew together. "Are you telling me that Andrew might not make it?"

"When I spoke to the senator, he told me the hospital had informed him that Andy had slipped into a coma. He's flying down to see him later today."

Logan saw her grab the back of the chair for support, and her face paled. She looked as though a feather could knock her down. There was a lost little girl quality about her, which elicited an enormous rush of sympathy from him. But just when he thought she was about to burst into tears, she surprised him with her composure.

"Isn't there some way I can see him? I know they said only family, but . . ." She shrugged helplessly.

"It's probably not a good idea. The press is bound to be sniffing around once the word gets out that it's the senator's son who's hospitalized. If you do go, you run the risk of creating a headline."

"Me?" She gave him a look of surprise.

He pulled out the newspaper that had been tucked under his arm and spread it open for her inspection. Timidly she closed the short distance between them until she stood directly in front of him. As he held the paper up for her perusal, he saw her eyes light on the picture of Peter. She took the newspaper from his hands and began to read the front page story. It only took a minute before she was rustling the pages to find the continuation of the article. Then came a gasp, and Logan knew she had spotted her own picture on page eight. He watched her read on, her face coloring with emotion at the press's interpretation of her relationship with her husband.

"Who told them all this stuff?" she asked, her blue-gray eyes flashing. "They've twisted practically everything they've written about me. They made it sound as though *I'm* a spy!" she told him with a look he could only describe as one of total bewilderment. As though she suddenly realized that perhaps Logan shared the newspaper's sentiments, she declared emotionally, "I'm *not* a spy!"

At that moment, Logan thought she could have been holding government secrets in her hands for all the world to see and he would have believed her. She made such a lovely picture standing before him, her cheeks flushed, her eyes sparkling, as she protested her innocence. He held up his hands defensively. "I didn't say you were." He realized as he spoke the words that he really didn't believe she was.

"When people read this, they're going to think I am." She waved the newspaper in disgust. "How can I expect strangers to understand any of this when I can hardly believe this is happening?"

Just then the phone rang. When Ronni hesitated before answering it, Logan said, "Aren't you going to get that?"

"It's probably another reporter," she replied, still not making any attempt to move.

"Do you want me to take it for you?" he offered.

Ronni sighed. "No, I'll get it."

Logan followed her across the room and stood beside her while she answered the phone. He was fast coming to know that Veronica Lang had a face he could read like an open book and this phone call was upsetting her. He was about to pull the receiver from her hands, when she slammed it down onto the cradle and thrust her fist close to her mouth. Logan put both hands on her shoulders to still her trembling.

"Who was it? What's happened?" he demanded, but she didn't say anything. "Veronica, tell me what's wrong."

When she looked up at him, it was with eyes that silently begged for comfort and understanding. "It was a woman. She said I have something she wants, something that doesn't belong to me, and that as long as I give it back to her, nothing will happen to me or Steffie." Her lip quivered and she immediately pulled it in beneath her teeth.

"Did she say what it is that you're supposed to have?"

"No. I was so frightened I hung up on her. Logan, what could I possibly have that she'd want?" Her fingers were clinging to his shirt sleeves. "Whoever it was had my phone number. That means they'll probably have my address, too."

This time her voice did break and Logan found himself wanting to choke Peter Lang for putting such a lovely lady into such a predicament. It was obvious she was caught up in a web he had spun.

"It could have been a prank phone call," he told her, knowing his explanation was feeble. "Now that your name has been in the paper, you're probably going to be the target of all sorts of kooky phone calls."

"Oh, that's just terrific," she moaned, letting go of his shirt and slipping out of his grasp. "It's bad enough that the public thinks I'm some kind of spy. Now I'm going to be the target of lunatics, as well."

"Maybe you should take your daughter and get away for a few days. Go somewhere the press can't find you," he suggested.

"I've never been one to run away," she told him, stiffening.

"It's not running away," he insisted, as the phone rang again. This time when he offered to answer it, she didn't protest. He smoothly got rid of the reporter, then turned to Ronni.

"Don't you have some friends or relatives you can go stay with for a while?"

Ronni shook her head. "My mother left this morning on a cruise. There really isn't anyone else I can turn to, now that Andrew's in the hospital." She tried to appear composed, but she felt so weary, so confused and so frightened. And worst of all, she felt alone. Dejectedly she dropped down onto the chair beside her desk. "Since all of this has happened, I don't even know who I can trust."

Logan hunkered down beside her and gave her an intense look. "You can trust me."

She responded with a nervous little laugh.

"I'm serious." His gaze moved slowly over her face.

"Are you inviting Steffie and me to stay with you?"

She gave him an incredibly beautiful look of disbelief that had Logan's insides doing gymnastic maneuvers.

"It's quiet and you'd be away from the nosy reporters and crank phone calls." His offer took him by as much surprise as it did her, and he immediately regretted his impulse. What in the world had possessed him to utter such an invitation? The last thing he needed at this point in his life was to be responsible for a woman and her child.

She gave him a look that was narrowly suspicious, before relaxing and smiling weakly at him. "It's very kind of you to offer, but I don't know you and you don't know me," she said.

"I feel as though I know you. Andy's spoken about you often enough." The second statement was a lie; the first wasn't. He did feel as though he knew her, and it wasn't because Doc had handed him a dossier on her. Her blue-gray eyes were softly disarming him, and he searched them for some clue as to why they should hold such an appeal for him. There was really nothing extraordinary about her eyes, yet they seemed to captivate him.

"I'm surprised Andrew talked about me to you." She seemed to be wondering what he could possibly know about her.

"Do you mean you're surprised he talked about you, or just surprised that he talked to me at all?" There was a hint of challenge in his voice.

"Both, I guess," she replied candidly, a bit uneasy he was able to read her mind. "It seems odd that he would discuss me with you, yet he seldom mentioned your name to me."

"Well, Andy can be rather odd at times." His mouth twisted wryly.

"That's not a very nice thing to say about a friend," she chided.

"You're not going to try to tell me that Andy's always spoken fondly of me, are you?" he asked with a lift of one eyebrow.

Her reply was a gentle toss of her blond head.

Looking at Logan, Ronni could understand why two men who had been best friends as children could be adversaries as adults. If they had been alike at all as children—which she seriously doubted—they were now as different as night and day. Quiet, timid Andrew would be no match for such an aggressive, virile man as Logan.

"Andrew seldom spoke about his family or his background," she told him, and was about to explain further, when the telephone rang again.

Once more Logan took the call. When he had gotten rid of yet another reporter, he said, "You really should try to get away for a few days. They're going to continue to call until all this business with your husband is settled."

"But those men from the FBI told me I wasn't supposed to leave."

"You have a right to your privacy." He could see that she was carefully weighing her alternatives. "Look, I'm not sure whether the FBI can do anything to stop the harassing phone calls, but if you'd feel safer contacting them, I understand."

For Ronni, it was strange that she should be more inclined to trust this man than the FBI agents, but she did. Despite the eye patch that gave him a sinister look, there was integrity in his face, and intuitively she knew that she could trust him. "Are you sure we wouldn't be imposing on you? I do have a toddler."

He shrugged. "It's not a problem. I live alone." He glanced down at his watch. "How soon could you be ready to leave?"

Ronni hesitated before answering. Despite his invitation, she wasn't convinced he really believed it was a good idea. She had the strange feeling he would have been pleased with either a yes or a no. Or was she simply projecting her own feelings on him? She wanted to say yes and she wanted to say no. She decided to go with her instincts.

"I guess I could leave as soon as Steffie wakes up from her nap and she's had her lunch." She looked down at her wrinkled sundress. "I'd also like to shower and change my clothes."

"I've got a couple of things to take care of, and I want to call the hospital and check on Andy. What if I come back in say, an hour and a half?"

"That should be fine." As she walked him to the door she said, "Thank you, Logan. I'm not sure what I would have done if you hadn't come by today. It's as though I went to sleep last night and woke up this morning in somebody else's life.''

One look into her delicate face convinced Logan that he had done the right thing by inviting her to his place. "It'll all work out," he promised.

There were two things on Logan's mind as he drove the short distance to the public phone in a nearby shopping mall. The first was the threatening phone call that Veronica had received. His gut reaction had been that it wasn't a prank. If he was right, she needed someone to watch over her—which accounted for his second thought.

She was a woman he *wanted* to watch over. Through the years he had met many women, but never one who aroused his interest the way Veronica did. There was something about her wide, sensual mouth that made him want to forget the reason he was with her. Whenever he was in the same room with her, he found himself wanting to believe every word she said. He knew now that his first instincts concerning her were right. She was no spy, but an innocent victim. Unfortunately she had hit the nail right on the head. She did wake up in someone else's life—Peter's life of espionage.

Doc had instructed him to find out about the baby and her involvement with Lang. He had found the answer to the latter question. Now all he needed to learn was the baby's paternity. Personally he hoped Doc was wrong. The thought that Veronica had had a child with Andy was not a possibility he wanted to consider, let alone accept. Just the notion that she could have slept with him was disturbing enough. It was only because he was certain that her relationship with Andy had been platonic that he would be able to find the answer for the senator.

Logan expected Doc to agree with his conclusion. Little did he know he would end up wishing he hadn't called the senator once more.

"I think you'd better leave the Lang woman alone," Doc advised him as soon as Logan told him what he had discovered.

"Leave her alone? I thought you wanted me to find out about the baby?"

"I do, but now that the feds are involved, it's probably better to leave it in their hands."

"I'm not so sure you're right. They've got Mahoney and Wicklund on the case, and they're more concerned about proving she's a spy than they are about protecting her and the baby."

"And you think she needs protecting?" Doc clicked his tongue disapprovingly. "Logan, you aren't telling me that you're going to be the one protecting her?"

"As a matter of fact, I am." Unbidden came the image of blue eyes appealing to him for help. "I'm going to take her down to my place for a few days."

"Logan, your job is over. Finished. You've told me you don't think she's involved in Lang's activities. That's all I expected of you after everything that's happened. If you want to find out about the baby, do so in Melbourne. I'm telling you, it's not a good idea to take her out of there—not with the feds involved."

"Doc, I know what I'm doing." He ignored the little voice in his head that wanted to argue that point.

"Ha!" The senator laughed sarcastically. "You're the last man I'd expect to be swayed by a pretty face."

"It's got nothing to do with her looks," Logan lied, as her face swam before him. "I've talked to the woman and I'm telling you she's not involved in this spy ring. She's an innocent bystander, only I have a feeling that she'll get dragged into it in a very unpleasant way if I don't help her.''

"I can't believe you're talking this way. A couple of hours with the woman and you're ready to absolve her of any guilt," Doc said impatiently.

"As far as I can see, her only crime was marrying a heel like Lang."

"I wouldn't be so sure of that. Smithson's uncovered some rather interesting information concerning your *innocent* Mrs. Lang."

Logan didn't like the feeling he had in the pit of his stomach. "What information?"

"Clara Summers and her daughter, Veronica, were killed in an automobile accident twenty-five years ago. It seems that your Mrs. Lang and her mother are using dead people's identities." There was a heavy silence until Doc finally said, "Logan, are you still there?"

"I'm here," Logan said wearily. "Doc, there's got to be an explanation."

"Yeah, I'm sure there is," the senator returned dryly. "I didn't think a smart boy like you needed an old codger like me to explain it to you, however."

"I'm telling you, you're wrong about her," Logan persisted.

Doc groaned. "From that tone of voice I know there's nothing I can say that will change your mind, is there?"

"You won't tell anyone where we are, will you?"

"Of course not." The words had the intensity of a promise.

"Thanks. I'll keep in touch—I'm going to probably need your help. There's some strange stuff going on."

"I'll say," Doc said under his breath.

"How's Andy? Has there been any change?"

"None. He's still comatose. I'm catching a plane down there in a couple of hours." There was a weariness in the senator's voice. "I feel as though I've already lost him, Logan. Even if he pulls through, I'm afraid of what the feds are going to uncover."

"Don't give up hope, Doc."

"You be careful, Logan. I may have already lost Andrew to a honey trap. I don't want to lose you, too."

Logan didn't want to think about Doc's warning, but the knowledge that Veronica and her mother had assumed identities was a fact he couldn't ignore. Long after he had hung up, he couldn't help but echo Doc's sentiments. Could he be wrong about Veronica? The fear, the concern for her daughter, the pleading of her innocence—were they all orchestrated for his benefit? He didn't think so. There had to be some explanation about her identity. But no matter who she was, he knew he couldn't just walk away from her.

She was like the apple Eve handed Adam. Only now there were two worms wriggling their way into his apple—the fact that she might have had Andy's child and the knowledge that she wasn't who she pretended to be. He knew that if the apple was going to be sweet and juicy, he needed to get rid of the worms.

Instead of returning to her house feeling protective of her, he felt annoyed. Doc had planted a tiny seed of doubt. Not even the beautiful smile of relief she greeted him with would ease his mind. He forced a smile to his lips, then quickly glanced away, not wanting to notice how appealing she looked.

She had changed into another sundress, but this one was a bright pink and had part of its back missing, exposing a lovely expanse of flesh. On her feet were a pair of thongs with a large daisy in the center of each, and her hair fell softly around her face.

"How's Andrew?" she asked, genuine concern in her voice.

The mention of Andrew's name in such an endearing tone reminded him that she might have been the man's lover, and that thought annoyed him more than the idea that she could be a spy. "There's no change. He still hasn't regained consciousness," he said curtly. "Are you ready to go?"

She was about to answer, when the sound of tiny bare feet thumping on the floor announced Steffie's arrival. Logan looked down and couldn't help but smile at the wobbly toddler. Steffie gazed up at Logan and burst into tears.

Ronni lifted her up into her arms, kissing her cheek soothingly, repeating softly, "It's okay, Steffie. This is Logan. He's a nice man."

But Steffie wanted nothing to do with him. She turned her face away from his inquisitive gaze and buried it in her mother's shoulder. When Logan attempted to take her hand in his, saying, "Hi, Steffie," she pulled her hand away and cried all the louder.

"She's recently become frightened of unfamiliar faces," Ronni said in an apologetic tone.

Logan simply shrugged. "Where are your things?" he asked brusquely.

"Everything's right there," she replied, nodding toward the hallway.

Logan took one look at the pile of things and rolled his eyes. "You're not bringing all that!" Besides the two suitcases, there was a playpen, a jumbo box of disposable diapers, the diaper bag, the car seat and a large catchall that was filled with toys.

"I do have a fifteen-month-old child," she reminded him with a thrust of her chin, wondering what had happened to the friendly man who had issued the invitation to his home.

"I'll have to make several trips," Logan said, picking up the suitcases.

Ronni went to check that the back door was locked. Passing through the kitchen, she noticed that the package containing Steffie's sterling silver medic alert bracelet still sat on the table. "We'd better take this along," she told her daughter, then slipped the package into the diaper bag.

"I'm not sure this is going to fit," Logan said a moment later, hoisting the folded-up playpen under his arm. "Does this have to go?"

"Unless you have a crib at your place. That's where Steffie sleeps."

"And that?" He pointed to the car seat.

"That's her safety seat. You'll need to attach it to the seat belts in your car."

"Pickup," he corrected her. "Let me get this monstrosity out first." He staggered through the doorway with the playpen under his arm and Steffie eyeing him suspiciously.

Ronni slung the diaper bag and her catchall over her free shoulder, so that when Logan returned for the final load, all that was left was the jumbo box of diapers. Scooping the box under his arm, he motioned for her to precede him out the door.

"Is that it?" he asked, as she managed to get the door closed behind them.

"That's it." When Logan relieved her of the diaper bag and carryall, she shifted Steffie to her other arm and inserted the key into the dead bolt.

"How far is it to your place?" she asked, walking toward the pickup.

"We should be there by dark."

"Dark?" She stopped beside the pickup and looked at him with questioning eyes. "Just how far is it?"

Logan had opened the door and was fiddling with the buckles on the car seat. "You can put her in. I think I've got all the straps in the right places." He gestured for her to place Steffie inside.

"Where *do* you live, Logan?" she asked, settling Steffie in her seat.

"Didn't I tell you?" He waited until she had climbed in beside Steffie, then he slammed her door shut and walked around the front of the truck to the driver's side. As soon as he was seated behind the wheel, he put the key in the ignition and said, "Key West."

CHAPTER FIVE

"KEY WEST? That's over three hundred miles from here," Ronni exclaimed.

"Yeah—Florida's a big state, isn't it?"

"You're taking us all the way down to Key West?" she asked.

"You said you wanted to go where you wouldn't be disturbed. I can guarantee you won't be disturbed in Key West." Noticing that her hand had moved to the door handle, Logan started the truck and pulled away from the curb before she could have any second thoughts about going with him. "Don't you like the Keys?"

"It's not that. It's just that I had assumed you lived in the Melbourne area."

"I'm only here because of Andy." He took the corner a bit faster than he should have, but only because he had spotted a suspicious-looking gray sedan in his rearview mirror. They were being followed.

Steffie had been fussing ever since he had climbed in beside her, and if it wasn't for the fact that his eyes were darting back and forth between the rearview mirror and the road, he would have made an attempt to pacify the child. Right now, however, he needed to concentrate on losing the tail.

"You missed the entrance to the freeway," Ronni commented when he cut in front of a bus in order to make it through a yellow light at the intersection.

"I'm not going to get us lost," he snapped, taking a quick left that had the tires squealing and Ronni complaining.

"Do you think you could slow down? Please keep in mind that you have a child riding with you."

"It's kind of hard to forget," he returned dryly. "She's been crying ever since I got into the truck."

"I think it must be a stage she's going through." Ronni had to raise her voice to be heard over Steffie's whining. "Normally she loves riding in the car. It usually puts her to sleep."

Logan shot a dubious look in her direction. By the time they finally reached the interstate, he had lost the gray sedan, but Steffie's whimpering had become a wail. When Logan reached up to adjust the rearview mirror, Ronni turned around to peer out the back window.

"Is there someone following us?" she asked. "Is that why you've been driving like a road warrior?"

"I think 'road warrior' is a little extreme," he said. "And no, there isn't anyone following us—at least not anymore."

"You mean there was?" She waited for him to elaborate, but he didn't. "Was it the FBI?"

"Probably." By now Steffie's crying was no longer easy to ignore. "Do you think she'd quit that bawling if I were to turn the radio on?"

"I doubt it," Ronni replied, bending over to dig into the diaper bag.

Logan looked at Steffie and wiggled his eyebrows. He gave her a smile, saying, "Coochie coochie coo," which only caused the little girl to cry harder. "My God, she's having a temper tantrum."

"Steffie doesn't have temper tantrums," Ronni insisted. She pulled a stuffed animal out of the diaper bag. "Here. Lookey, Steffie. Here's your favorite Pooh bear." She jiggled the mustard-colored stuffed animal in front of her daughter, who was twisting and stretching in an attempt to get closer to her mother and farther away from Logan.

"I don't think she's going to shut up as long as she's sitting next to me," Logan remarked. "Maybe you ought to take her on your lap."

"I can't. It's not safe."

"Well, maybe we ought to forgo safety for the sake of sanity," he retorted.

Again Ronni reached into the diaper bag, and this time withdrew a pacifier. "Lookey, Steffie—here's your plug," she said, trying to force the rubber nipple between screaming lips. Steffie grabbed the pacifier with her little fist and threw it up in the air. It ricocheted off the ceiling and landed with a thunk somewhere near the gas pedal.

"That's not a temper tantrum?" Logan asked sarcastically before reaching down to retrieve the pacifier. "What about giving her a piece of candy? I've got some Lifesavers in the glove compartment."

"Soothing a child with sugar is not healthy," Ronni returned primly.

"Having a child screaming for six hours in a car is not healthy, either," Logan countered, nearly out of patience.

"Maybe you should pull off the highway at the next exit and I'll take her out of her seat until she calms down," Ronni suggested.

Without another word, Logan shot off the next exit and brought the pickup to a screeching halt on the side of the road. He climbed out, slammed the door, then stomped around to Ronni's side and pulled her door open in a dramatic gesture of chivalry. Ronni unfastened Steffie's seat belt, then climbed out of the car, murmuring soothing words to Steffie, who was clinging to her neck for dear life.

"What are you doing?" Ronni asked when Logan started to unstrap the car seat.

"Moving this contraption next to the door. She's not going to ride peacefully as long as she's sitting beside me. You'll have to sit in the middle," he told her.

As much as Ronni hated to admit it, he was probably right. When Steffie was finally quiet and Logan had finished strapping the seat onto the passenger side, he looked at Ronni and said, "Got any ideas on how you're going to get her back in?"

"No problem," she replied with a look that bordered on hostility. "See, Steffie. You get to ride next to the window," she told the toddler as she attempted to slide her back into the car seat. Steffie's response was to tighten her arms around Ronni's neck and squawk.

"She's bucking again," Logan said smugly.

Sighing, Ronni backed away from the truck with Steffie in her arms.

Logan glanced around the area where they were parked. "You wait here," he said, then started off toward a roadside café about fifty yards away. With his departure came silence from Steffie, and Ronni wondered how on earth they were going to make it all the way to Key West when Steffie was so obviously frightened of Logan.

It wasn't long before he returned, carrying three large paper cups, three plastic spoons and a bundle of napkins.

"How about some ice cream, Steffie," he said softly, handing Ronni two of the paper cups, two long-handled plastic spoons and the pile of napkins. "A milk shake isn't unhealthy, is it?"

"No, she loves ice cream," Ronni replied graciously. "Thank you." As soon as Steffie realized she was going to get the milk shake if she was strapped in, she willingly went into the car seat.

When all three of them were back in the pickup, Logan started up the engine and drove back onto the highway. Ronni was grateful her daughter had stopped fussing, although she wasn't so sure she was going to be any more comfortable sitting next to Logan than Steffie had been.

The cumbersome car seat forced her to sit closer to him than she would have chosen. His shoulder was touching hers, his half-naked thigh pressed against her cotton-covered legs. She could smell his after-shave—at least, she figured it had to be after-shave, for he didn't look like a man who wore men's cologne. She tried to disregard the tiny dark hairs that covered his forearms and legs, the large fingers that were wrapped around the steering wheel, and especially the dark patch over his eye, a patch that gave him a mysterious look.

While Logan drank his milk shake through a straw, she fed Steffie with a red plastic spoon. Now the only sounds in the pickup were the air conditioner fan, Logan occasionally slurping through his straw and Steffie humming as she savored each spoonful of ice cream. Before the cup was even half-empty, Steffie's head began to droop to one side, and she soon fell asleep.

Before long the silence became uncomfortable, as Ronni sat with Steffie's half-consumed milk shake as well as her own full cup. Several times she glanced in Logan's direction, hoping he'd initiate some sort of small talk, but he didn't. It was only when she finally spoke that he turned his head to look at her.

"Would you like some more?" she asked, as he stuffed his empty cup in the litter bag hanging from the radio knob. "Steffie didn't finish hers and I haven't even touched mine."

"If I'd known ice cream would put her to sleep we could have stopped sooner," he commented, his voice low.

"As I said, she usually falls asleep in the car, but she was crying so hard she couldn't relax. It's been a stressful day for both of us," she explained.

"I think she's a little scared of me, Veronica."

"I wish you'd call me 'Ronni.' All my friends do. In fact, my mother's the only one who calls me 'Veronica.'"

He shrugged. "Then 'Ronni' it is."

"I really don't think Steffie's afraid of you because you're you." She chuckled nervously. "What I'm trying to say is she seems to have developed an aversion to men in general. Just last week when we were in the grocery store she burst into tears when this kindly old gentleman said hello to her."

Ever since they had been in the truck, Logan had been wondering if she was aware that in order for him to see her he needed to turn his head. He wanted to give her the opportunity to ask about his eye patch if she was curious about it. "Well, I can't really blame her for being scared. My patch does have a piratical touch."

"What happened to your eye, Logan?" she asked gently. "Was it an accident?"

As much as he hated talking about his injury, Logan felt a bit relieved that she had come right out and asked him about it. The injury was too recent for him not to feel self-conscious, yet he appreciated her directness. His response was just as straightforward.

"Yes, it was an accident," he said soberly. "There was an explosion. I could have been badly burned, but I was fortunate in that regard. Debris went flying in all directions and several small particles became embedded in my right eye. I didn't lose my eye, only my vision."

"Then you can't see out of it at all?" Again there was a gentleness in her voice, which made it easy for him to talk to her about a subject he usually avoided.

"Not at the moment, but the doctors tell me that could change. Only time will tell for sure."

"Does it bother you?"

"If you mean does it hurt, the answer is no. If you're asking if it bothers me to be without the sight in my eye, the answer is yes. I bump into things because I'm not used to being blind on my right side and I've had a hell of a time adjusting to having no depth perception. It's one of those things you take for granted until you try to catch a baseball or you go to park your car and discover you're three feet from the curb."

Ronni closed one eye and found herself surprised at how her vision became altered. For one thing, she was acutely aware of the outline of her nose.

"Is it a strain for you to be driving such a long distance?" she asked.

"Not as long as there isn't a child crying all the time," he said, the charm of his smile taking the sting out of his words. He wished it would have been possible for her to be sitting on his left side so he wouldn't have to turn to see her. He wanted to be able to look at her without it being so damn obvious.

"I'm sorry. I was simply going to offer to drive part of the way."

"It's not necessary," he told her smoothly, then adjusted the rearview mirror, positioning it so that he could glance into it and see her face, rather than the traffic behind him. That way he wouldn't have to keep turning his head to get a glimpse of her. He would also be able to read her expressive face when he questioned her about Andy, a subject he was eager to discuss.

"Have you known Andy long?" he asked casually.

"About five years. Why?"

He shrugged. "I was just curious about how the two of you became such good friends."

Ronni heard the emphasis on the word "friends" and felt a bit defensive. "Actually he was a friend of my husband's. Peter and Andrew worked together at Bartron. I only met him because I took a computer class."

When Logan didn't respond, Ronni felt the need to explain. "You see, Bartron offers an evening program of computer classes for employees and their spouses. When I took the introductory course, Andrew was my instructor. He's a whiz with computers."

"Yes, I know."

"When it came time to take the second course in the series, I had a scheduling conflict, so Andrew offered to teach me at home. Since he was living alone, I cooked him dinner in exchange for his helping me with my computer instruction."

"I see."

"And that's how we became good friends." This time it was she who emphasized the word "friends."

"And your husband didn't object?"

"There was nothing to object to," she lied, knowing full well that Peter had more than objected to her friendship with Andrew; he had accused her of having an affair with him. Yet she wasn't ready to reveal anything so personal to Logan.

Logan was watching her in the rearview mirror and knew by the expression on her face that she was lying. Either Peter Lang was as jealous as hell of her friendship with Andy, the computer whiz, or her relationship with Andy was more than a friendship. Logan preferred to believe it was the former. No man in his right mind would welcome a woman who looked like Ronni having a friendship with another man—even one as meek as Andy.

"Andy told me he's Steffie's godfather," he said, watching her closely in the mirror.

"Yes." She wanted to say that Andrew had been more of a father to Steffie than Peter had ever been, but there was something in Logan's tone that disturbed her. "He's very good with children. I often tell him he would have made a wonderful schoolteacher."

"Is that the voice of experience talking?"

"You do know I'm a teacher, don't you?"

"Yes. I saw that paperweight on your desk—the one that said 'A teacher's three favorite words are June, July and August.'"

"That was a gift from one of my students." She smiled in recollection. "Even though I love teaching, it's nice to have the summer off, especially now that I have Steffie."

"You don't teach summer school then?"

"No. I never have. Before Steffie was born, I always spent my summers as a volunteer at a summer camp for mentally handicapped children," she answered quietly.

That was something that hadn't been in the senator's file on her, and made him realize how little information the file had actually contained. "It sounds like an admirable way to spend a summer."

She appreciated his praise. "Unfortunately Peter didn't share your sentiment. He couldn't understand why I would volunteer to teach kids when I could get paid for it."

"That type of work probably has rewards greater than any of those with monetary value," Logan remarked.

"Oh, it did," she assured him, her eyes sparkling as she talked about a subject dear to her heart. "I can't tell you how exciting it is to see a child who has been struggling for weeks with something so simple as printing a letter of the alphabet finally succeed. It's true I gave a lot of time to those children, but what they gave me in return was something I wouldn't haven't given up for anyone—not even Peter."

He didn't miss the determined angle of her chin or the decisiveness flashing in her eyes. "Did you have to make sacrifices for him?" he asked.

Ronni nearly answered candidly, but she stopped herself, a bit embarrassed at how easy it would be to reveal her private life to a near stranger. "I'd really rather not talk about Peter, if you don't mind."

Logan shrugged. "It's all right with me. He's probably not worth talking about."

Again there was an uncomfortable silence, until Ronni finally said, "You're right. He's not worth talking about, and just the mention of his name makes me angry. I should have divorced him two years ago.''

"Then what the paper said was true? You are still legally married?''

"I was a signature away from being free of him," she confirmed.

"It's too bad you weren't free of him before he defected. It might have saved you a lot of grief.''

"You don't think the press would be hounding me if I were his ex-wife?''

"You probably wouldn't be under suspicion the way you are now.''

"I'm not a spy, and I don't understand why you offered to help us if you think I am.'' She looked up and met his gaze in the mirror.

He was the first one to turn away. "I haven't said you are.''

"Well, I'm not," she insisted, suddenly feeling too tired to be arguing with him. She'd had little sleep the night before and the motion of the vehicle was causing her eyelids to droop. Suppressing a yawn, she looked first right, then left, wishing for something soft to lean against. Sitting in the middle, she had either Steffie's car seat or Logan's shoulder to turn to. She placed her arm along the back of the car seat, turning her chin into her shoulder. Within a few minutes, she was asleep.

Logan wondered why she had stopped trying to convince him of her innocence. He glanced in the rearview mirror and once again saw traffic. When he turned his head and saw Ronni's neck bent awkwardly over the car seat, he wanted to reach out and pull her into his arms, cradling her so that her creamy smooth cheek would be cushioned against his shoulder rather than the plastic molding on the car seat. But the picture the two of them made was one he was loath to disturb.

Again he found himself questioning his judgment in offering to help her out. He could feel himself being drawn into their predicament, and if he wasn't careful, he could easily lose his objectivity. So far, he hadn't learned who she really was or whether Steffie was Andy's daughter. What he had discovered was that she was as genuine a woman as he had ever met. Despite what Doc had told him about her identity, he found himself attracted to her and wanting to know everything about her—and not for Doc's sake. From what he could see, she had become entangled in a web of intrigue and he was going to do everything in his power to get her untangled.

He thought about that web of intrigue as the truck ate up the miles and miles of coastal highway on the way to Key West. The beauty of the palm-lined beaches and the sparkling waters of the Atlantic Ocean were lost on him, for his mind was preoccupied with trying to connect the information Doc had given him with the woman sleeping beside him.

After several hours of silence, Logan began to wonder just how exhausted mother and daughter could be. Not even the noisy congestion of rush-hour traffic on the Miami interstate had aroused either one of them.

It was Steffie who woke first, uttering a few words of gibberish. Logan turned to look at her, giving her a quick grin. "Hi, Steffie." He waited for the tears, but there were none.

Craning her little neck in his direction, she simply said, "Ba."

Ronni shot upright, straightening the bodice of her sundress as she did. She greeted Steffie with a lip-smacking kiss that Logan could hear but didn't see. It had, however, the power to arouse all sorts of images in his mind.

"Where are we?" she asked, looking out and seeing water everywhere as the truck ventured across a long bridge toward a cluster of cottages and wharves reminding her of a New England fishing village.

"We're in the Middle Keys."

"Already?"

"It's after six," Logan told her.

Ronni checked her watch. "I can't believe we slept that long. Do you think we could find a rest stop? Steffie needs to have her diaper changed and she's probably hungry."

"I should stop for gas, anyway. We're not far from Grassy Key, which is where a friend of mine owns a small resort. Actually it's more of a fishing club, but I know the restaurant serves kids' portions."

Cooter's Fishing Club was located just off the main highway and was comprised of waterfront cottages, a saltwater lagoon and an informal restaurant that overlooked the marina. As it turned out, Cooter, Logan's friend, was out deep-sea fishing, but the restaurant staff treated Logan with an easy familiarity.

While Ronni took Steffie to the rest room to freshen up, Logan managed to get a table on the patio and arranged to have a high chair brought outdoors. He was sipping on a beer by the time she and Steffie had finished washing up and joined him.

"Care for anything to drink?" he asked, getting up to help her settle Steffie in the high chair.

"Iced tea, please," she told him, as he signaled for the waitress. "And milk for Steffie." She sat down across from Logan and opened the soda crackers that had been sealed in plastic wrap on the high chair tray.

"It's lovely here, Logan," she said, looking out across the lagoon to where a flock of egrets stood in stark white contrast to the blue-green water, patiently waiting for their prey.

"You should see it at sunset. The water changes colors so many times it's impossible to describe or even photograph. It has to be experienced." He handed her a menu. "The specialty is fresh shrimp steamed in beer. There should be a children's menu slipped inside there, too."

Ronni found the extra sheet of paper indicating what choices were available in children's portions and gave her order to the waitress as soon as she brought their beverages. "With Steffie one learns to be fast," she told Logan, with a faint smile.

Once their food arrived, it didn't take long for him to see what Ronni was referring to. She spent more time attending to the toddler's food than she did her own. Steffie smeared applesauce all over the high chair tray, as well as herself, tossed several mushy French fries in the direction of the diners across the aisle and splattered her milk on everything within a three-foot radius. When it was obvious that Steffie was no longer going to sit quietly in her chair, Ronni warned Logan that they should probably leave.

"But you haven't finished. Maybe you should get her some ice cream," Logan suggested, and before she could reply, he had signaled the waitress and was ordering a dish of vanilla ice cream.

Steffie's fidgeting ceased the minute the tulip-shaped dish of ice cream was set on the table. When Ronni reached for the spoon, Logan said, "Do you think she'd let me feed it to her? That way you could finish your meal."

Ronni hesitated, looking apprehensively from Logan to Steffie, whose little fingers were reaching impatiently for the glass serving dish.

"I think she's probably used to the patch by now," Logan told Ronni in an aside.

She's not the only one, Ronni thought, noticing for the first time how really handsome Logan was. With or without the patch he would be devilishly attractive. He didn't, however, look the type to be spooning ice cream into a toddler.

"If we weren't in a public place she could try to feed herself," Ronni said, then reluctantly passed him the spoon. She watched as he slid his chair closer to Steffie's, then thrust the spoon into the small mound of ice cream.

"I'm afraid I haven't had much experience with this kind of thing," he said, looking a bit uneasy as he gingerly held the spoonful of ice cream out in front of Steffie, who quickly opened her mouth and accepted it with an appreciative hum.

"You don't have any children of your own?" Ronni asked, surprised at how easily Steffie had become accustomed to Logan's presence.

"No. I've never been married," he replied.

"Why not?" The words seemed to pop out before she could think about them. "I'm sorry. That's a rather personal question."

He shrugged. "It's all right. I haven't married because I guess what they say about some careers and marriage not mixing is true."

"What do you do, Logan?" she asked, suddenly feeling as though she'd done all the talking during their ride in the car. "Andrew never mentioned what your career was, only that you were the best at everything you ever did."

He gave a sardonic chuckle. "Hardly the best. If I were, I wouldn't have this," he said, gesturing at the patch. "At the moment I don't have a career. I guess you might say I'm in one of those mid-life crises. Of course, I have an excuse, since I was injured on the job and I'm down here to recuperate." He was toying with the neck of the empty beer bottle. "Since I'm not very good at doing nothing, I've been dividing my time between helping a friend get his boat seaworthy and exploring the reef."

"Snorkeling or scuba diving?"

"A little of both, but I prefer snorkeling."

"Me, too, although I haven't been able to go very often since Steffie's birth."

As if Steffie could tell her mother was talking about her, she began to squirm and wiggle her way out of the high chair.

"I think it's time to leave," Ronni said, dropping her napkin on the table. "I'd better wash her up in the rest room."

"I'll take care of this," Logan said, picking up the check, "and meet you back at the truck."

In the ladies' room, Ronni set Steffie on the vanity top, then found the square piece of terry cloth she carried in a plastic bag for emergency cleanups. "Let's get all that sticky applesauce off that pretty little face," she said aloud, moistening the cloth and dragging it across Steffie's rosy cheeks. "Let me see those hands, too," she coaxed, swabbing in between each of the little fingers.

Lifting the Medic-Alert bracelet, she dabbed at the irritated skin underneath. "Mama's going to have to put some cream on that before you go to bed tonight," she told Steffie, them remembered she had stuck the sterling silver Medic-Alert bracelet in the diaper bag.

Ronni groped for the package. "Aha. Here it is," she said, quickly tearing open the brown wrapping paper. "Lookey, Steffie." She dangled the new bracelet in front of her daughter's wide-eyed face. "A new bracelet!"

Carefully she unclasped the old chain, then fastened the new one in place. "Now you won't get any more itchy rash." Steffie briefly fingered the silver links. "Isn't that pretty?" Ronni asked, holding the little wrist up in the mirror for inspection.

She almost tossed the old bracelet in the waste receptacle, but changed her mind and dropped it into the side pouch of the diaper bag. "We'd better not throw that one away, Stef. You never know when we might need it."

Steffie responded with her usual "Ba," then reached for her mother's outstretched arms, and together they went to find Logan.

CHAPTER SIX

THE EVENING AIR was balmy and Ronni could hear the
faint sounds of calypso coming from somewhere farther down the beach as she stepped out of the pickup
and onto the gravel drive beside Logan's house. Like
many of the homes in Key West, it was painted white,
with flamingo pink shutters. Although a bit awed by its
location, she was disappointed by its size. The house
had a veranda extending around three of its sides, but
they were tiny sides. As Logan led her through the gate
in the wrought iron fence and past a towering poinci-
ana that appeared to be larger than the house itself, her
first thought was that there wasn't going to be enough
room for the three of them.

Once inside, her suspicions were confirmed. There
were only four rooms—a kitchen, bathroom, living
room and bedroom. Logan deposited her things in the
latter.

"You don't have to give us your room," Ronni told
him, eyeing the sparsely furnished bedroom. "I could
sleep on the sofa and Steffie has her playpen."

"It might be easier for her to get to sleep if you can
shut the door," he reasoned.

Ronni shrugged, then looked around the room, trying
to visualize where she could put the playpen. "We'll
probably have to push the bed up against the wall to fit
the playpen in here."

Logan gave first one end of the bed a shove, then the other. "I'll get some clean sheets for you as soon as I've brought in the rest of the stuff."

"Let me help," she offered, but he dismissed her with a wave of his hand and disappeared out the door.

Ronni did a quick visual inventory of the room, which seemed to lack any personal touches that would identify it as Logan's habitat, and she wondered how long he had been living here. It could have been a hotel room; there were no traces of his occupancy other than the pair of running shoes next to the dresser.

Logan returned lugging the cumbersome playpen under one arm and the box of diapers in the other. "I think one more trip ought to do it," he told her, unfolding the mesh playpen, then wiping the dampness from his forehead with the back of his hand.

Ronni acknowledged his efforts with a nod. There was something about seeing Steffie's playpen in this hotellike room that brought the stark reality of her situation into focus. Despite the fact that Logan was practically a member of Andrew's family, he was virtually a stranger to her, yet here she was, sleeping in his bed, sharing his home. Unconsciously she tightened her arms around Steffie, who grunted in protest. Ronni kissed her cheek, then set her on the bed so that she could rummage through the suitcase for her nightgown. When Logan returned with the rest of their things, she was wrapping a sheet covered with rainbows around the playpen pad.

"If it feels a little warm in here it's only because the landlord didn't get the air-conditioning working until late this afternoon." He pulled the chain on the ceiling fan and the blades whirled faster. "It should gradually cool down."

"I think I'll let Steffie sleep in her diaper," Ronni said as she continued to make the playpen into a bed, tossing Steffie's Pooh bear and a lightweight blanket onto the pad.

Logan stood in the doorway watching her, admiring her gracefulness, her beauty. "Do you want to feed her anything before she goes to bed? I think there might be some ice cream in the freezer."

Straightening, Ronni smiled at him. "I think she's had enough ice cream for today. She usually has a bottle of milk before she goes to sleep."

"I'm afraid I don't have any milk, but it'll only take me a couple of minutes to run to the convenience store. There's one right around the corner. What about in the morning? What will you need?"

"Maybe some juice? I brought her cereal and fruit along." Steffie was clinging to her mother's leg in an appeal to be picked up. "I'll give her a bath while you're gone," Ronni said, scooping the child up into her arms.

"Make yourself at home, and I'll be right back."

Ronni waved a weak hand in his direction, then turned her attention back to Steffie, who had crawled across the bed to the nightstand and had discovered a paperback novel. Before she could mangle any of the pages, Ronni gently eased the book from her grasp, noting that the author was one of her favorites, too. When Steffie made a grab for the cord of the clock radio, Ronni scooped her into her arms and went to look around the rest of the house.

"Lookey, Steffie." She paused next to a life-size statue of an old sea captain that appeared to be standing guard at the entrance to the living room. "Now where do you suppose this came from?" she mused aloud, giving the wooden statue a thorough appraisal.

"I guess it does sort of fit the decor," she added, noting the eclectic assortment of furniture in the room. One look at the rattan couch had her doubting that Logan would be able to use it for a bed.

Near-empty bookshelves lined the walls, and Ronni wondered if the house had been some writer's retreat. There was a calendar featuring the artwork of Georgia O'Keeffe, but it was last year's calendar. A cassette player sat on one of the shelves, and when Ronni pressed Play the sound of Al Jarreau filled the room. "He can't be all bad if he likes Al Jarreau," Ronni whispered to Steffie, punching the Stop button.

Although sparsely furnished, the house was neat and clean, with pine floors throughout except for a sea-green linoleum in the bathroom and the kitchen. Like the rest of the house, the bathroom was small, with enough room for a shower stall only—no tub. The compact vanity top was cluttered with shaving things, shampoo and a can of men's hair spray. There were no feminine traces anywhere, which made her suspect that what Logan had said was true. He did live alone. She opened a louvered closet door and found a stack of linens, all neatly pressed and folded. "He probably has a cleaning lady," she told Steffie, whose wide eyes looked around the place with the same curious gaze as Ronni's.

Stepping into the kitchen, Ronni saw a drop-leaf table and apartment-size appliances. She opened the refrigerator door and made a face. Two shelves of imported beer, a roll of salami and a partially disintegrated head of lettuce greeted her. The usual condiments lined the shelves of the door, but there was no butter in the butter keeper. "At least there aren't any creepy things growing inside,'' she said to Steffie, then closed the door.

A peek into the freezer compartment revealed one lonely frozen dinner entrée. Investigating the cupboards, she found sparse contents, as well, and Ronni knew she would have to go to the grocery store in the morning if they were going to stay for any length of time.

Since there was no tub, she was giving Steffie a bath in the kitchen sink when Logan reappeared with a bag of groceries. His first thought was that the two could have been a Norman Rockwell picture. Steffie's little feet and hands were busy splashing playfully while Ronni attempted to wash her slippery body. Logan reflected he had never seen a more heartwarming scene. ''Don't you ever take her bracelet off?'' he asked, noticing Steffie was still wearing the silver chain around her wrist.

''It's a Medic-Alert bracelet,'' Ronni explained, lifting Steffie out of the sink and onto the towel draped across the countertop. ''She needs to wear it at all times so that if she's ever in an accident the medical personnel will know that she's allergic to penicillin.''

''What would happen if she did accidentally receive penicillin?'' he asked.

''She'd probably only get a severe case of hives, which is what happened when we first discovered the allergy. When she was six months old she had an ear infection that the doctor treated with a form of penicillin. But there's always the possibility of more serious complications, which is why I have her wear the Medic-Alert bracelet.'' Ronni wrapped the towel around Steffie and lifted her into her arms. ''I'm going to get her ready for bed. Would you mind filling that bottle with milk?'' She nodded toward the table, where Logan saw a plastic bottle with a Minnie Mouse figure painted on its side.

"Skim? Whole? Two percent?'' He raised his eyebrows inquisitively.

"Whatever you bought is fine.''

"I got one of each,'' he said with a crooked grin, producing three cartons of milk from the brown sack and setting them on the table. "I wasn't sure which one was best.''

Ronni couldn't hide her smile. "Whole for tonight.''

Logan filled the bottle, screwed on the nipple, then handed it to Ronni, who bestowed the most beautiful smile of thanks he thought possible. While he put away the groceries, he could hear her reading Steffie a bedtime story, and at one point, he couldn't resist peeking around the corner to get a glimpse of the two of them. They were lying side by side on the bed, Steffie with the Minnie Mouse bottle clasped in her hands, Ronni holding the book of nursery rhymes. Listening to the gentleness in her voice, he knew it was impossible that she could be involved in Peter Lang's activities.

Ever since Doc had told him of her false identity, he had been reviewing everything that had happened in the past twenty-four hours, thinking he must have missed a clue somewhere. His intuition told him she was innocent, yet he'd been an agent for too many years to totally disregard the fact that two and two weren't adding up to four.

He didn't want to admit it, but the truth was he was letting his feelings cloud his judgment. He'd always prided himself on his ability not to get emotionally involved in any case. But, then, he'd never felt so overwhelmingly protective of anyone. Only it wasn't just protectiveness Ronni aroused, he was thinking when she returned to the kitchen, where he was sitting at the drop-leaf table, drinking a beer.

Seeing that Logan had opened a bottle for her, Ronni sat down across from him. "This tastes good," she told him, after taking a sip of the cold liquid. "Thanks." She trailed her fingers down the side of the moisture-laden bottle.

"You look tired." He didn't want to be concerned about her, but he couldn't help it. She did look tired.

"I didn't sleep very well last night."

"I don't suppose you did." He hadn't intended the words to sound quite so sarcastic, but from the slithering expression she gave him, he knew she thought he had.

"The reason I didn't sleep well last night was that Steffie was in the hospital," she stated quietly, her chin lifting just a fraction as she spoke.

"The hospital?" he repeated.

"Yes. She accidentally swallowed some cough syrup, so we both spent the night there. For your information, Logan, I didn't know about Peter's defection until this morning."

"The newspaper article implied—"

"The newspaper was wrong," she cut in. "I heard about Peter's defection the same way millions of other people did—on the morning news—only I was at the hospital waiting for Steffie to be released. Now it seems her accident was a blessing in disguise."

"Why do you say that?"

"We were supposed to fly to Vienna yesterday and meet Peter. He agreed to the terms of the divorce, but he wanted to see Steffie one more time before it became final. Now I think he was planning to steal her from me and take her with him when he defected." When her bottom lip began to quiver, she stilled it with her teeth.

Logan studied her intently, wanting to believe her. The woman was gentle and compassionate. He could see it in her face; he could feel it in his bones. There was no way she could ever be cunning and ruthless.

After taking another swallow of beer, he asked, "Ronni, do you know what a honey trap is?"

She looked at him with eyes as innocent as Steffie's. "No. Should I?"

"Not unless you're pretending to be somebody you're not." He wanted her to be the one to tell him who she really was. But if he was expecting an admission of anything, he couldn't have been more wrong.

She was up and out of the room in a flash. Just as quickly she returned, clenching her shoulder bag. "This isn't the first time you've insinuated I'm not Ronni Lang!" She reached into her purse and pulled out her wallet, whipping out several credit cards before extracting her driver's license. "Look. That's me! Veronica Summers Lang." She slid her license across the table. "Five-foot-five, one hundred ten pounds, twenty-eight years old."

Logan stared at the photo and saw a beautiful, innocent face—as innocent as the eyes that were pleading with him across the table.

"I don't understand any of this." Her expression was troubled. "Why did you bring me here if you're suspicious of me?"

"Because I..." He nearly said *because I saw a woman I was attracted to*, but he stopped himself. "Because I knew you were a friend of Andy's and I didn't believe you could be involved in anything as nasty as the newspaper implied."

"I'm not!" she denied. "If I'm guilty of anything, it's marrying a man for all the wrong reasons."

"You weren't in love with Peter?" He knew he wasn't asking the question from a professional perspective.

"I thought I was at the time, but it didn't take long for me to see that the things I thought I loved in him were things I'd hoped to find in a father." She slowly put her credit cards and driver's license back in her wallet, then sat down again and faced him across the table.

"At nineteen I was looking for a man to tell me what to do, to take care of me," she reflected. "I guess as time went on, I realized I didn't need a father, I needed a husband. Peter wanted to be in complete control of my life. If he'd had his way, I would have been staying home with babies right from day one of our marriage. I wanted to finish my education and teach a few years before we started a family."

"He disapproved of you working?"

"'Disapproved' isn't a strong enough word." She frowned, then shook her head slightly at unwanted memories. "He always blamed our troubles on the fact that I wanted a career, when the truth was he's a very manipulative person. It's funny I didn't see that when we first started dating."

"Maybe because at nineteen you didn't want to see it," Logan suggested.

"I wouldn't be honest if I said I didn't enjoy having a man in my life who wanted to take care of me," she admitted. "Not having a father, I never had someone to do that for me."

"Is your father dead, Ronni?"

"Umm-hmm. He was killed in a car accident when I was a child. I don't even remember him." She sighed and lowered her eyes. "I know that doesn't excuse my marrying a man much older than me. I really tried to make the marriage work, Logan."

There was a weariness in her voice, Logan thought, as though the struggle hadn't been worth the effort.

"We were separated for more than two years before I finally contacted an attorney," she finished.

"It sounds as though you gave it a fair chance," he commented, not wanting to be drawn to her, but unable to stop himself.

"I didn't want to make any hasty decisions, especially not where Steffie was concerned. I grew up without a father and I know what that's like. I wanted her to at least have the opportunity to know hers, to choose to see him if she wanted." Her mouth curled cynically. "Now look what he's done to us. He's got kooks and weirdos calling our house...the government's questioning my integrity..." Her voice cracked until it was barely a whisper. "Our lives could even be in danger." Then she lost what little control she still possessed and began to cry.

Logan was normally not a man to succumb to a woman's tears. But when it came to Ronni, he found he wasn't behaving normally. He rose from his chair and pulled her into his arms, smoothing a hand over her blond head as he murmured, "It's all right. We've gotten rid of the kooks and the weirdos...and the government agents will soon get to the truth."

"If he's done anything to put my baby in danger..." she said, sobbing.

"I'm not going to let anything happen to you or Steffie. Look at me, Ronni." He held her at arm's length and raised her chin with his forefinger. "You're safe with me." He wiped away the tears under her eyes with his thumbs. Ronni's gaze held his, then much to his surprise, she kissed him.

It was a kiss salty with tears, a kiss Logan would have liked to last longer than the time it took to say thank you. But as her lips moved lightly over his, he realized that that was exactly what she was doing—expressing her gratitude. She ended the kiss just as his libido kicked in.

"You do believe me, don't you?" She gazed up at him with pleading eyes.

This time his answer was a kiss, not sweet and gentle as hers had been, but demanding and intimate, surprising both of them with its intensity. A powerful surge of desire spread through him as her lips softened and opened beneath his. While her hands found his nape, his were moving up her back, drawing her closer, until he could feel her body burning hot with a pleasure he wanted to share.

Somewhere in his brain a tiny warning sounded, but he couldn't bring himself to let her go, not when she was matching each rhythmic stroke of his tongue with an incredible caress of her own. When he felt her nipples tighten against his chest, every muscle in his body seemed to harden. But the tiny warning kept growing stronger, burrowing its way into the desire that was sending tremors through his body. Reluctantly he pulled his mouth from hers.

He tried not to notice that her lips were rosy from his kisses or that she was breathing just as raggedly as he was. From the way she was looking at him he knew she had been as hungry to taste him as he had been for her. Not trusting his self-control, he turned away from her.

"You'd better get some sleep." Unlike his insides, his voice was surprisingly cool. "If you need anything, I'll be in the next room."

"Thank you—for everything."

Her voice was like soft velvet, threatening to unravel his resolve.

"Do you need to get anything from the bedroom before I . . ." Her voice trailed off.

"No, I'm fine." He avoided meeting her eyes. "Just try to relax and get a good night's sleep."

Later, it wasn't Ronni who was having trouble sleeping but Logan. The sounds coming from his bedroom provided his imagination with vivid images of the woman sleeping in his bed. Every time the old iron bed squeaked he had visions of her rolling over. Was she, too, like Steffie, sleeping without a nightgown? The problem was, he knew how appealing she looked asleep. Her full lips parted ever so slightly, her golden lashes created a thick fringe on creamy smooth skin. And her even breathing caused her chest to heave ever so slightly—just enough to remind him that it was indeed a most noticeable chest.

He grumbled, then shifted his cramped legs, trying to find a more comfortable position on the rattan couch. But each position felt more uncomfortable than the previous one. He knew it wasn't only because he was scrunched up like a pretzel that he was miserable. No matter how many explanations he arrived at regarding Ronni, there was still the unanswered question of who she really was and why she and her mother were using dead people's identities.

He didn't need for Doc to tell him it was common practice for a Russian female spy to assume the identity of a dead person as a cover for clandestine activity.

Could Ronni be a Russian? He didn't want to even consider the possibility. She'd looked so innocent when he asked her if she knew what a honey trap was. And he certainly didn't want to think she might have responded to his kisses in an attempt to entrap him with her sexual wiles. If she was a honey trap, he was falling very neatly into it. Look at what a couple of kisses had done to him.

He punched his pillow. He wouldn't think about it. There had to be a logical explanation for her false identity. As for the tail he'd lost leaving her home—was there a logical explanation for that? He had an uneasy feeling that it wasn't the feds—which left the KGB. If the Russians were interested in her, it could mean that the threatening phone call she'd received wasn't simply from some prankster. She and the baby could be in real danger... another reason for him to be worrying.

He'd put himself in a position to protect the two of them. Logan McNeil, one eyed and still a little weak in the knees, was now responsible for the safety of a mother and child. He'd already caused one child to be killed. What made him think he could protect this one? His reflexes were slow, he was blind in one eye and he was sorely lacking confidence in himself as a protector of anyone.

There was only one thing for him to do. He knew several people in the CIA with contacts in the Soviet Union—agents who owed him more than the time of day. It was time he called in his markers. While Ronni and Steffie slept, he made a few important phone calls. When he did finally manage to fall asleep, it was only after he'd decided that he wouldn't become emotionally involved with Ronni until he'd proven her innocence.

RONNI AWOKE the next morning to the smell of freshly brewed coffee. She glanced at the digital clock on the nightstand and was surprised to see it was after eight. Usually Steffie was her alarm clock—waking every morning at six-thirty on the dot. Ronni's eyes automatically moved to the playpen. It was empty.

She quickly threw back the sheet and scrambled out of bed, slipping into her cotton kimono as she crossed the room. Barefoot, she made her way to the kitchen— and breathed a sigh of relief. Logan was seated at the kitchen table, balancing Steffie on his knee and trying to feed her breakfast. Steffie, with a dish towel wrapped around her neck for a bib, had little clumps of scrambled eggs oozing through her fingers. There were blobs of grape jelly smeared all over the tabletop, as well as all over Logan's white slacks.

Ronni's first thought was that Peter would never have bothered to feed Steffie at all, especially if it meant holding her on his lap. Unless Ronni could assure him that Steffie wouldn't make a mess, Peter hadn't wanted to hold her period.

"Good morning." Logan was the first to break the silence.

"Hi." He was gazing at her rather curiously, and suddenly Ronni was conscious of the fact that she'd just climbed out of bed and her hair probably looked as though a bird had been nesting in it. Self-consciously she smoothed a hand over her head. "I'm sorry. I usually wake up when Steffie does."

"It's all right," he told her, still giving her a rather close scrutiny.

"From the look of things, it's hard to tell who's been feeding whom." An involuntary smile tugged at her lips. "I'm afraid she's made a mess of your clothes," she said apologetically, trying not to notice the firm muscles shaping the tank top he wore.

Logan glanced down briefly. "Yeah, well, other than a couple of days around the holidays when I usually go visit my brother and his wife, I haven't had much experience with kids. I made her scrambled eggs because that's what my nephews always seem to be eating whenever I'm there."

Ronni eyed the remains of the breakfast on the table. "That's fine."

"She didn't eat much," he said, then set the squirming toddler down so she could greet her mother.

Leaving a trail of scrambled eggs in her wake, Steffie wobbled toward Ronni with arms outstretched. In one hand she carried a soggy piece of toast, which she held up for her mother's inspection.

Ronni lifted her into her arms and kissed the only part of her that wasn't covered with food—the top of her head. "Good morning, Steffie. I bet you have more breakfast on you than in you," she said, walking her fingers playfully across chubby arms. She looked over at Logan. "I think I'd better take her in the shower with me."

"You go ahead and I'll clean up here." He stood and began clearing away the dishes, grateful for the diversion. When Ronni had lifted Steffie into her arms, Steffie's foot had caught the hem of the kimono, giving him an enticing view of bare thighs and weakening his resolve not to regard Ronni in anything but a platonic manner.

The memory of how she had felt in his arms last night and that image of bare flesh stuck with him as he heard the sound of the shower running. To take his mind off such thoughts, he decided to cook breakfast, so that by the time Ronni and Steffie were dressed, the aroma of green peppers and onions wafted tantalizingly through the house.

"You didn't have to go to any trouble for me," Ronni told him when she saw that two places were set at the table.

He shrugged away her comment. "It's no trouble. Aren't you hungry?" he asked, reaching over to turn down the volume on the portable television that sat on the countertop.

"It smells wonderful," she admitted. "Is there anything I can do to help?"

"There's fresh juice in the refrigerator and the coffee's over there." He waved toward the space-saver coffee maker suspended beneath the cupboard.

Ronni filled two mugs with coffee, then poured two glasses of orange juice, while Logan slid an omelet onto each of the plates, then gestured for her to be seated. As soon as she sat down, Steffie wanted to climb onto her lap. Knowing the child would be in her food unless she had toys to keep her occupied, Ronni went to find the large plastic carryall.

"That ought to keep her busy for a few minutes at least," she told Logan when she'd returned and dumped its contents in the middle of the floor.

"She's quite a bundle of energy for such a little thing," Logan commented, as an awkward silence seemed to crop up between them.

"Yes, she is," Ronni replied, wishing she could think of something more clever to say, but after last night, she was feeling self-conscious. Had she been so lonely that a simple kiss could ignite such a reaction? Actually she wasn't sure it had been simply a kiss, which was why she felt compelled to discuss it with him. "Logan, about last night."

When he looked up from his food, his face had a neutral expression. "You needed a little comfort and I provided it," he said with a slight lifting of his shoulders. "Maybe that's all we should say about it."

All morning she had fretted over what had happened, wondering if he, too, had experienced the powerful sexual attraction she'd felt for him. Now that he was telling her he'd kissed her to comfort her, she felt disappointed.

When she didn't speak, he added, "I'd be lying if I said I didn't find you attractive, Ronni. But right now there are two things preventing me from letting that attraction grow. At this particular time in your life you're very vulnerable. You're also still married—at least legally."

"And I've Peter to thank for both of those things, don't I?" she said with a brittle smile.

Logan reached across the table to cover her hand with his, but she slipped it out of his grasp.

They continued to eat in an uncomfortable silence for several minutes before he said, "I called the hospital earlier this morning."

Ronni held her fork poised in midair. "Is Andrew worse?"

"There's been no change in his condition. He's still comatose. Senator Potter wanted me to tell you he would call us if there was any news."

"I still can't believe Andrew had a heart attack. He's too young and he's also heart smart. He's the one who's always telling me I eat the wrong foods and that I should watch my cholesterol."

Logan didn't want her to know what he suspected—that Andrew's heart attack might have been induced as a means of silencing him permanently. At least the police had been able to confirm that Ronni had arrived after the paramedics. He didn't want to even consider that she might have tried to eliminate Andrew, although the possibility that someone else had loomed largely at this point. It was a disturbing thought—not only because it could mean Andrew was a traitor, but because it could mean that Ronni had been his honey trap.

"This is really very good," she said between mouthfuls of food. "It isn't exactly what I expected for breakfast—not after I saw the contents of your refrigerator last night."

"Breakfast is about all I can handle—farm-boy skills, I guess. Normally my idea of cooking is to pop frozen lasagna in the microwave." He pushed his half-empty plate aside and wrapped both hands around his coffee mug. "Actually I haven't had much of an appetite since my accident."

His mood had changed again—something Ronni was coming to expect. One minute he was friendly, the next he was aloof. There was another silence, with the only sounds in the room Steffie banging a squeaking rubber hammer on the floor, Ronni tapping her fork against her plate and the hum of a commercial jingle on the television.

Finally Logan got up and scraped the remainder of his food into the garbage disposal. When he dropped the plate and cup into the sink with force, Ronni knew she had to say something. She quietly got up from the table and approached him from his right side. Unable to see that she was coming up behind him, he unwittingly turned around and bumped into her.

"I told you I can't see on my right side," he snapped, angry with himself more than her for feeling like a clumsy clod. "Are you all right?"

"I'm okay," she assured him. "I'm sorry if I startled you."

He sighed. "No, I'm the one who's sorry." He wanted to tell her how frustrated he was feeling, but the picture on the television had captured his attention. Reaching across the counter, he turned up the volume.

Ronni followed his movement, then her eyes widened in horror as she recognized the man on the black-and-white screen. Seated at a table with two other men, an array of microphones in front of him, was Peter.

She moved closer to the television, her face paling at the sight of her husband. Blue eyes that had been sparkling just moments ago became cloudy, as her long, thin fingers grasped the edge of the counter for support.

As flashbulbs went off and television cameras rolled, Peter Lang held his press conference. So great was Ronni's anger, she found it difficult to breathe. Never in her life had she felt such a rage toward another human being. But, then, never before had anyone ever assaulted her character in such a despicable manner.

In a most convincing tone Peter told the world, "I want it made public that I chose to make my home in the Soviet Union. I was not forced to leave the United States. All I ask now is that my wife and daughter be allowed to join me as they had originally planned."

CHAPTER SEVEN

"HE'S LYING!" Ronni exclaimed, her fists in tight balls. "We weren't going *with* him. We were going over to visit him so that he could see Steffie and I could get the divorce papers signed. That's all!"

She stared at the television contemptuously while Peter continued with his statement.

"I want to send a message to my wife, and that is this—Ronni, you must know how much I love you, and how much I want both you and Steffie here with me. Please don't keep my daughter away from me."

Several reporters asked questions. Peter gave vague responses, but it wouldn't have mattered what he said, for all Ronni could think of was how he'd lied about her joining him. As soon as the news segment was over, she switched off the television angrily.

"How can he even think I'd let him have Steffie?" She shook her head in amazement. "He hasn't wanted to have anything to do with her in fifteen months. Now all of a sudden he's trying to make it sound as if he's a devoted father."

"Maybe since he's given up his freedom he's realized how important the two of you are to him," Logan suggested.

Ronni's response was a guttural sound of disbelief. "I don't understand why he's doing this to us. I never thought he would be vindictive, but what other reason would he have to lie like that? Everyone is going to think that I'm one of...of...*them*." She said the word as though it were bile in her mouth. Reaching for her purse, she dug through it until she found what she was looking for—the FBI agent's number.

"What are you doing?" Logan asked, as she picked up the telephone and started to dial.

"I'm calling the FBI."

Logan crossed the kitchen and took the phone from her hand. "If you think the FBI was hard on you yesterday, what do you suppose they're going to say after this?"

"But I'm innocent, Logan," she declared vehemently. "I don't have anything to hide. Oh!" she groaned in frustration, rubbing fingers across her temple. "I should have never left my home. Now I probably look guiltier than ever."

"But you're not guilty." He realized that as he said the words, he wasn't simply trying to console her, but that he truly believed them. "And if you had stayed in Melbourne, you would have had to worry about the press hounding you, crank phone calls and who knows what else."

"But what am I going to do? Hide out here?" She felt totally confused.

"I wouldn't exactly call it hiding, Ronni. You simply chose to get away for a few days rather than subject yourself to harassment," Logan reasoned.

"To me it feels like I'm hiding and I shouldn't be. I've done nothing wrong." Her eyes sought his, and found the trust she so desperately needed. "You really are a friend, Logan, and I'm sorry about sounding so ungrateful. I do appreciate you helping us. The next time I see Andrew, I'm going to tell him his suspicions about you are unfounded. I don't know what Steffie and I would have done if you hadn't chosen yesterday as the day you were going to make amends with him."

Logan felt more than a twinge of guilt. He debated whether he should tell her his real reason for going to see Andrew. What would she think if she knew that in addition to being a close friend of the Potters, he was also an ex-agent—an ex-agent whose initial interest in her was for the same reasons as the FBI. He knew that emotionally she was getting close to the breaking point. Revealing his identity now might only confuse her further. Besides, his interest in her went beyond Doc's inquiry. The memory of the taste of her lips made the decision for him.

He took her hands in his. "You've got my help if you want it, Ronni. You can stay here as long as you like."

She bit her lip indecisively. "You really don't think I should call the FBI?"

"Why don't you let me see what I can learn from Senator Potter? He's on the Senate Intelligence Committee, so he should be able to find out if the government is close to cracking the spy ring Peter was involved in."

"How long do you suppose that will take?"

"Hopefully not more than a couple of days. As soon as the government uncovers Peter's contact, your name will be cleared. It won't matter what Peter does or doesn't say."

She looked skeptical. "It's just not fair. I shouldn't need to have my name cleared."

"I know that, and it won't be long and the rest of the world will, too." He lifted her chin with his finger. "Trust me, Ronni. It'll all work out."

Ronni studied his face and wondered why just looking at him made her want to believe that everything would be all right. To her surprise, she did trust him. "Do you really think the senator will be able to tell you anything?"

"He's in a position that affords him information unavailable to the FBI."

She could only nod her agreement.

"Does that mean you want to stay?" he asked.

Again she nodded.

"Good." He took her hands in his. "The first thing I think we ought to do is clear your mind of any thoughts of Peter the Terrible. How would you and Steffie like to see where I've been spending most of my time lately?"

"You don't need to entertain us, Logan."

"I want to, Ronni," he said sincerely. "I'd like to take you out on the reef and show you some sea life."

"That sounds wonderful, but Steffie hasn't learned how to swim yet."

"I'm not talking about diving. When I said I was helping a friend of mine get his boat seaworthy, I didn't mention what kind of boat it was." He reached for the captain's hat that sat atop the refrigerator and slipped it onto his head. "Ever been on a glass-bottom boat?"

"No, I can't say that I have—despite having lived in Florida almost all my life."

"You've been to Key West before, haven't you?"

She shook her head. "I've been to Key Largo, but that's as far I've made it down the Keys."

"Then we should play tourist. I think it'll do you both good to get out on the Gulf, in the fresh air, and forget about everything that's been happening on the television and in the newspapers."

The thought was too appealing to even consider refusing. She simply agreed.

And she was glad she did. Logan took them past picturesque old buildings, fresh with paint and framed with hibiscus, to Mallory Square, where statues of bearded fishermen and sea captains much like the one in Logan's living room graced the sidewalks. There they boarded the Old Town Trolley for a sight-seeing tour of the city. For lunch, Logan chose an outdoor café with picnic tables overlooking the marina; the specialty of the house was conch chowder and key lime pie. He also managed to find a quaint ice cream parlor, much to Steffie's delight.

At the marina, Logan introduced her to Casey Stevens, a friend of his who not only operated the glass-bottom boat, *Rosemary's Baby*, but ran a charter seaplane service, as well. When Casey offered to take the three of them on an aerial tour of the Keys, Ronni took a rain check, uncertain whether Steffie would be a good flier.

Once they'd boarded the glass-bottom boat, Ronni was happy with her choice. The two-hour narrated cruise from the Gulf of Mexico to the Atlantic Ocean took them into a fascinating world of underwater beauty. It wasn't long before Ronni discovered that Logan had more than a passing interest in aquatic life.

Steffie, as it turned out, was a better sailor than her mother, giggling and cooing as the boat churned its way through the reef. Most of her attention was on the large group of children, who enthusiastically vocalized their excitement at seeing big basket sponges and schools of porkfish and grunts. Ronni's attention was on Logan, who enthusiastically pointed out the variety of corals on the reef, as they looked through the glass panels in the ship's hull. Throughout the trip, she couldn't help but be impressed by his knowledge of the reef.

Ronni learned a lot about Logan that afternoon. As patient as he was with Steffie, he could also be rather intimidating, especially in a crowd. Part of his uneasiness in public she knew was due to his lack of sight on his right side. He was careful to make sure she was always on his left, and although he didn't seem self-conscious about his eye patch, she could see that he was uncomfortable with the crowded sidewalks and streets, where getting bumped and jostled about was common even for those who had full vision. By the end of the day, she knew that had it not been for his wanting to show her and Steffie a good time, he wouldn't have mingled with the tourists.

She brought up the subject later that evening after Steffie had been bathed and put to bed. "Thanks for today, Logan," she said when they'd finished the chicken and barbecued ribs he'd ordered from a local carryout restaurant.

"It was my pleasure," he responded, lifting his wineglass in a salute.

He'd changed into a white knit shirt, and Ronni noticed how it made his tanned skin appear even darker.

"I know it's not always easy with a child Steffie's age in tow," she continued.

"Steffie was one of the bright spots," he told her with an indulgent smile.

"You don't like crowds, do you?"

He shrugged. "I can tolerate them."

"You should have said something. We could have just as easily gone to the beach, or even stayed here." She looked at the man seated across from her and wondered how she could know so little about him, yet at the same time feel as though she knew so much.

"There aren't many uncrowded beaches in Key West. And I wasn't lying when I said I enjoyed today. In fact, it's been a long time since I've laughed so much." He was looking at her as though she'd accomplished some miraculous task.

"Steffie does have a way of creating funny scenes," Ronni agreed lightly, not wanting to see in his face that same tenderness she'd seen the night before—just after he'd kissed her. "I've always said that to be a parent one must have a good sense of humor." She promptly rose and began clearing away their empty plates, for she'd caught a glimpse of that tenderness and it frightened her.

She was at the kitchen sink when she heard his chair scrape against the floor. Next he was at her side, only inches from her; yet Ronni could feel her skin tingle as though he were touching her.

"You're fun to be with, Ronni," he told her. "Your students are lucky."

Like the gentle ocean trade winds that carried the scent of frangipani and wild orchid, his compliment carried a sweet, heady fragrance that affected Ronni in a manner that was more intoxicating than any perfume. "Thank you," she said softly. She stole a look at him, then wished she hadn't, for there was no levity in his face, but an intensity that left no doubt in her mind that he was very much attracted to her.

Unconsciously her lips parted, and had she known he could read every emotion on her face, she would have turned away from him. The way he was looking at her made her feel as though her stomach were smiling, and even if she'd wanted to look away, she wouldn't have, for his expression had her mesmerized.

When he caught her face between his hands, she felt sapped of any rational decision-making powers. He lowered his head to taste her mouth with his own, a feather-light kiss that began as gently as a whisper, caressing her lips with the promise of intimacy.

It was that promise that made Ronni forget she hadn't known Logan but a few days, made her forget she'd vowed not to let what had happened the night before repeat itself. With a shiver of pleasure, she instinctively opened her mouth to his, not wanting the kiss to end before she had felt the warmth of his tongue moving over hers.

When it did finally end, they were both trembling. Cheeks that were already flushed deepened to a rosy bloom as Ronni realized how her body had moved sinuously against his in a sensuous quest. She tried to pull free of him, but his arms firmly stopped her.

"Look at me, Ronni," he commanded, when her eyes focused on his feet. When she raised her eyes to his, he brushed his lips gently over hers. "There's no point in denying we're attracted to each other."

"You said this morning—"

He raked a hand through his hair. "I know what I said," he cut in impatiently, as though he wished he could forget the words he'd uttered. "Unusual circumstances have more or less thrown us together, but had I met you under ordinary circumstances, I'd still have the same feelings for you."

"Do you have feelings for me?"

For an answer, he caught her mouth with his, not gently tasting, but hungrily taking possession. Ronni responded with equal passion, shuddering at the intense need his touch created. He moved his hands over her, stroking, caressing, pulling her closer so that she could feel his need for her. His warmth seemed to seep into her bones, causing her to quiver with desire. She heard him groan, but it was only as he pushed her away that she realized it was a groan of displeasure. The phone was ringing.

Ronni watched him reluctantly inch his way backward to answer it, never taking his eyes off her. Upon hearing the voice on the other end of the line, however, he turned his face to the wall. When he glanced at her over his shoulder, she realized he was uncomfortable with her listening to his phone conversation. Awkwardly she motioned to him, indicating she would wait for him in the living room.

He didn't stop her, which made her wonder who it was on the telephone. If it had been the senator, wouldn't he have wanted her to stay and hear the report on Andrew? Although Logan deliberately kept his voice low, Ronni could make out bits of his conversation. Unconsciously she found herself straining to hear more, especially when she caught such phrases as "take her to Russia" and "disobey orders."

Ronni's pulse sped up. Who was Logan talking to? And why was he talking about going to Russia? She crossed the living room, then pressed herself to the wall, following its path until she was next to the open archway. Holding her breath, she leaned as close as she could to the entrance, and listened. Logan's voice was low, but there was a hint of impatience in it that caused it to carry.

"I'm here with the baby and her mother. You're going to get what you want."

Ronni bit down on her lower lip. Why was he talking about her and Steffie, going to Russia and disobeying orders all in the same conversation? Fear as she'd never experienced swelled inside her, making her legs tremble and her throat tighten. Suddenly Andrew's words echoed in her mind like a broken record: *"Don't trust anyone. Don't trust anyone."* She tried to push away the recollection of how distressed he'd been to see Logan, but the memory forced itself to the front of her thoughts, and she found herself questioning Logan's integrity as fear clouded her thinking.

By the time he joined her in the living room, she was seated on the sofa, trying to appear composed. She was hoping he would tell her about his conversation and erase all the doubts that had materialized from the bits and pieces she'd overheard. He didn't.

He took one look at her sitting like a frightened child on the sofa and his tone became distant. "That was the senator. He told me to tell you there's still no change in Andrew's condition." Unaware that she had overheard parts of his phone call, he could only draw one conclusion from her obvious discomfort: she was unhappy about what had happened before the phone rang, and was worrying that he would expect her to take up where they'd left off.

Ronni could see that Logan was avoiding her eyes and guessed it was because he was lying about the phone call. "Did you ask him about the investigation?"

"Yes. They still don't know who Peter's contact is." He had thrust both his hands in his pockets and was jiggling his loose change.

"Did he say how long he thought it would take for me to be cleared?"

He shook his head. "All he could tell me was there had been a couple of leads they were checking out."

"Does he think it's a good idea for me to be here with you?"

"He's not going to send the feds down here, if that's what you're worried about," he snapped.

If she was worried, it wasn't because she was troubled about the FBI finding her. She was confused over her feelings for Logan. Just minutes ago she'd been in his arms, trusting him completely. Now a single phone call was responsible for the doubts that filled her head, unsettling her so that she questioned whether her trust was misplaced. He was looking at her oddly, which only made her more apprehensive.

"It's getting late," she said, glancing nervously at her watch. "Well, actually, it's not late, but it's been a long day and..." Slowly she got to her feet.

Sensing her uneasiness, he said, "I think I'm going to go out for a walk."

"Then I guess I'll say good-night now," she said stiffly, avoiding his face.

His good-night was equally stiff. As soon as he'd gone, Ronni began searching the small living room. What she was looking for, she wasn't sure. Maybe something that would put to rest the doubts the phone conversation had created. Glancing through the few titles on the bookshelves, she found nothing out of the ordinary. She noticed, however, that there was something sandwiched between two of the hardcover novels. When she pulled down one of the books, several pieces of paper fell to the ground. Bending to retrieve them, she discovered that they weren't simply pieces of paper, but envelopes containing letters.

There were three of them, each looking as though it could easily come apart at the seams. A glance at the addresses told her they were indeed Logan's letters, but they hadn't been sent to him here in Key West. One had an East German address, whereas the other two had been sent to him in Czechoslovakia. What on earth would Logan have been doing in Czechoslovakia?

With shaky fingers she removed one of the letters from its envelope, carefully unfolding the fragile paper, only to discover she couldn't read its contents. The letter was penned in a foreign language—one she didn't recognize. A quick glance at the other two letters revealed they'd been written by the same person—someone who identified himself simply by the letter A. Again she scrutinized the envelopes, but there were no return addresses. Who was this "A" and why was he writing to Logan in what looked to her like it could be Russian?

Once more she felt a growing wave of panic threaten to rob her of her breath. Logan couldn't have anything to do with the Russians...he was Andrew's friend—wasn't he? Of course he was. Andrew had mentioned him on several occasions, although he hadn't ever shown her a picture of Logan McNeil. Maybe this man was an impostor—a Soviet impostor. Could that have been why Andrew was so upset when Logan had appeared?

Now the panic wasn't just taking her breath away, but her composure, as well. She shoved the letters back in between the books and looked around in confusion. "We have to get out of here," she said aloud to the empty room.

No. She was overreacting. Rubbing her palms up and down her bare arms, she paced the room. Logan couldn't possibly be a spy. He was trying to help them. Then a frown wrinkled her forehead. Was he really helping them, or simply attempting to keep them away from the government agents?

She had to leave, but how? Steffie was asleep, and even if she were awake, Logan had the keys to his pickup in his pants pocket. She'd have to think of a plan—a safe escape for her and Steffie.

While she prepared for bed, she tried out and rejected dozens of ideas. She came to the conclusion there was only one way she would be able to leave Logan, and that was to take his pickup. But she needed to get hold of his keys.

Since she couldn't risk leaving in the middle of the night, she'd have to wait until morning. If she loaded everything—including Steffie—into the pickup while Logan showered, she could sneak into the bathroom and lift his keys from the pocket of his slacks. Because there was no lock on the bathroom door, all she had to do was slip in and slip out. He wouldn't even have to know she'd been there.

It seemed easy enough. But as she climbed into bed and thought about what lay ahead, she began to have doubts. *If* he was a spy, she and Steffie were in terrible danger. What if he caught her trying to leave? Would he have a gun? He didn't wear one, but that didn't mean there wasn't one in the house.

She reached for the flashlight on the nightstand, then crawled out of bed, stubbing her toe on the playpen as she groped around in the dark. She searched through each of the dresser drawers but found nothing except underwear and socks. Next she went through the narrow closet, where she uncovered a few shirts and some snorkeling gear, but no gun. That left only the front hall closet. Expecting Logan to return any minute, she hated having to look there, but fear gave her no choice.

It was in that closet that she found it—a small silver handgun, hidden behind a shoe box on the top shelf. The gun was no bigger than the palm of her hand, but to Ronni it looked too large even to grasp. She'd never handled a weapon before and she certainly didn't want to start now. Again fear made the decision for her.

Gingerly she picked the piece up, holding it away from her as though it were a stick of dynamite. She carried it into the bedroom and carefully stuck it in her purse, which she in turn placed atop the tall dresser. She wouldn't even pull the gun out of her purse unless it became necessary. Oh, God, how she hoped it wouldn't be necessary, for she wasn't sure if she would be able to point it at another human being. All she wanted was to take her daughter and leave.

WHEN RONNI WOKE the next morning after a restless sleep, the first thing she did was check to see if the gun was still in her purse. It was and she heaved a sigh of relief. She'd half expected Logan to come storming into the bedroom the night before, demanding to know what had happened to the gun. Since he hadn't, she could only hope he had no idea what she was planning.

She wished she didn't have to face him at all, but while she was quickly packing up her belongings, she could hear him moving around in the kitchen. Taking a deep breath, she opened the bedroom door and called out to him, "If you want to use the shower first, go ahead. I'm going to feed Steffie her breakfast before I have mine." She closed the door and leaned against it, then nearly jumped out of her skin when he rapped on the other side.

"I need to get some clean clothes," he told her as she slid the door open a fraction of the way.

"Oh! Sorry," she said with a weak grin, then reluctantly swung the door wide open. At first she was worried he would notice her suitcases standing beside the door, but he went straight to the dresser and pulled out a pair of briefs from the drawer, giving her an idea. When he had what he needed, he tossed her a faint smile and went straight to the bathroom.

As soon as she heard the shower running, Ronni flew into motion, pulling open the closet door and grabbing every pair of slacks inside. Then she rummaged through the drawers of the dresser until she'd pulled out every pair of briefs and shorts she could find and added them to the pile on the floor. She raced out to the kitchen to get a large green plastic garbage bag, then rushed back to the bedroom, where she frantically shoved the pile of clothes into the bag.

She didn't think her heart could beat any faster than it was when she dragged the suitcases, the big green bag and Steffie's carryall past the closed bathroom door. When everything was loaded into the back of the pickup, she grabbed Steffie and the diaper bag and installed them in the cab of the truck.

"You wait right here for Mama, pumpkin," she told Steffie as she strapped her into the car seat. "Let's hope this isn't one of those mornings when he takes a short shower," she said, then gave Steffie a bottle filled with juice and hurried back into the house. She went straight to the bedroom, where she pulled the gun from her purse before slinging the leather bag over her shoulder.

Taking a deep breath, she squared her shoulders and headed for the bathroom door. The sound of water running bolstered her confidence, and with gun in hand, she made her move. The minute she opened the door she saw that the keys weren't in Logan's pants pocket but on the narrow wooden shelf below the mirror. She didn't realize she'd been holding her breath until her lungs practically collapsed with relief. She wouldn't have to step into the bathroom at all. She could snake her hand in and snatch the keys. What she hadn't counted on was the shower curtain being zipped open and a drenched Logan catching her in the act.

He stood there stark naked, soapsuds cascading down his tanned body as the hot water continued to bounce off him in miniexplosions of moisture. Just who was more startled was a toss-up. Ronni let out a shriek; Logan appeared to be at a loss for words. The gun was in her left hand, while her right hand seemed frozen, inches from the wooden shelf and the keys. It was in that instant that Logan's eyes met hers, and before she could grab the keys, his voice was booming in her ears, stopping her hand's progress.

"Are you looking for something?" There was a seductive quality to his voice, and Ronni realized he thought she'd come to beguile him.

She tried to keep her eyes from running down the length of his body, but he was a fine specimen of a man and it wasn't every day she accosted a man in the shower. It was also the first time she'd seen him without the black eye patch, and except for a slight bruise under his eye, there was no evidence of a loss of sight. He had a hint of a smile on his face and Ronni noticed he made no effort to cover himself with either the washrag or the shower curtain. For a brief moment she found herself wanting to indulge in the pleasure of looking at his body, but she quickly brought herself back to her senses and nudged the door open, exposing the gun in her hand.

When Logan saw the weapon his provocative smile disappeared. ''What are you doing with that thing?'' he demanded.

Carefully she transferred the gun from her left hand to her right. ''I don't want to have to do this, Logan, but I need the keys. I'm taking Steffie and leaving.'' She was surprised at how steady her voice sounded, considering how fast her heart was beating.

''Leaving?'' He turned the water off. ''And where do you plan on going?''

''Just away,'' she said shakily.

''Away from me, isn't that what you mean? Ronni, you must know I'd never hurt you or Steffie.'' He made a move as though to step out of the shower.

''Logan, please. Don't move.'' She raised the gun until her arm was nearly straight out in front of her. ''Just let me take the keys and leave.''

''I'm hardly in a position to stop you, am I?''

Again he smiled, and Ronni had to fight hard not to listen to the voice in her head that told her she was being ridiculous to think Logan could be one of the bad guys.

Slowly she reached for the keys, expecting that Logan would try to stop her. But he didn't. Nor did he move when she took his clothes and tucked them under her arm. ''I'm sorry,'' she found herself mumbling, then immediately chastised herself for feeling guilty about leaving. She raced through the kitchen and out the back door.

Despite the fact that her hands were shaking so badly she could barely get the key in the ignition, she managed to start the engine and back out of the driveway. She half expected a naked Logan to come running out of the house after her, but he didn't. As she headed toward the highway, she kept seeing images of him naked, remembering the feral look on his face as she surprised him in the shower. It was difficult to believe that he was on the wrong side, that he could have been part of a scheme involving Peter. But because of Steffie, it was a chance she couldn't take.

By the time she reached the highway, Steffie had almost finished her bottle and was looking peacefully content, unlike her mother, who felt as though a war were going on in her head. There was only one road out of the Keys and she was on it, and so far, she'd seen nothing to indicate that Logan was following her. How could he? Even if he were to find a pair of pants and somehow manage to borrow a car, he would have a hard time catching up with her. Yet as she drove across the series of bridges connecting the Keys, she continually checked her rearview mirror, keeping her foot steady on the gas pedal.

More miles stretched between her and Key West, and she began to believe she was actually going to escape Logan. As she followed the road signs toward Miami, she relaxed a bit and thought about the next step in her plan. She would stop at Evelyn and Marshall Lang's home in Miami, and from there contact the FBI.

When Steffie began to fuss, Ronni reached into her purse and withdrew a small plastic bag filled with teething biscuits. "Here, sweetie. Munch on this until Mama finds us a nice place to eat," she said, handing one to Steffie.

Steffie eagerly grabbed the hard biscuit and immediately began gnawing on it, humming as she did so.

Ronni looked back over her shoulder one final time. "It won't be much longer and we'll be far away from Mr. Logan McNeil. Then we won't have to look back anymore," she said, wondering why the thought was not a comforting one.

CHAPTER EIGHT

LOGAN BANKED the seaplane slightly and squinted through his aviator sunglasses at the highway below. Despite his altitude and the fact that the automobiles looked like crawling bugs, he'd been able to spot the bright orange pickup easily and had been following it as it sped across the highway. Several times the truck had left the highway, cutting down side roads, then doubling back, as though its driver were trying to determine whether she was being followed.

Logan could imagine her looking everywhere. To her left. To her right. Behind her. Everywhere. Everywhere but up—which was why he'd been able to tail her without being noticed. It also helped that he was an experienced pilot who knew how to vector from time to time and stay in her blind spot.

He still couldn't believe she'd pulled a gun on him. It had been a humbling experience for an ex-agent, although he didn't know which was worse—her pulling the gun or leaving him without any pants. He wondered what she'd done with all of them. Were they in the pickup? They certainly weren't hidden in the house—he'd made a thorough search and hadn't found a single pair. Even his swim trunks were gone. He was a bit surprised that she'd left him his underwear.

If it hadn't been for Casey, he might still be sitting in his skivvies. Instead he was sitting in the cockpit of a seaplane in a pair of Casey's walking shorts. Glancing down at the baggy shorts, he wondered if it wouldn't have been smarter to wear his skivvies. Although Casey was the same height as Logan, he was probably a hundred pounds heavier. On Logan, Casey's baby blue walking shorts looked like oversize boxers and had probably produced just as many smirks as his underwear would have.

"Beggars can't be choosers." He could still hear Casey's mocking tone as he'd handed him the pants. Logan would have loved to wipe the grin off of his friend's face, but he really couldn't afford to be ungrateful when the man had offered him the use of his seaplane. Rather than try to catch her in Casey's Jeep—which Logan knew had a tendency to stall at the most inopportune times—he'd accepted the offer. With only one route out of the Keys, it hadn't taken long for him to spot the orange pickup.

He thought back to the day he'd leased the vehicle, remembering how he'd debated whether it might not be better to lease a car rather than drive around in what the salesman had called an "ultra orange machine." But he'd wanted a pickup, so despite its color, it had become his. Now it was because of that color that he was able to maintain his position tracking Ronni.

And track her he did until she reached the bridge at Plantation Key. At that point he flew on ahead and landed at a marina in Key Largo. There a friend of Casey's handed Logan a set of keys to a silver Mazda. The marina was situated right off the highway, so all Logan had to do was move the car to the edge of the parking lot and wait for the pickup to come by. He didn't have to wait long. As it went cruising by, Logan started up the Mazda and was soon driving behind it.

He stayed far enough back, so that even if Ronni saw the silver Mazda, she wouldn't be able to recognize him. Compared to some of the routes he'd traveled while tailing suspects, following Ronni was relatively easy. Except for a brief stop at a gas station, where she had the attendant fill the tank while she took Steffie into the rest room, she continued to follow U.S. 1. Instead of taking the exit going north, however, she surprised Logan by heading toward Miami.

At first he thought she must have missed the turnoff that would have led her to Melbourne. But when she left the highway and began traveling down a residential section of the city, he knew she hadn't planned on returning to Melbourne—at least not right away. So where was she going? More important, who was she going to see?

He still didn't understand what he'd done to frighten her into running away. Ever since the phone call from Doc she'd been uneasy in his presence. Even if she had overheard his end of the conversation, he didn't think he'd said anything that would have precipitated her leaving. Which left the other possibility—the one that gave credibility to Doc's assertion about Veronica Lang. Logan hated to think he could be wrong about her, but as he followed her into the city of Miami, he had to admit that the possibility that she'd left to meet a contact did exist.

He tailed her for several miles until she finally pulled the pickup into the cement driveway of a modest brick home across the street from a church. Logan drove into the church parking lot and watched Ronni get out of the car with Steffie in her arms. Up to the front door the two of them went, where Ronni rapped on the brass knocker. After several minutes she rapped again, but still no one came. Frowning, she hustled Steffie back to the truck. When she didn't start the engine, Logan wondered if she had decided to wait for the residents of the brick house to return.

He didn't have to wonder for long. Within minutes Ronni was out of the pickup and walking over to the mailbox at the foot of the driveway. Logan watched her slip a piece of paper inside, then get back in the truck and drive away. On his way after her, Logan passed in front of the mailbox. He debated whether he should intercept the message. But then he saw the name stenciled on the mailbox: Mr. and Mrs. Marshall Lang. Peter's parents. They were as straight as an arrow according to Doc's report.

He breathed a sigh of relief. Ronni *wasn't* a spy looking for her contact. She was simply searching for someone she could turn to. He didn't look at the message Ronni had left for her in-laws. Nor did he glance around to see if anyone else was interested in it. If he had, he would have seen the gray sedan that was parked around the corner.

But Logan was too worried about following Ronni to suspect that anyone would be following him. They were in the midst of rush-hour traffic and several times he nearly lost her. He was relieved when she finally pulled into a motel parking lot. Steffie appeared to be fussing as Ronni hauled her out of the car, and he could only surmise that the little girl was probably the reason she was looking for a place to sleep.

He watched her come back out with Steffie, who didn't seem any happier than when they'd gone in, then get in the truck and drive around to the side of the building, where she parked directly in front of room 112. As soon as she had unlocked the door and taken

Steffie inside, Logan went to see the clerk at the registration desk.

Minutes later, he emerged with a hotel key and two cans of soda. He pulled the silver Mazda into the spot that was directly across the courtyard from the pickup, then unlocked the door to his room, which by no coincidence was directly across from Ronni's. Next he turned the knob on the air conditioner to high, then closed the red-and-blue plaid drapes on the large window.

As was typical of economy-motel drapes, when closed they left a gap of about half an inch either in the center or at the sides. He chose to have the gap in the center. Then he turned on the radio on the TV set, settled himself in a square chair and propped his feet up on the other square chair. Through the gap in the curtains he was able to observe Ronni's room without any problem.

Although there was little to observe. Logan watched her carry the two heavy suitcases into the room, one at a time. A member of the motel staff came by with a crib. Then there was no movement until around dinnertime, when room service brought her a tray. Logan, too, ordered room service, then groaned when the tray arrived and he got a look at the economy-motel cuisine. Hungry, he ate the food, anyway, still keeping an eye on Ronni's room through the gap in the curtain. He was washing the meal down with his third cup of coffee when Ronni and Steffie emerged.

For the first time since he'd known her, Ronni was wearing shorts. Other than the quick glimpse of thigh he'd caught yesterday morning, he hadn't seen much of her legs, for she usually kept them hidden beneath the long, flowing skirts of the sundresses she liked to wear.

The sight of slender bare legs was enough to cause his pulse to dance. Ronni and Steffie headed for the children's playground connected to the swimming pool area. Again Logan was able to observe simply by sliding his chair to the end of the window and adjusting the gap in the curtain.

He watched Ronni place Steffie in the dolphin-shaped swing and push her back and forth until the child giggled merrily. Then they both climbed the elephant slide and slid down its metal trunk, shrieking with glee. When Steffie toddled toward the large sandbox, Ronni followed her. She plunked herself down to one side and began scooping sand into a plastic bucket nestled between Steffie's legs. Logan wished he could run outside and join them, but until he was certain she wasn't making contact with anyone, he couldn't risk it.

As the sun began to sink low in the sky, Ronni brushed the sand off Steffie, then carried her back to room 112. Again Logan found himself wishing he could join them. Images of Steffie's red head covered with suds and Ronni's wet shirt clinging to her breasts as she bathed her daughter in the kitchen sink filled his mind, only to be replaced by the memory of how her body had responded to his during their brief but passionate embrace.

He found himself glancing at his watch more frequently as every hour seemed to get longer and longer. After watching the room for nearly seven hours, Logan was tired and there was a dull throbbing in his right eye. He was tempted—even in an economy motel—to stretch out on the bed. It was obvious from the absence of light in Ronni's room that she had gone to sleep. She wasn't a spy. He'd bet his life on it. So what did he expect was going to happen in room 112 tonight? Of one thing he was certain. If anything was going to happen, he wasn't going to miss it. So he popped the top on his second can of soda, which was now warm, propped his feet up and watched some more.

By midnight the neon Full sign on the motel's carport was lit, and there was little activity anywhere. Logan decided to stretch his legs and go for a walk around the parking lot. He crossed the asphalt driveway, stopping to lean against the fence surrounding the kiddie playground, where just hours earlier Ronni and Steffie had frolicked. He regretted not confronting her when it was still daylight. If he were to go pounding on her door in the middle of the night, she would really be frightened. After much deliberation, he decided that first thing in the morning he was going to get things straightened out.

As he was about to step out of the shadows and into the light, he noticed the gray sedan parked across the street. A chill began at the base of his spine and his heart started to beat a little harder as he recognized the car that had been following him when they'd left Melbourne. When two men materialized onc big, one small—Logan's eyes darted to Ronni's darkened room before quickly returning to the two men. The prickly sensation along the back of his neck told him they weren't there by invitation.

They started across the motel parking lot, and Logan's heart began to pound even harder. He watched them slip into the shadow of the overhang and walk the entire length of the motel until they came to room 112. There they paused, as though searching for a key, and Logan felt his body go rigid before a shot of adrenaline electrified him into action.

Logan knew his catlike footsteps wouldn't betray his presence, but he wasn't so sure about his heart. It beat so hard in his chest he felt he could have aroused the sleepiest guest in the motel. As he hurried across the parking lot, he could see they were picking the lock, but before he could reach Ronni's room, the bigger man had slipped inside. Just as he lunged at the man standing guard outside Ronni's room, he saw the light go on and heard Ronni frantically cry out, "Get away from my baby!"

Logan easily took care of the smaller man with a blow to the stomach that caused him to double over in pain. Another quick left sent him to the ground, where he lay half in and half out of the open doorway. But the bigger man caught Logan by surprise, coming at him from his blind side and landing a fist to his jaw that sent him reeling backward.

Flat on his back and momentarily stunned, Logan struggled to clear his head. Slightly dizzy but aware that Ronni and Steffie were in danger, he willed his weak muscles to work together and staggered to his feet, only to see the big man's fist coming at him again. Only this time his fist never had the chance to connect with Logan's flesh, for brittle words split the air.

"Stop or I'll shoot!"

Logan looked past the man's shoulder and saw that Ronni had both her hands wrapped around his gun and was aiming it in their direction. The big man slowly backed away from Logan, who by now was steady on his feet. With deliberate steps, Logan moved closer to Ronni.

"Are you all right?" he asked, noticing the wild expression in her eyes.

She nodded, swallowed with difficulty, then said, "Steffie's crying."

Logan glanced over to where Steffie sat, looking lost and forlorn in the crib, then gave Ronni a reassuring nod. "She's okay and everything's going to be fine. Just keep the gun on these two." Then he turned his attention to the intruders and snapped, "You...up against the wall...both of you." He quickly patted each of them down in a thorough search that produced two weapons.

"Well, well, well," Logan slowly said as he carefully examined the guns. "What have we here? Looks to me like Russian-issue automatics."

"Did Peter send you to take my baby?" Ronni demanded, her cheeks flushed and her eyes flashing as the gun wavered unsteadily in their direction.

Neither man uttered a sound.

"I think you're wasting your breath, Ronni. They look like the silent types to me." Logan pulled out the bigger man's wallet and checked the identification inside. "It says here this is Fred G. Miller. He's even got a union card that says he's a member of the local carpenters' union. Pretty authentic-looking stuff, *Fred*," Logan remarked dryly. "These automatics must come in handy when you're building houses, eh?" He tucked one of the guns into the waistband of his shorts, then handed the other one to Ronni. "Either one of you got anything to say to the lady before she leaves?"

Again both men remained silent, until Logan finally said, "I didn't think so." He shoved Fred's wallet back into his pocket, then ordered, "On the floor, both of you, and put your hands behind your backs." As both men fell facedown on the floor, Logan turned to Ronni. "If either one so much as bats an eyelash, shoot him."

Then he moved over to the bed and began ripping apart a sheet.

"What are you going to do?" Ronni asked nervously.

"I'm going to tie them up and then we're going to get the hell out of here," he said, as his fingers worked quickly tearing the sheet into long strips of cloth. In a matter of minutes he had bound and gagged each of the men until they reminded Ronni of mummies.

"There. That ought to hold them," Logan said soberly. "You can put those down now," he told her gesturing to the guns she still held tightly in her hands.

Ronni gave them a distasteful glance before handing them to Logan. Then she went over to the crib and lifted Steffie into her arms. With eyes closed, she rocked the whimpering child in her arms, whispering soft words of comfort as she clung desperately to her daughter.

Logan wished he could have wrapped both of them in his arms, but he knew that what was important right now was for the three of them to leave. "Come, we'd better go," he advised, placing a hand on her shoulder. "Where are your things?"

"In the closet…and some are in the bathroom," she replied anxiously.

"You've got five minutes to get everything together. I'm going to go settle our bills. When I get back, we'll leave." He started toward the door.

"You're not going to leave me alone with them, are you?" she called out in near panic, motioning to the two men on the floor.

"They are tied up," he reminded her. His words, however, were of little comfort to her, he saw, especially after the trauma she had just experienced. "All right," he conceded. "You take Steffie and go settle the bills and I'll pack your things. You'd better get dressed first."

Ronni glanced down at her cotton nightgown and blushed. "I'll only be a minute," she told him before disappearing into the bathroom. When she returned, she was wearing the same pair of shorts and top she'd had on earlier in the evening, which Logan found was an even greater distraction than the two intruders. "I'm ready," she said, carefully stepping around the two bodies on the floor, then shivering when one of the men groaned. "I've got to get out of here."

Logan opened the door and gestured her outside. After he had pulled the door shut behind them, he said, "I want you to wait for me in the lobby. As soon as I have everything loaded into the truck, I'll drive up to the front door, all right?"

"Logan, about those men...are they really Russians?"

There was a faint tremor in the fingers that reached for his arm.

"Ronni, I don't think this is the right time to be discussing this. Once we're out of here I'll answer all of your questions." He tried to steer her toward the reception area, but she hesitated, confusion clouding her eyes.

Suddenly she started to tremble, and Logan wondered if the shock of what had just happened was finally making itself felt. "They were going to kidnap Steffie. If you hadn't come along..." Her voice quivered with emotion.

"What's important is that I did come along and you and Steffie are safe. But, Ronni, that might not be the case if we don't leave," he snapped a bit impatiently.

For several moments Ronni just stared at him, then, as if she suddenly realized the gravity of their situation, she dug into her purse and pulled out the keys to the truck. ''Please hurry'' were her parting words.

CHAPTER NINE

"WHERE ARE WE GOING?" Ronni asked as the pickup pulled away from the motel, this time with Steffie sitting between Logan and her.

"Someplace you'll be safe," Logan replied.

"I'm beginning to wonder if there is such a place," she said wearily.

"You can quit looking over your shoulder," Logan told her as he headed north on the interstate. "No one's following us."

"How can you be sure?" Ronni asked, wishing she could be like Steffie, who was already drifting off to sleep.

"Those two thugs weren't in any condition to hop in their car and come after us," Logan said dryly. He winced as he rubbed his jaw.

Ronni caught the action and said, "You probably should have put some ice on your face. It looks like it might be a little swollen."

"It would have looked a lot worse than this if you hadn't pulled the gun out when you did," Logan told her, assessing the damage in the rearview mirror. "That big guy had an iron fist."

"If you hadn't come along I wouldn't have had time to get the gun out of my purse. They would have taken Steffie." Her voice was choked with emotion. "I don't know how to thank you."

"You could start by trusting me, Ronni," he said bluntly.

"That seems like a fair request," she agreed. "Logan, how did you manage to find us?"

"I borrowed Casey's seaplane. While you were driving the pickup on the highway, I was flying overhead." A smile played with the corners of his mouth. "I've been following you ever since you left the Keys."

"I thought it seemed too easy," she said, sighing.

"Ronni, why did you run away?" He shot her a puzzled glance.

For several seconds she stared at him, before finally saying, "Because I was frightened."

"Of me?" he asked in disbelief.

"I was so confused. And you weren't making it any easier," she replied, feeling rather foolish now.

"Confused about what?"

"About who the good guys and the bad guys are," she said impatiently, throwing her hands up in frustration. "The FBI said one thing, Andrew said something different, then you said something else. I didn't know who to believe."

"Why didn't you just tell me you were confused? Why did you have to run away?"

"I overheard your phone conversation last night. You were saying something about orders and having to go to Russia."

"I was talking to the senator about your predicament. Is that why you were so nervous when I came back into the living room?"

"You were acting so secretive, and then when you went for your walk, I found several letters on your bookshelves.... Letters that were addressed to you but sent to places in Czechoslovakia and East Germany. Unless I was mistaken, they were written in Russian."

"You thought *I* was a Russian spy?" He punctuated the question with a laugh.

"After everything that's happened in the past few days, can you really blame me?" she asked, her voice rising. "Why were you getting mail written in Russian at an East German address?"

Logan shook his head and exhaled a deep sigh. "Ronni, there is absolutely no reason for you not to trust me. East Germany and Czechoslovakia are only two of the many foreign countries I've lived in working for the government. That career I told you about—the one I left behind—was with the CIA. I'm an ex-agent. You don't need to fear me."

Instead of being reassured by his admission, she was dismayed. "You're a spy?"

"Not a spy in the sense that your husband is a spy," he said defensively, resenting the look of distaste that had spread across her face. "I spent most of my career as a counterintelligence officer, tracking down double agents or agents who defected."

There was a silence while she seemed to be digesting what he'd just told her. When she did finally speak again, her voice was small and distant. "Is that what you're doing now? Tracking down Peter?"

He shook his head. "Peter was never one of our agents. His isn't a case of a U.S. agent gone bad," he explained. "He was recruited as a civilian. And as I told you, I no longer work for the CIA."

"If you're not tracking down Peter and you're no longer with the agency, why did you come after me and Steffie?"

Logan had been asking himself that same question, and had only learned the answer when he'd seen those two thugs breaking into her hotel room. He wondered what she would say if he told her that he was falling in love with her and didn't want to lose her. He doubted she'd be very receptive to such a declaration at this time. There hadn't exactly been a flash of admiration in her eyes when he'd announced he was an ex-agent. So instead of telling her he was finding it difficult to stay away from her or that he wanted to be her hero, he decided simply to tell her the truth—at least, part of the truth.

But before he could say another word, she was angrily demanding, "Were you hired to spy on us?"

"No!" he denied vehemently.

He might as well not have said anything, for she continued on as though she hadn't heard him.

"That's why you were so suspicious of me, isn't it? You were supposed to be finding out if I was a spy. All this stuff about being a friend of Andrew's and wanting to help us out was just a way to find out if I was working with Peter."

"Initially, yes," he admitted, "but that was before Andy had his heart attack, before the feds became involved and before I met you." He wished she would at least look at him instead of staring out the window. "Senator Potter asked me as a personal favor if I would do a little investigating to find out if Andy was in any way connected to Peter. He wanted to know if there was any evidence that could possibly link his son to the spy ring."

"Are you saying that Senator Potter thinks Andrew is involved in this mess?" Her eyes widened as this time he did manage to get her attention.

"Before Peter's defection it was only speculation," he said solemnly. "Now it appears that it's probably true."

"True? How could it possibly be true? Andrew is a good, honest man. I've known him for five years. I even lived with him for a short period. I would have known if he was involved in anything clandestine."

Her defense of Andrew annoyed him. "You mean the way you knew about your husband's clandestine activities?" Immediately he regretted his words. "I'm sorry, Ronni. That wasn't fair. The truth is, one thing that all spies have in common is an ability to dissemble. They're capable of leading two separate lives at one time. I don't want to think that Andrew is involved in this mess, either, but until I hear officially, one way or the other, I have to tell you, it doesn't look good."

"Is that why you went to see him the day of his heart attack? To *accuse* him of being a spy?"

"I wanted to prove he wasn't," he insisted. "The senator has been like a father to me. If there's any way I can spare him pain, I will. I'm on your side, Ronni. I hope Andrew is innocent, too."

She studied his face, wanting to believe him. "But you don't think he is, do you?"

"It might be a case of Andrew having to clear himself. Until he's well enough to be questioned, he'll remain under suspicion. The FBI knows what I know—that he worked for Bartron the same time Peter did, that they were friends...." He paused, as though deliberating whether he should say more, then finally added, "that you two are quite close."

She gave a mirthless chuckle. "That explains the treatment I got from the FBI. I must be their number one suspect, although for the life of me I can't understand why."

"They're only doing their jobs," he rationalized.

"And you would know all about that, wouldn't you, Logan?" She laughed bitterly. "Oh, damn. Why did you have to be one of them?"

"One of them?" He thought it was a good thing he was driving, or else he would have been tempted to shake her. He tightened his grip on the steering wheel. "You make it sound as though I should apologize for wanting to protect our right to freedom. I'm an ex-one of them," he reminded her. "And because I am an ex-one of them I was able to prevent those two goons from kidnapping Steffie." This time he was the one who laughed sarcastically. "You're going to have to forgive me for not understanding this, Ronni, but for some reason I thought that if you knew I was an ex-agent you'd be able to trust me."

"I do trust you," she told him. "It's just that…" She wondered how she could explain her disappointment in learning his real identity. The truth was, she had wanted to believe he had helped her and Steffie because of a personal interest, not because of some favor he owed a senator. She had foolishly let her emotions sway her into believing he had risked his life because he cared about her, and now he was telling her his presence in their lives had nothing to do with his feelings for her.

"What do you want to do, Ronni? I can either take you to stay with me or I can take you back to Melbourne," he stated simply.

"We'll go with you, Logan." She surprised herself with her quick response.

Other than an indolent shrug accompanied by a muttered "Good," he made no effort to indicate he was pleased with her decision. "You'll be safe with me, Ronni."

"I know." She lowered her eyes, acutely aware of the change in his tone. She wished she knew what he was thinking, but unlike her, he was so good at masking his emotions. "Logan, what about those men we left back at the motel. Won't they try to find us?"

"They'll try all right. That's why I don't want to return to my place. Men like that seldom give up until they get what they want."

"They want Steffie," she said, her voice faltering. "I think Peter sent them to take her away from me."

"Ronni, it's not likely that KGB agents would attempt a kidnapping simply because an American defector wants his daughter with him," he reasoned. "There must be more to it than that. I'd have to say that phone call you received wasn't simply a prank. It's possible they hoped to use Steffie as a bargaining tool to get what they're really after."

"And what would that be?"

Logan shrugged. "If we knew, we wouldn't have to be driving around in the middle of the night, looking for a place to sleep."

"Just where are we going?" she asked.

"A friend of mine who is no way connected to the government has a place in Fort Lauderdale," he answered. "That's about an hour's drive. Maybe you should try to get some sleep."

She wanted nothing better than to take his suggestion, but every time she closed her eyes she saw the big, muscle-bound man standing over Steffie's crib. As exhausted as she was, what she needed more than sleep was the assurance that Steffie and Logan were right beside her. Rather than watch the Florida coastline speeding by, she fixed her eyes on Steffie's face, appreciating the serenity in the delicate features. Occasionally she'd glance at Logan's expressionless face and wonder what would have happened had he not followed her to Miami, and such thoughts would bring a shudder.

The remainder of the trip to Fort Lauderdale was accomplished in silence, but it wasn't an uncomfortable silence. When Logan pulled off the interstate and slowed for a blinking amber light in a deserted intersection, Ronni straightened in her seat and asked, "Where are we?"

"About five minutes from our destination," he told her, taking a road that led into a residential section.

Except for the streetlights, the neighborhood was dark until they came to a bungalow with a small illuminated yellow globe over its door. Logan parked the truck in the driveway, then offered to carry a sleeping Steffie inside. Ronni followed him up the narrow walk to the door, where she saw two doorbells, and she realized that the house was actually a double bungalow.

Expecting to see a man who had been a classmate of Logan's at the Naval Academy, Ronni was surprised when a woman answered the door and welcomed them inside. She reminded Ronni of a petite version of her mother, only she had a much warmer smile and a very soft, soothing voice. She didn't seem to be the least bit put out that she'd been awakened at three in the morning, and Ronni could only wonder if Logan had previously brought over other visitors under such strange circumstances.

"I'm sorry to get you out of bed, Mabel," Logan apologized, bending to press a kiss on her cheek as they stepped into the hallway separating the two apartments.

"You know I don't mind," she said, brushing aside his apology with the wave of a wrinkled hand. She unlocked the apartment door on the left. "I've put clean linens on the beds, but I'm afraid the refrigerator is empty. You didn't tell me you were bringing a baby," she admonished gently, looking lovingly at Steffie, who was still asleep on Logan's shoulder.

"Mabel, this is Ronni and her daughter, Steffie," he said casually.

"Such a beautiful baby," Mabel crooned affectionately.

"Thank you." Ronni felt an instant rapport with the older woman and began to relax just a bit. "And thank you for fixing the beds."

"If there's anything you need, I'm just across the hall." She pulled the key out of the lock and handed it to Logan, but addressed her words to Ronni. "Would you like some milk? I'm sure Steffie'll want to eat as soon as she wakes up in the morning." She lowered her already soft voice to a near whisper.

"You're right, Mabel. I would like to borrow some milk if you don't mind," Ronni replied gratefully.

"Not at all. I'll get some for you right away."

"While you do that, I should get the bags out of the truck," Logan said. "Should we put her down on one of the beds?" He was looking at Steffie as he spoke.

"I've got an old crib I keep in the garage, but I'm afraid it's all dusty and will need a cleaning before you can use it," Mabel offered.

"Maybe we can get it in the morning," Ronni suggested. "She'll be all right with me for tonight."

"We can move the bed up close to the wall in this room," Mabel told her, leading the three of them into one of the bedrooms. Instead of flicking the switch to the ceiling fixture, she turned on a small brass lamp sitting on the nightstand between the twin beds. In no time, both beds were rearranged so that together they formed one large one against the wall. While Ronni turned back the covers, Mabel fetched two more pillows from the closet.

"Maybe if you put these along the side, she won't roll off," she suggested, aligning the pillows lengthwise after Logan had gently deposited Steffie on the bed.

"I'm sure she'll be fine until I lie down with her," Ronni said softly.

"Which means I'd better get the suitcases so we can all get to bed," Logan stated in a low voice.

"You wait here with the baby and I'll go get that milk for you," Mabel insisted in a whisper.

During the few minutes they were gone, Ronni casually surveyed the apartment. Like Logan's house, it had only one bathroom, which meant they would be sharing, but at least now that Logan had his own bedroom she wouldn't have to worry about getting up in the night and running into him asleep on the couch. The apartment itself seemed less intimate than his house, a feeling that disappeared the minute he came back inside.

As he carried in her suitcases, she wondered how long she would be staying with him. Some of her uncertainty must have shown. After setting the luggage in the bedroom, he took her hands in his.

"I wish I could erase that frightened look from your face," he whispered.

It felt so good to have his concern, his gentleness. She wondered what he would say if he knew she wanted nothing better than to curl up in his arms and retreat from the world. She wished now she hadn't made such a fuss over his being an agent. But the truth was, she had hoped his interest in her had been responsible for his offer to help them.

She was attracted to Logan McNeil in a way she'd never thought it would be possible to be attracted to a man, and during their drive from Miami, she'd found herself tempted to tell him she wanted him to care about her, not simply feel responsible for her. If there was a frightened expression on her face, it was because being with him was a danger—a danger to her heart.

She was saved from having to say anything by the appearance of Mabel, who brought not only a carton of milk, but a plate of cinnamon rolls, as well. If the older woman hadn't looked so tired, Ronni would have invited her to stay awhile. The air between her and Logan had become charged with emotions she wasn't sure she was ready to face. But after slipping the milk in the refrigerator, Mabel said good-night and Ronni knew she was going to have to face being alone with him.

She told herself they really weren't alone. Steffie was in the other room. Then she looked at him and remembered what it felt like to be kissed by him and she shivered.

Logan mistook the shiver for fear. "I'm going to keep you safe, Ronni. Both of you."

"I know you will," she said softly.

He walked over to a wooden cabinet in the corner of the living room and slid open the door to reveal several glass decanters. "Why don't you let me pour you a brandy? It'll help you sleep."

Ronni didn't object, sinking down onto the leather sofa while Logan filled two glasses with the amber liquid. "This is a nice place," she said, glancing around the room.

"It belongs to Mabel's son, Josh, my old college roommate. He uses it as a winter retreat when he needs to get away from the snowy cold in Maine."

"How long do you think we'll be here?" she asked when he handed her a snifter of brandy.

"It should only be a matter of days before the government uncovers Peter's conspirators." He sat down beside her. "I've been in contact with a couple of our agents overseas and I'm expecting to hear something shortly."

"Does the FBI know we're here?"

Logan shook his head. "No one does, not even the senator. I think it's better that way—at least until we can figure out what it is those men wanted from you. What I'd like to do first thing tomorrow is go over all your recent conversations with Peter, and hopefully something you'll tell me will give us a clue to what it is they're after."

Ronni pushed the hair back off of her forehead with a tired hand. "We can do that, Logan, but I honestly don't think it'll help. Peter and I haven't exactly had lengthy telephone conversations recently. And when we did talk, it was usually to argue over our divorce agreement."

"Until either the feds or my contacts come up with something, it's the best we can do."

She sipped the brandy, letting it warm her insides. "Tell me something, Logan. What causes people to become traitors? As many faults as Peter had, I'm still having trouble understanding why he would do something like this."

Logan shrugged. "There could be any number of reasons, but I'd say the number one lure is money. Unfortunately trading secrets can be very profitable. Was Peter in debt?"

"Probably not more than any other person, although I do know that he had a Swiss bank account. I came across it one day when I was cleaning."

"That doesn't surprise me. As for the other reasons, often the people recruiting spies will look for someone with an alcohol or drug problem, or someone who's dissatisfied with a job."

"Peter had a lot of problems, but as far I know, he was never into drugs. And he seemed to get along all right with his employer, although he always seemed to resent authority." Ronni swirled the brandy in her glass pensively. "He often talked about getting even. I just never thought I'd be the one he wanted to get even with." She couldn't prevent the shudder that overtook her.

"You should get to bed," Logan said, taking the half-empty glass from her. "Listen to me, Ronni." He helped her to her feet so that she was facing him. "You're safe here. No one, and I repeat, no one, knows where you are. You can trust me."

"I do trust you, Logan. And I'm sorry about running away. It seems so foolish now...especially the way I did it." She could feel her skin warm at the recollection of catching him naked in the shower. He smiled, and she knew that he remembered those few minutes, too.

"By the way, where are all of my pants?"

She dropped her gaze to the baggy blue shorts, and felt a giddy sort of guilt that made her want to giggle.

"They're in the back of the pickup in a large green trash bag."

"Great. That means I won't have to go out in public like this again." He managed a big foolish grin. "I have to confess, it was rather humbling for an ex-agent to be caught not only with his pants down but with his own gun."

"I can't believe I did it. I'd never even held a real gun in my hands, let alone point it at someone," she confessed.

Logan laughed.

"What's so funny?" she asked.

"That gun wasn't loaded. I haven't used it in years. Contrary to what the public believes, agents seldom carry guns."

"If you knew it wasn't loaded, why didn't you try to stop me?"

He shrugged. "I guess because at that point I still wasn't convinced you weren't working with Peter." He paused, then added with a half grin, "And there was the possibility that you had found the bullets."

"You mean we stopped those KGB agents with an empty gun?" Again she shuddered, and a wave of weariness washed over her. "I was fortunate you were there," she said softly, her eyes misting over with emotion. "And it doesn't matter why you were there. I'm just grateful you were. I don't know how I'll ever be able to thank you."

"I thought we'd already settled that."

He encircled her in his arms, and the space between them disappeared. "It's called trust."

Then he lowered his head until his lips were only inches from hers, and she could feel his breath caressing her cheek.

She wrapped her arms around his waist and in the seconds before his lips found hers, her eyes looked trustingly into his, telling him much more than words could ever say. Need, desire and promise were all there, and Logan could see that she wanted him the way he wanted her.

His lips moved slowly over hers, softly at first, as though he were reassuring her that he'd never hurt her. For Ronni, it was a kiss that seemed to warm every tiny hollow in her body, yet at the same time reminded her there were places that needed more than warmth; they needed his touch. She moved her arms upward and slid them around his neck, pulling him closer to her as those other places in her body began to ache with her longing for him.

Not quite sure whose body was trembling, Logan responded to the suggestive thrust of her body against his, tightening his hold on her with hands that pulled her intimately against him. Her mouth opened beneath his, and the kiss was no longer sweet but provocative, echoing the hunger they were both feeling for each other.

A groan came from deep in his throat as Ronni let her tongue find his, and instinctively she moved against him in an intimate invitation. Had he wanted to, Logan wouldn't have been able to resist. This time he heard no warning bells, only the wild beating of his heart. Her skin was warm and delectably sweet as he feverishly kissed her neck and her ear, inhaling the ambrosial scent that was hers alone.

Ronni whimpered as his hand inched its way downward and found a burgeoning breast. Through the thin cotton of her shirt, he caressed the beaded tip, while she exhaled a shuddering sigh. When he slipped his hand inside her blouse, her knees threatened to buckle.

"If you keep kissing me like this, I might just melt away," she said breathlessly, her eyes smoky with passion.

Logan eased himself down onto the sofa, deftly pulling Ronni on top of him so that she was cradled in his arms. Then his mouth was crushing hers, and soon they were no longer sitting but lying side by side, legs entwined on the sofa.

"I want you, Ronni," he said thickly.

"I want you, too."

Her voice was whisper soft, yet radiated sensuality. Her admission made him forget she was still legally Mrs. Peter Lang and that she was using a dead woman's identity. It made him forget that she could have been Andy's lover and that the FBI suspected her of being a spy. It made him forget that she could be a honey trap. Right now all she was was a woman he wanted to be a part of, a woman he needed to be a part of him.

While fingers frantically fumbled with buttons and zippers, Logan thought of nothing but what it was going to be like to love her. His breath nearly stopped when her fingers found the hardness of his desire. The last vestiges of self-control were slipping away and Logan's breathing became hoarse as his body moved in an involuntary response to her exploring hands. Sounds of love were all around them...the sound of clothes being removed...the sound of lips trailing kisses across warm flesh...the sound of sighs created by caresses...the sound of Steffie crying.

As if they both became aware of her whimpering at the same time, Logan and Ronni raised their heads.

"Steffie's crying," he said aloud, as though he couldn't quite believe it himself.

"Yes."

Logan didn't think he'd ever heard the word uttered with such anguish. For a couple of seconds, they stared at each other, then both laughed. "I'll be right back," she whispered before getting up from the couch.

Logan slowly sat upright, taking a long, deep gulp of air as he watched Ronni walk out of the room. Although it was only a few minutes, it seemed like an eternity before she returned. Only she wasn't alone. Steffie was in her arms, her face red from crying, her eyes narrowed to tiny slits as she came from the dark into light. Logan silently groaned.

"I think she needs a drink of water," Ronni explained, her eyes telling him she was just as disappointed as he was that Steffie was awake.

Logan remained seated on the sofa, waiting while Ronni took the child into the kitchen. He heard the cupboard open, the faucet being turned on, the soothing words of comfort—and Steffie's stubborn whining. The two of them came back through the living room, Ronni looking frustrated, Steffie looking wideawake.

"I'm going to put her back down," Ronni told him as they passed by.

Logan nodded. "I'll wait for you."

"Ba?" Steffie stretched an arm out toward Logan, who returned the gesture saying, "Bye-Bye."

The two of them disappeared into the bedroom, and almost immediately he heard Steffie begin to cry. It wasn't a sound one could easily ignore, and after a few minutes, he got up and walked into Ronni's room.

"Is she all right?" he asked from the doorway.

"I think it's the strange bed. I'm afraid she's not going to fall back to sleep unless I lie down with her," she said apologetically.

Logan didn't think he'd ever been more disappointed about anything in his lifetime. But Steffie was scrambling across the bed, gurgling and smiling at the sight of him, dissolving his frustration into an almost comic relief. He leaned over and planted kisses on both Steffie's and Ronni's cheeks, then tossed a "Sweet dreams," over his shoulder and sauntered out of the room.

CHAPTER TEN

"LOOK WHAT I FOUND. Not only did Mabel have an old crib in the garage, but this high chair, as well," Logan told Ronni when she waltzed into the kitchen the next morning with Steffie on her hip. He proudly displayed the worn but sturdy wooden high chair he'd just finished scrubbing, tossing his sponge into a bucket of soapy water. "It's missing the pad, but I stuck a towel in here so she won't slide out." He rapped on the wooden seat hidden beneath a blue terry-cloth hand towel, then slid the high chair up to the table.

He was dressed in khaki trousers and a salmon knit shirt that was unbuttoned at his throat, and to Ronni he'd never looked more attractive. "That'll be fine," she said, suddenly self-conscious about what had happened the night before.

Logan reached for Steffie, who willingly went into his arms and received a "Good morning" and a kiss smack-dab in the center of her nose, producing a gleeful sound from the toddler. Ronni looked on enviously.

As though he could read her mind, Logan asked, "Does Mom want a good morning kiss, too?"

She laughed softly. "Not on my nose."

"What about right here?" he asked, trailing his thumb across her lower lip.

No part of him touched her except for his thumb and his warm breath, yet she trembled. Before she could answer, his lips captured hers briefly—too briefly for Ronni, who after last night knew how long a kiss could be.

"Good morning, Ronni," he said with a lazy drawl.

"Good morning," she repeated, swaying slightly as she folded her hands behind her back.

"You smell good...like apples and sunshine," he told her, his breath just a bit more irregular than it had been. "Did you sleep well?" he asked, turning away from her to slip Steffie into the high chair.

"Did you?" she countered. The two words had the power of a magnet, drawing his attention away from Steffie to her.

"I had a little trouble falling asleep," he confessed with a wry smile. For several moments neither one of them spoke, as though silently commiserating about what hadn't happened the night before. Steffie's fussing brought them both back to the present. "Can she have some of this?" he asked, reaching for the box of cereal on the table.

"I'm going to give her some oatmeal, but she can munch on those until I get it ready," Ronni told him, moving over to the refrigerator.

Logan sprinkled a small mound of the toasted O's on the high chair tray. "It's probably a good thing Steffie awoke when she did last night," he said, pulling out a chair and sitting down at the table.

Of all the things he could have said, those were not the words Ronni expected or wanted to hear. She masked her disappointment, however, focusing her attention on the task before her. "You could be right," she said evenly, despite feeling very uneven at the moment.

"We shouldn't be rushing into anything we both might end up regretting."

There was silence except for Steffie's soft familiar hum—the one that accompanied her munching on the cereal. Ronni emptied the packet of instant oatmeal into the bowl, grateful now that she hadn't gone and told him she'd nearly knocked on his door last night after Steffie had fallen asleep.

"You're vulnerable right now, and I'm probably the last man on earth you should be getting involved with," he continued in a tone that sounded as though he were not only trying to convince her, but himself, too.

"It's all right, Logan," she managed to croak, furiously mixing the required amount of water into the cereal before sticking it in the microwave. "You don't need to let me down easy. I understand." Although she really didn't. For the first time in her life she felt as though she might have found a man who was right for her, only to have him tell her he was wrong. Her eyes filled with tears, and before she could stop them, they trickled down her cheeks. When she turned, he was standing next to her, having crept up behind her. She tried to move away from him, but he caught her by the shoulders.

"You don't understand," he said, brushing a silky strand of hair away from her face. With a sense of urgency, he pulled her into his arms. "I'm sorry, Ronni. I don't want to hurt you."

"You're not," she mumbled into his shirtfront, trying to push out of his arms, but he held her forcefully, possessively.

"Look at me," he ordered, and she lifted her tear-stained face to his. "All I'm saying is that maybe we should take it slower. We don't have to come to a complete stop." The tenderness in his expression held her more tightly than the brute strength of his arms. "You've been through so much these past few days, right now I think we should concentrate on getting things back to normal. Why don't we take things slow and easy?"

"Slow and easy," Ronni agreed, forcing herself to ignore the way her mouth ached for his.

As though he knew what she was thinking, he gave her a quick, hard kiss, then eased himself away from her, putting some distance between the two of them in the small kitchen. When the timer on the microwave chimed, he said, "Why don't you get Steffie fed and then after breakfast we'll work at normal, okay?"

During the next few days, Ronni was surprised at how normal everything did seem. It was almost as though she and Steffie had planned a vacation and met Logan and Mabel along the way. Together the four of them would walk to the ocean, which was only a few blocks away, with Logan carrying Steffie on his shoulders. At the beach he'd build castles in the sand that Steffie would mischievously demolish with her shovel and a gleeful shriek.

Other than an occasional phone call from a public telephone booth, Logan gave no indication that he was involved in solving a spy case. After the first morning, when he'd questioned her extensively about her relationship with Peter, he hadn't spoken of the defection or any of the possible consequences. He was acting as though they were on some sort of holiday. They spent days at the beach and evenings playing three-handed cribbage with Mabel.

Ronni was grateful for the older woman's presence, for she enjoyed the stories Mabel told about Logan and her son, Josh. Ronni could tell that Logan was uncomfortable being the subject of conversation, but short of taping Mabel's mouth shut, there wasn't much he could do. Despite Mabel's frail appearance, she was a lot like Ronni's mother—strong willed.

Mabel's presence also helped alleviate the tension between Ronni and Logan, a tension that seemed to be growing with each passing day as Ronni found herself becoming more anxious about her feelings for him. Living together provided an intimacy neither one could deny, yet he managed to keep his distance from her, while an inner battle constantly waged in her between wanting and not wanting him. The better she got to know him, the more she was attracted to him. She often found herself wondering if it was because he was someone she could lean on, which only complicated her feelings for him. If there was one thing she had learned from her marriage to Peter, it was not to be dependent on a man.

At first she'd found Logan's attentiveness reassuring, and she'd wanted him to be the rock she could cling to while she floundered in uncertainty. But as she became more dependent on him, she began to worry that she was enjoying having him take charge of her life. The thought was frightening, since it reminded her of her relationship with Peter and the control he'd exerted over her. She wanted to tell Logan how she felt, only the problem was, how could she explain it to him when she didn't understand it herself?

Her frustration finally surfaced one evening after she'd bathed Steffie and put her to bed. Instead of telling Logan her fears, she confronted him on a totally different issue.

As usual, Logan could tell by a glance at her face she was upset about something. He'd been sitting at the table, doing the *New York Times* crossword puzzle, when she'd swept through the kitchen, banging cupboard doors along the way.

"What's up?" he asked innocently.

She stopped banging long enough to prop her hip against the table and say, "You don't fold your towels correctly."

"I beg your pardon?" Logan looked up, pencil poised.

"In the bathroom." She cocked her head. "The towels ... when they're wet. You fold them over at least four times before you hang them up and then they don't dry."

"At least I hang them up. Isn't that better than leaving them in a pile on the floor?" He grinned, then realized she was not amused.

Without another word, she spun around and vanished out of the kitchen. Logan followed her, easily overtaking her shorter stride. He grabbed her by the hand and pulled her into the bathroom.

Good-naturedly he said, "If you show me the *proper* way to fold a towel, I'll make sure it won't happen again." Once more he tried the grin. Again it failed.

"Just forget it," she retorted somewhat sullenly. "It's not important."

"If it wasn't important you wouldn't have brought it up." He still had a hold of her hand, and was gently massaging her palm with his thumb. He could feel the tension in her. "Go pour us a couple of brandies and I'll refold my towels."

She pulled her hand out of his. "Will you please stop telling me what to do? You're taking charge of my life as though you were my... my..." she stammered.

"Husband?" Logan supplied, arching one eyebrow.

There was a gleam in his eye that dared her to deny the sexual attraction between them. She did.

"No, my father," she shot back stubbornly, stalking out of the bathroom.

Logan followed her into the living room. "There's not a paternal bone in this body where you're concerned."

"Then quit hovering over me like I'm a child who needs to be told what to do."

"I'm not trying to tell you what to do," he denied calmly. "I'm trying to protect you."

"Protect?" she repeated. "Do you realize that when we're not in this apartment, you don't let us out of your sight for a single minute? If anyone even glances at Steffie, you look as though you're ready to sprout fangs. Sometimes I have to peek over my shoulder when I go use the ladies' room just to make sure you haven't followed me in there. Logan, I appreciate your trying to protect us, but you're suffocating me."

Unbidden came the memory of a little girl with blond curls being enveloped by the flames of the explosion. He winced, then turned away from Ronni, the color slowly draining from his face.

"Logan, what is it?" she asked, seeing him sink down onto the couch, his head in his hands. She dropped down on her knees beside him, propping herself at his feet. "I'm sorry. I didn't mean to sound ungrateful," she apologized, placing a hand on his thigh. "It's just that after being married to a very possessive man who tried to run my life for me, I'm not very good at dealing with someone wanting to protect me."

"If I seem overprotective, it's only because I'm trying not to make the same mistake twice." He raked a hand through his hair.

"What mistake, Logan?"

For several moments she thought he wasn't going to tell her, for that neutral expression of his was back in place. But then he said, "The explosion I told you about—the one where I injured my eye—also caused the death of a five-year-old child. A little girl named Michelle Donet."

"And you feel responsible for her death?"

He made a guttural sound. "I was responsible."

"But I thought you said it was an accident?"

He made another derisive sound. "'Carelessness' would have been a better word."

There was no mistaking the emotion in his voice. It was pain—the pain of a man who couldn't let go of guilt, and it brought an ache to Ronni's chest. "Tell me what happened, Logan," she gently urged.

"Ever hear of a dead drop?" he asked. When she shook her head, he continued. "That's when an agent will leave something in a prearranged spot to be recovered by another agent. It's a way of passing information, which is what I thought I was doing when I arranged to pick up a package in a park in the south of France. What I didn't know was that the agent who was passing the intelligence information wasn't only working for the U.S. The package I was supposed to retrieve carried explosives, courtesy of another foreign government." He shook his head at the painful memory.

"And the little girl?" she carefully prodded.

"I had arranged for the exchange to take place in a newly remodeled section of the park that wasn't yet open to the public. And it was deserted, except for one little girl who'd somehow managed to get into the closed area. Before I had a chance to recover the package, her ball rolled under the bench where my package sat. When she went to fetch her ball, she bumped the package, triggering an explosive that was meant for me."

"Oh, Logan, I'm sorry." The words felt so inadequate, but she didn't know what else to say.

"I tried to reach for her, but it was like grabbing thin air. I couldn't save her from the fingers of fire that seemed to swallow her up right before my eyes." He rubbed his hands across his face as though he were trying to erase the memories.

"Surely you can't blame yourself for her death, Logan?"

He shot her a look that told her he did. "I should have been more careful. As I look back now, I see so many things I could have done differently," he reflected, staring absently into space. "I should have figured it out that he was a double agent."

"You were betrayed, Logan. It's sad that an innocent child was killed, but you can't blame yourself." She wanted to ease his pain, but she felt as helpless as someone trying to put out a forest fire with a bucket of water. "You have to accept that it was an accident."

"I want to, but I keep seeing that angelic face." He shook his head in remorse.

"Is that why you quit the Agency?" she asked.

He sneered. "Quit? They retired me. Oh, I could have had some desk job at headquarters, but my field-work days were over. Now I'm not even sure if I'd go back if my eyesight were to return." He absently rubbed several fingers across his jaw. "Sometimes I wonder if subconsciously I didn't slip up because I was tired of living on the dark side of humanity."

"You didn't enjoy intelligence work?"

He considered her question seriously before he answered. "At one time I did." He shrugged. "Maybe one can only do that type of work for so long. It's a murky world, one of deception and betrayal."

"Whatever made you go into it?"

"That was the senator's doing. I guess I had always wanted a career in the government. Politics wasn't for me, so I chose a field where I thought I could make a difference. Save lives, protect our freedom."

He sounded like a disillusioned little boy, and Ronni couldn't help but respond. "You *were* protecting our freedom, and now, you're protecting me and Steffie," she told him, reaching for his hands.

He sighed heavily. "The problem isn't protecting you and Steffie."

He looked at her, and for once she didn't see the unfaltering assurance that was usually there. Gently she asked, "Then what is the problem?"

"I'm afraid I've developed an obsession."

"Are you obsessed with protecting us?" she asked in a husky voice.

Slowly he trailed the tip of his finger across her cheek until he found her mouth. It had been three days since he'd kissed her, yet her lips felt moist, as though his mouth had just brushed hers. He wanted to feel those lips again, and he knew that she wanted it, too.

He leaned forward until his face was only inches from her. "I'm obsessed with wanting you."

The words caressed her cheeks, like silken whispers of longing. "That doesn't sound like a bad obsession to me," she murmured. Her lips parted in anticipation of his kiss, but it didn't happen.

With a groan, he slumped back against the couch and dropped his arm across his eyes. "It's a fantastic obsession," he said in an almost agonized drawl. "Except we agreed to take things slow and easy."

She closed her eyes, wanting to scream in frustration. For days she'd been fighting her feelings for him, denying the longing that swept through her whenever he touched her or came near her. How could he even think slow and easy after so much had happened between them? Infuriated by his self-control, she wanted to yell at him, *I don't give a damn about what we agreed to do. I need to be loved by you.* However, she wouldn't have been able to bear the humiliation should he reject her a second time. Instead she swallowed her frustration and slowly got to her feet.

"It's late. I think I'll turn in."

She paused, giving him the opportunity to say something, but he remained silent, and her hopes that he would change his mind and ask her to stay with him were dashed when he finally uttered, "Good night."

She crept into the bedroom, where Steffie lay sleeping in the green glow of the numerals on the digital clock radio. Instead of undressing right away, Ronni sat down on the end of the bed, mulling over her conversation with Logan. She'd known that he was self-conscious about his eye, but he'd always seemed so sure of himself; she never expected that he would lack self-confidence. For the first time since they'd been together, she felt as if she were the stronger one, and it gave her hope that he might need her just as much as she needed him. She wished now that she hadn't been so quick to say good-night. Hoping that he would still be up, she tiptoed out of the bedroom, only to find the living room empty. It took her a couple of seconds before she realized that he was in the shower—his second shower of the day.

A smile inched over Ronni's face at the thought. She hurried toward the door and, before she could change her mind, turned the knob. This time when she entered the bathroom, there was no gun in her hand. Unlike the house in Key West, where there had been only a shower stall with a plastic curtain, this house had a tub with a glass enclosure. Billowing clouds of steam rose above the top of the panels, but she didn't notice, for her eyes were drawn to the male silhouette discernible through the tinted glass.

Softly she closed the door, then leaned back against it, mesmerized by the blurred naked image. Arms lifted, hands rubbed, and Ronni stood there staring, And absorbing. And appreciating. And anticipating. While she watched, she peeled off her clothes. Hers did not join his neatly folded ones on the vanity, but fell in a heap on the floor. She placed her watch beside his, then took a deep breath.

With a trembling excitement, she quickly closed the distance between her and the tub. Heart hammering, skin tingling, she slid the glass door open and was greeted by a rush of steam. At the movement of the glass panel Logan swung around, and Ronni's breath caught in her throat.

Soapsuds were coasting down the sleek sheen of tanned flesh like icing on a cake. Wet, his hair looked almost black, but it was his eyes that were responsible for the fluttering in her stomach. After their initial look of surprise, they had darkened with another emotion, and were making a thorough assessment of every inch of her naked body. Whether or not he saw out of his right eye didn't matter; she felt as though he did, for both eyes were blazing with desire.

A fine mist had begun to glisten on her skin, when she heard him say, "Aren't you going to come in?"

She turned away long enough to step in behind him. Logan slid the glass door shut, then pulled her under the pulsating stream of hot water, maneuvering her so that her backside was fitted close to his front side.

"Ah! It's hot!" she exclaimed, and she wasn't only talking about the water temperature. She was wrapped so tightly in his arms she could feel the evidence of his arousal burning against her flesh.

"Too hot?" he asked, as rivulets of water ran down her breasts and his hands molded her to him.

"Uh-uh" was the only reply she was capable of uttering, for in his hands was the bar of soap, and he was gliding his lathered fingers across her swollen breasts.

Ronni leaned back against him, and his hands slid lower until she felt their circling motion on the flat of her stomach. She closed her eyes at the exquisite sensations his large hands created as they worked a magic of their own on her skin. He pressed kisses into her neck, nipping at her earlobe before saying, "Does this mean you don't want to take it slow and easy?"

"Uh-uh," she moaned, shivering as his hands slid even lower. "Do you?" She heard the bar of soap drop, then he was turning her around to face him.

"I just want to take you," he said, before crushing her mouth with his. As they kissed, she pressed hard against him, wrapping her arms around his neck.

"Here?" She managed to pull her lips away from his long enough to ask the question.

Logan's answer was to place his hands around her trim waist, then with one swift movement lift her up. Her legs slid around his waist as he guided her down onto him. Holding tightly to him, she cried out his name in a moan of pleasant surprise at the ease at which their bodies were united.

In her mind she had already lived this moment, but never had she expected such exquisite joy as her body moved with his, establishing a private rhythm that only the two of them would ever share. Deliberately, intently, they moved together with a hunger they both understood, a hunger they couldn't have leashed had they wanted to.

It was dazzling, it was delightful, and it was all too soon done. Although they had tumbled over the edge of ecstasy, neither one wanted to still the shuddering, and it was with spent sighs that their heartbeats slowed.

He nuzzled his face in her wet breasts, savoring the sweetness that was threatening to fade. Ronni felt her feet touch the bottom of the tub, and she groaned.

"What's wrong? Did I hurt you?" Logan asked as his hand snaked around her to turn off the faucet.

She opened her eyes and touched his face with a kind of wonder. "Uh-uh. I just don't want it to be over."

He smiled, a devastating smile that held more than a hint of wickedness. "Did you forget? I'm the one who said we were going to take this slow and easy." He slid open the glass doors and reached for a large fluffy towel, then began to dry her skin, smoothing the towel over her shoulders and down her arms. When he reached her breasts, the tips hardened. "They don't think it's over yet, either," he said, pressing a kiss on each nipple.

He continued to towel her dry, arousing all sorts of feelings that never really had a chance to be put to rest. She gasped as the towel slid across her bare thigh, then journeyed up and down each leg. Weak and trembling, she watched him take several quick slashes at his own wet body before dropping the towel on the floor.

"Now it's time for *slow and easy*," he said huskily, then picked her up and carried her into his bedroom.

IT WASN'T STEFFIE who woke Ronni the next morning, but Logan, as he attempted to slip from under her without disturbing her sleep.

But after the night they'd shared, even asleep Ronni was in sync with him and she stirred the minute the warmth of his shoulder disappeared. "Where are you going?" she murmured, pressing her hand against his bare back as he sat up.

He leaned over on one elbow and smiled down at her. "Just thought I'd better test my legs. I'm not sure I can still walk."

A lazy, dreamy grin lit up her face. "It was wonderful, wasn't it?"

Logan kissed her twice, first on the lips, then on her breast, where he pillowed his head. "Unbelievably wonderful. I still can't believe you came into the shower."

"Actually I was going to show you how to fold your towels, but you insisted on showing me soap tricks," she teased, her fingers rumpling his dark hair.

He chuckled and positioned himself so that he had a hand on either side of her head and was looking into her eyes. "I have no scruples when it comes to finding naked women in my shower...." He lowered his face even closer and whispered, "Or in my bed."

"You're not sorry, are you?"

"Does this feel like a remorseful man?" he asked, shifting so that she could feel his arousal.

She laughed seductively as she felt desire flare—loving the power she had over him—loving the power he had over her.

"What about you? We didn't exactly act like two responsible adults," he said softly.

"If you're worried about any possible consequences, you don't need to be. I'm on the Pill," she told him with an understanding smile, while her hands, as if long familiar with his body, were finding his erogenous zones. "Now wouldn't it be wonderful if we didn't have to get out of this bed all day?"

"Ummm-hmmm. It would be," he agreed, his breath growing ragged. "I'm surprised your daughter isn't awake."

"Her biological clock is a little off schedule—probably because of all the moving around."

"Your biological clock sounds perfect," he said, pressing his ear to her breast.

"I've never felt this good—not in my entire life," she said when he looked up at her.

"Me, neither," he admitted, gazing into her eyes. "Who said obsessions can't be healthy?" He gave her one more long, satisfying kiss before hauling himself out of bed.

"Do we really have to get up?" she asked with a cat-like stretch, admiring his naked form as he moved around the bedroom in search of some clothing.

"We promised Mabel we'd take her to the botanical gardens this morning," Logan reminded her, slipping into a pair of pants. "She wanted to be there when they opened."

"Then the botanical gardens it'll be," Ronni declared, wrapping the sheet around her body toga-style as she marched past him, a crooked grin on her face. "We'll be the first ones in line."

As soon as Ronni glanced outdoors she doubted there would even be a line. A heavy rain relentlessly pelted the streets, and after talking to Mabel, Logan decided they would save the gardens for another day. He did, however, suggest that he and Ronni take Steffie for a drive. When they stopped at a gas station, Ronni knew their outing was serving a dual purpose—Logan needed to use the pay phone. There was no telephone in the apartment they were occupying, and she could only guess that to protect Mabel, he never used hers. He still hadn't told Ronni if he'd heard anything about Peter, and she realized that she could no longer pretend the entire problem would go away if she refused to think about it.

"Are you going to call the hospital?" she asked as he parked the truck.

He paused with his hand on the door handle. It was the first time in several days that she'd mentioned the hospital and it reminded him that she had feelings for the senator's son. "There hasn't been any change in Andrew's condition. I would have told you if there had been," he said, an edge to his voice.

"I know that." She saw the defensive look on his face and wondered why the subject of Andrew always created such tension between them. "Maybe I'm just feeling a little guilty. I mean, Andrew's lying in some hospital, fighting for his life, and I'm here with you in what seems to be almost paradise."

The fact that she'd alluded to the night before as "almost paradise" made Logan want to take her straight back home to bed. But her concern for Andrew raised the same old questions in his mind. Automatically his eyes flew to Steffie's red head. Had Ronni found "almost paradise" in Andrew's arms, too? After last night he could no longer ignore the questions he had concerning her relationship with Andy. He needed answers and he needed them now.

"If Andrew is fighting for his life, it's probably because of his own making. And before you waste any more energy feeling sorry for him, maybe you ought to consider that he could be one of the reasons Steffie was nearly kidnapped." The words came out more harshly than he'd intended.

"You have heard something, haven't you?" she accused.

"No, I haven't. And I don't have any concrete evidence, only my gut reaction. But if I'm right, I have to tell you, Ronni, it disturbs the hell out of me to think of your relationship with him."

"And what if you're wrong?" she countered, her voice rising.

Once again her defense of Andrew irritated him like salt on an open wound. "Well, I don't think I am, but even if Andy is innocent, that still doesn't make it easy for me to accept your relationship with him." At this point he didn't care if the whole world knew he was jealous.

"My relationship with him?" she repeated. "What could you possibly object to in my relationship with Andrew?"

"You need to ask me that after last night?"

She looked out the rain-splattered window and quietly said, "Logan, don't do this."

"Don't do what?"

"Don't try to control every aspect of my life for me. I've already been in a marriage where my husband tried to tell me who I could and could not have as friends. I won't let anyone control me that way ever again."

"Friends? Is that how you describe your relationship with Andrew?"

"What else could it possibly be?" She gazed at him, totally perplexed.

"What else, indeed!" he answered sarcastically.

"Logan, you know Andrew." She dismissed his statement with a laugh.

"And according to Senator Potter, you knew him quite well yourself," he retorted.

"I don't know what it is you're accusing me of, but I don't like the sound of your voice." The tilt of her head challenged him.

Logan drummed his fingertips on the steering wheel. When he finally spoke, he looked not at Ronni but Steffie. "One of the reasons Senator Potter asked me to investigate you was that he wanted to find out if Steffie was his grandchild."

Her blue eyes widened. "Steffie his granddaughter? Didn't you tell him that's highly unlikely."

"Highly unlikely? Andrew's got pictures of the two of you all over his house. You were living with him at the time of Steffie's conception. What's so unlikely about someone assuming the child is Andrew's?" he argued.

"You may be a friend of the senator's, but you don't know Andrew if you need to ask me that question." Seeing his puzzled frown, she said, "Logan, Andrew is gay. When I moved in with him, he was involved in a relationship with another man."

Logan was momentarily stunned by the information. After a lengthy silence, he finally said, "I didn't know."

"Neither does his father. Andrew has always been concerned that it might somehow affect the senator's political career," she said quietly. "I thought you would have known, since the two of you were once close."

"Not *that* close," he said under his breath. He sat staring out the front window. "I can't imagine how Doc is going to accept this."

"Does he have to find out?"

"Wicklund and Mahoney might not be the smoothest investigators, but they are thorough."

"Andrew's private life is his own business," Ronni declared in his defense. "He's never hurt anybody with his actions."

"Not that you know of," Logan added grimly.

"Why are you so critical of him?" she demanded.

"Why are you always defending him?" he countered.

"Because I happen to believe Andrew is a good person. When my reconciliation with Peter ended in an ugly scene, he was the one person who was there for me. He's been like a brother to me, and more of a father to Steffie than Peter ever wanted to be. And right now I'm having a very hard time accepting that he could be anything but a friend of ours." Her voice broke and a trembling hand covered eyes wet with unshed tears.

"Look—" he leaned over Steffie's car seat and pulled Ronni's hand from her eyes "—I don't want him to be guilty any more than you do. And if there's any way I can prove he's innocent, I will." He raised her fingers to his lips. "You wait here while I make a couple of phone calls, okay?"

Ronni nodded, holding back her tears as Logan climbed out of the truck and dashed into the public phone booth. He'd parked as close as possible so he could keep his eye on Ronni and Steffie. First he tried calling the senator. When there was no answer, Logan felt relieved. He knew it was going to be difficult to keep information from his mentor, and he wasn't ready to discuss the reason he was certain Steffie was not the senator's granddaughter.

He had better luck with his second phone call, which was to one of his agency contacts. "What do you have for me, Max?" Logan asked, keeping his eye on the pickup.

"Your suspicions about a honey trap were right, Logan." The voice came as sharp as a lightning bolt and Logan felt a prickly sensation along the back of his neck. He wouldn't have been able to keep from staring at Ronni's face had he wanted to.

"It seems our Peter Lang took himself a mistress—a Russian female agent who went by the American name Holly Conrad." Logan closed his eyes and breathed a sigh of relief. "Whether or not he knew she was an enemy agent at the time he started fooling around with her is debatable. At any rate, she's one of the reasons for his defection. But I think the main reason was his son."

"His son?" Logan frowned.

"Yeah. It seems Holly—or I should say Svetlana—was pregnant when she was ordered back to her country. Lang was promised the three of them would be together in Little America. As a linguist, he'll be useful to them there, teaching all those Russkies how to speak like homegrown Americans."

"How old is the baby?" Logan asked.

"Less than a year. Pretty good leverage to use to get Lang to defect, wouldn't you say?"

"Yeah, if he needed to be coerced," he said sarcastically. "Do you know how long he's been working for them?"

"Intelligence estimates maybe as long as five years. At least, that's how long it's been since he was first seen with Svetlana."

Logan glanced over to where Ronni sat looking as though she couldn't hurt a single soul if she wanted to, and he felt an eruption of anger at Peter Lang. How could any man have cheated on someone like her? "What about the public plea for his wife and daughter?"

"Probably staged by the KGB. Word's out Lang left some valuable information behind. She must be in possession of it."

"She doesn't have the foggiest idea what it could be."

"It's got to be something big. They've got their top agents working on this one."

"I'll check with Doc and see if he's come up with anything. And Max, thanks." Logan replace the receiver with a grimace. In less than an hour he'd heard enough to make his stomach feel like the inside of a volcano. Andy was gay and Ronni's husband was an adulterer. How could he relay such information to two people he cared about? The senator was hundreds of miles away; Ronni was several feet from him. He was going to have to tell her something.

He ran the short distance back to the pickup and quickly climbed inside. He didn't start the engine, but turned to look at her.

His concern for her must have shown on his face, for she said solemnly, "You've heard something, haven't you?"

"There's no news from the hospital, but I did find out some information about Peter," he told her honestly. "Have you ever heard of Little America?"

Ronni shook her head.

"It's an intelligence training school in the Ukraine where Soviet spies are taught to think and behave like Americans. It's a model of a small American city, complete with department stores and fast-food restaurants. Newspapers are American, so is the currency, and English is the only language spoken, so that when the trainees are sent to the U.S., they'll know how to talk and act like Americans. Peter's going to be an instructor there."

"Peter a teacher?" She blinked at him, surprised. "That's rather ironic."

"Why do you say that?"

"He always scoffed at the teaching profession—at all levels. One of the reasons he went to work for Bartron was that he said there was no money in teaching."

"It could be that as an instructor in Little America he'll hold a position of honor. Although he's going to discover that honor has different meanings to different people."

"He's always been the kind of man who's done what he wants, when he wants. It's hard to imagine him in such a rigid environment," she said pensively. "What if he doesn't like it and wants to come back?"

"You mean redefect?" At her nod, he said, "There have been instances where we've traded jailed operatives for our own people. In Peter's case he would probably face criminal charges if he were to return to the U.S." She had a faraway expression in her eyes, and for just a brief moment he felt threatened by her feelings for another man. "Would you want him to return?"

"No."

The response came swiftly and firmly, pleasing Logan. "I don't think it's something you need to worry about. I doubt he'll be back," he told her confidently.

"I'm wondering what's going to happen with our divorce. He never signed the papers," she said unhappily.

Again Logan felt a surge of anger at Peter Lang. "It'll all work out," he said, then turned his attention to the key in the ignition.

"Is that it? Was that all you learned?"

"That's it," he lied, looking out the windshield rather than at Ronni. As they drove home, he debated whether he should have told her everything he'd found out about Peter. Even if she was through with the marriage, how would she react to learning that her husband's defection was the result of a honey trap—that it wasn't simply a case of greed driving him to become a traitor. Personally he didn't want Ronni to know that Peter had been having an affair with a Russian spy while he was married to her. Or that he'd had a son with that spy. Or that the son was the reason he'd chosen to give up his citizenship. Because if she did react strongly, he just might think she still harbored feelings for the man, and that thought was unbearable.

Parts of the puzzle were slowly falling into place, although one of the pieces he'd found today troubled him. If Peter Lang had such strong paternal feelings, why would he leave without his daughter?

CHAPTER ELEVEN

AFTER HIS CONVERSATION with Max, Logan knew that as much as he dreaded calling the senator, he had no choice. When he finally managed to reach him the following afternoon, Doc was able to confirm Max's information, and Logan learned the reason for the KGB's interest in Ronni. When Peter Lang had defected, he'd taken classified information on several strategic defense weapons. He had left behind, however, the code that would access electronic control of the weapons. According to Doc, that information was on a computer microchip stolen from Bartron. Despite Logan's assertions that Ronni knew nothing about any missing microchip, Doc wasn't convinced she wasn't somehow connected to its disappearance. Logan assured the senator that he would speak to her about it. Because of Mabel's presence, however, that wasn't possible until late that evening.

"We need to talk." He stilled Ronni's hands, which were busy clearing glasses off the kitchen table. Just minutes earlier he and Ronni had been playing cribbage there with Mabel.

"Something's bothering you, isn't it? I thought you seemed rather preoccupied during dinner." A frown transformed her serene expression into one of apprehension. "What's wrong?"

Logan wished he could tell her that everything was all right—even though he knew it wasn't. He nudged her toward the living-room sofa and pulled her down onto his lap.

"I was finally able to reach Doc this afternoon."

"And?" She looked at him expectantly.

"I know why the KGB are following you. Apparently when Peter defected, he made off with a pile of military secrets. For some reason, though, he left behind the one piece of information that would make those secrets worth anything."

"Why would he do that?" she asked, puzzled.

Logan sighed. "If only we knew the answer to that question. Right now all we do know is that the information everyone is looking for is on a programmable computer microchip that is so small it's not even easily seen with the naked eye. And from everything that's happened, you're the primary candidate for having it in your possession."

"That's ridiculous! I don't have any computer chip!" she protested. "I haven't even seen Peter since last Christmas." She dismissed the idea with a toss of her head.

"He's been back to the United States at least three or four times since Christmas, Ronni."

Surprised, she said, "I had no idea." Slowly she shook her head. "He must not have wanted us to know he was here. I can understand he didn't want to see me, but why wouldn't he want to see Steffie?"

He squeezed her hand in an effort to reassure her. "It doesn't make sense to me, either, unless he was so deep into espionage he couldn't risk it. There's a strong possibility Peter didn't obtain that information without inside help. Someone who was an expert in computer technology.''

Ronni sighed. ''You mean Andrew, don't you?''

''Whoever it was at Bartron, he was clever enough to prevent the theft from being discovered until after Peter defected.''

She nibbled on her lower lip thoughtfully. ''There's something I think you ought to know, Logan. Peter once questioned whether Steffie wasn't Andrew's child—just as the senator did.''

''He didn't know Andy was gay?''

She shrugged. ''Oh, he knew all right, but in his perverse mind he couldn't understand how any woman could live with a man and not sleep with him. Then, when Steffie was born with red hair, he drew his own conclusions.''

''He doesn't deserve a beautiful child like Steffie,'' Logan told her quietly.

''No, he doesn't,'' she agreed, a lump starting to form in her throat. ''And I can't tell you how many times I wished he wasn't her father. I still remember when the doctor told me I was pregnant. I burst into tears. Not because I didn't want to be a mother, but because I knew that my baby hadn't been conceived out of love.''

Logan reached out to gently stroke her hair, then pressed his fingers across her cheek. ''Did he force himself on you?''

''No, but it was an unpleasant, meaningless act that left little doubt in either of our minds that there was nothing to salvage from our marriage,'' she said, keeping her voice low. ''I didn't see him again until he came to the hospital the day after Steffie was born. And I can count the number of times I've seen him since, which is why I don't understand how anyone could think I have knowledge of some missing microchip.''

Right now her eyes were more gray than blue, Logan noted, as they became cloudy with alarm.

"What about by mail? Did he send you anything recently... any packages?''

"No. He didn't even send Steffie a present on her first birthday," she answered, unable to hide her disappointment at his thoughtlessness.

Logan absently rubbed his thumb over her hand while he stared into space. "I keep thinking that your not going to Vienna must somehow be the key to all this. At first I thought Peter deliberately left the microchip behind as a type of insurance for you and Steffie joining him in Little America. But he had no way of knowing you weren't going to be on that plane." He paused, then added, "Did he ask you to bring him anything in Vienna. A package of any sort?''

"There was only one thing I was supposed to bring him—the divorce papers," she said sharply. "I just don't see how I could possibly have any connection with this microchip.''

"Unfortunately the KGB believes you do have some connection to it, which would account for the kidnapping attempt," he said soberly.

"And what about the U.S. government? Do they think I have it, too?''

He wished he could tell her the FBI believed her story, but he knew how important it was to be honest with her, so he answered truthfully. "I'm afraid they do."

"But do they think I have it because I'm working with Peter—or do they think I have it but don't know I have it?''

Logan couldn't help but smile at her innocence. "I don't think they're sure themselves. You *were* scheduled to meet Peter in Vienna, which by the way is a nest of KGB activity. I've done everything in my power to convince Senator Potter you're innocent."

Anxiously she asked, "And do you think he believes you?"

"He's not as convinced of your innocence as I am," he admitted. "But, then, he doesn't know you the way I do." He twirled a strand of her blond hair around his finger. "With everything that's happened to Andy, I think he's letting his emotions cloud his judgment. Of course, he thinks I'm letting my feelings for you cloud my spy common sense."

"And just what are those feelings, Logan?" she asked, her eyes searching his.

He brought the strand of hair to his lips. "Do I need to tell you after last night?"

His voice had become husky, reminding her of how it had sounded when he'd murmured words of endearment and passion.

"Some things can never be overstated," she said softly, her eyes on his mouth.

The vulnerability on her face tugged at his heart. He wrapped his arms around her, hugging her close as he burrowed his face in her hair. He wanted to tell her that he loved her, but he wasn't quite sure if he was ready to admit it to himself. It had all happened so fast. He hadn't expected their lovemaking to unleash such an overwhelming need for her, an all-consuming desire to be with her.

"Let's go to bed," he whispered into the perfumed hollow of her ear.

"Yes," she said simply, then giggled as he attempted to rise with her in his arms, but somehow in the process managed to send them both tumbling back against the cushions.

"Some kind of hero," he grumbled as Ronni playfully slid off his lap and got up.

"I don't need a hero. I need you," she told him with desire dancing in her eyes.

Logan stood, too, and this time easily lifted her into his arms, then carried her into the bedroom.

IT WAS HOURS LATER when Ronni awoke. Slivers of moonlight were tracing patterns on the wall and she wondered what it was that had caused her to wake from such a peaceful sleep. Warm and secure in Logan's arms, she could hear his even breathing. But it wasn't enough to feel the powerful muscles of his chest. She needed to see him, to look at his face, softened by repose. As she gingerly attempted to reverse her position, she felt the hand on her hip caressingly move across her thigh and a pair of lips nuzzle her nape.

"Can't sleep?" he murmured, raising his head to examine her face.

"I'm sorry. I didn't mean to wake you." She traced the outline of his lips with her fingertip.

"I love waking up next to you," he whispered, pulling her closer, his hands gently stirring the embers of passion, barely extinguished from their earlier lovemaking.

Ronni sighed dreamily, shifting her hips to welcome his touch more easily. They'd only been together a little over a week, yet what she was feeling for him was so strong she couldn't bear to think of what would happen to them once she was no longer in any danger and she could return to her home in Melbourne. "What's going to become of us, Logan?"

"We're going to find the missing microchip and return it to the U.S. government. My contacts are working on this, Ronni, and it's only a matter of time until we learn who Peter's conspirator here in Florida is."

He sounded so confident, so optimistic, she couldn't do anything but nod in agreement. His words, however, did little to ease her concern. More important than unraveling the mystery she'd been caught up in was her worry over what would happen to their relationship after that mystery was solved. Right now, she didn't want to think that she might lose Logan, for that would be a greater danger than any other peril she'd encountered.

"I really don't think it'll be much longer," he told her, his hands traveling across her naked flesh.

"Do you still believe that Andrew's involved?"

The mention of Andrew's name stilled his roving hands and he shifted uncomfortably. "Ronni, I think you should know that Andy saw Peter when he was in the States in May."

"Yet he never told me." Sadness etched her words. "Why would he do something like that—especially when he knew that Peter was behind on his child support payments?"

He wished he could get her to accept that Andy wasn't the paragon of virtue she thought he was. "The obvious reason would be that he, too, was trying to keep Peter's visit secret."

She sighed. "Maybe. Have you told Doc about Andrew being gay?"

Logan exhaled a ragged breath. "I couldn't . . . not with everything else that's happened. He's worried enough over Andrew's physical condition." He propped himself up against the pillows, pulling her into the crook of his arm.

"But you did tell him Steffie wasn't his granddaughter, didn't you?" she asked, resting her cheek against his chest.

"Yes. I think I was able to convince him Andrew isn't Steffie's father, although it wasn't easy."

"If the senator believes that I'm a spy, I would think he'd be relieved to know that his son didn't father my child." Bitterness laced her tone.

"Don't be too hard on the man, Ronni. He's only seen pieces of the puzzle. If he knew you the way I do, he wouldn't have a doubt in his head." His hand was again tracing patterns on her skin, traveling to places warm and soft. "On second thought, I don't want him knowing you the way I do. I don't want any man knowing you the way I do."

"No man ever has, Logan." His hand had found the now familiar spot where he could reawaken desire with a tender caress. "You've touched me places I never even knew existed. You've created such a hunger in me I find myself lost in erotic daydreams, wishing for nighttime to come so that we can be together. We've only known each other a week, yet you know me more intimately than anyone ever has. I have no secrets from you," she whispered. "You seem to be able to see right through me. Only you know the real Ronni."

"The real Ronni," he repeated. He slid his hands to her breasts, where he gently circled her nipples with his thumbs. "You definitely are real." Then he looked deep into her eyes and said, "Even if you aren't really a Ronni."

Despite the fact that he was nearly driving her insane with his touch, she was lucid enough to hear him clearly.

She stiffened, but he didn't seem to notice. "Umm, you taste good," he said, replacing his thumbs with his lips.

"Logan, what did you say," she asked, shifting beneath him.

"I said you taste good," he repeated.

"No, before that."

Puzzled, he looked up at her.

"You said something about even if I'm not Ronni." She was frowning. "What did you mean?"

He could see that she was more than curious, she was disturbed. "I just meant that it doesn't matter to me what your real name is. There are good reasons for people to change their names. I know you're not a spy," he continued. "That's all that matters."

Ronni sat up and reached for the lamp. "Change my name? Logan, what are you talking about?"

The sudden burst of light caused Logan to squint uncomfortably. Ronni had pulled the sheet up over her breasts and was looking at him inquisitively. As Logan gazed into her bewildered face, he realized that she had no idea what he was talking about. Could it be that her mother had never told her the truth? Twenty-five years of using an assumed identity meant that Ronni was only three when she became Veronica Summers.

"Logan, tell me what you meant!" she demanded, pulling her knees up to her chest and clutching the sheet.

There weren't enough derogatory adjectives to describe what he thought of himself at that moment. Reluctantly he said in a low voice, "You and your mother are using assumed identities."

She laughed nervously and brushed a strand of hair away from her face in an almost childlike gesture. "That's absurd! Where would you get such a crazy idea?"

"Because you've been under investigation by the government," he said in an even lower voice. "The day Andy suffered the heart attack, Senator Potter informed me you and your mother were using false identities. That's one of the reasons I was so suspicious of you when we were traveling to Key West."

"I don't understand. Are you trying to tell me that my mother and I aren't Clara and Veronica Summers?" Again there was disbelief in her face, and the color was slowly disappearing from her cheeks.

"Clara Summers and her daughter, Veronica, were killed in an automobile accident in Madison, Wisconsin, twenty-five years ago."

Her face grew even whiter. "No!" She shook her head defiantly. "I'm Veronica Summers," she insisted. "You're wrong! I've got a birth certificate and..." Her eyes met Logan's and tears slowly began to spill down the paper-white cheeks. "Tell me it isn't true," she pleaded.

"I'm sorry, sweetheart. I thought you knew." He tried to pull her into his arms, but she stiffened and pushed him away.

Impatiently she swiped at the tears with the palm of her hand, then said, "My mother's best friend lives in Madison. We're originally from Eau Claire, which is where my father died." Her brows drew together in a frown. "That is, if he was my father. If I'm not me, then maybe he's not him." The look she gave Logan was almost desperate. "Oh, my God, if I'm not Veronica Summers, who am I?"

He took both her hands in his. "You're still you, Ronni. A name doesn't change who you are. It's the person inside that counts. You're bright, compassionate, beautiful, and it doesn't matter what name your mother gave you."

"But everything she told me about my family must have been a lie!" she sobbed. "That must have been why she never wanted to talk about my father." She wrenched her hands free of Logan's, climbed out of bed and started to pull on her clothing. "This is horrible!"

"What are you doing?" he demanded.

"I'm getting dressed." Restlessly she prowled the room, searching for the garments that only hours earlier had been scattered about in passion. "I need to talk to my mother." She was trembling so badly she had to sit down on the bed to pull on the lacy underwear. "She'll be home the day after tomorrow and I intend to be in Melbourne when she arrives."

"Ronni, it's after midnight." Logan got up and donned his pants.

"I don't care what time it is," she said irrationally, then shrugged away from his second attempt to take her into his arms.

This time Logan was not about to be rebuffed. Lovingly but firmly, he gathered her trembling body close, cuddling her in the same way he'd learned to soothe Steffie when she was having one of her temper tantrums. "I know this has been a shock, and I'm sorry, Ronni." He kissed the top of her head. "I would never have mentioned it to you if I had thought you didn't know about it."

"Logan, please take me back to Melbourne," she cried, as the tension slowly eased out of her body.

"I wish I could." He continued to massage the back of her head, holding her tenderly, gently rocking her. "But until that missing microchip turns up or the feds crack the case, it's just not safe for us to leave here."

When the tears were spent and she appeared to be back in control, Logan loosened his hold on her.

Ronni eased herself from his grasp and put a little distance between them. "I've got to go back, Logan. Don't you see? I don't know who I am. All this time I've been thinking I'm somebody I'm not."

Calmly Logan asked, "So what are you going to do?"

"I'm going to go to my mother's apartment and search until I find something—I don't know what—but something that will tell me who I am."

He watched her flitter around in search of her shoes. "And are you going to wake up Steffie and drag her out of here in the middle of the night, putting her life in danger because you have to search your mother's apartment?" He raked a hand through his sleep-tousled hair. "Ronni, have you forgotten that the KGB caught up with you when you stopped at your mother-in-law's house? Don't you think they'll have someone watching your mother's house, as well?"

"You tell me. You're the spy," she said nastily, kicking his shoe out of her way with a vengeance.

He ignored her gibe. "What if you go there and you don't find what you're looking for? You'll be putting two lives at risk for nothing."

"Nothing? Finding out who I am is certainly not *nothing* to me, Logan."

"Of course it isn't," he said consolingly. "But you don't know if your mother has any documents that will tell you what you want to know. As far as you can tell, she's the only one who knows the truth, and she's not even there. All I'm asking is that you give me a couple of days. If I haven't heard something by then, I'll take you to see your mother in person...I promise."

He could see her prickly edges softening. He extended a hand to her and said, "Come on, Ronni. Trust me. I haven't let you down yet, have I?"

She placed her hand in his and let him pull her back down beside him on the bed. Her body slouched against his.

"First thing in the morning I'll call the senator and my other contacts, all right? Maybe there'll be some good news and we'll be able to leave tomorrow." Slowly he began to ease the cotton shirt from her shoulders. Ronni didn't protest, but allowed him to undress her as though she were a child.

When she was once again naked, he gently laid her back on the pillows.

"Don't leave me, Logan," she called out softly when he would have gotten up from the bed to fold her clothes.

He moved her skirt and blouse to the end of the bed, then climbed in beside her. "I'm right here, Ronni." He placed a butterfly kiss on her forehead. "Don't worry about a thing. I'm going to take care of everything. I promise."

She snuggled down close to his bare chest and murmured, "Right or wrong, I'm glad."

"Shhh. It's definitely not wrong." He kissed the top of her head.

But as right as it felt to be in his arms and let him take care of her, Ronni couldn't help but wonder why she seemed destined to have a man take charge of her life for her. At the moment, however, she was too emotionally drained to deal with those feelings. Right or wrong, she needed Logan, and clutching him to her, she fell asleep.

RONNI AWOKE to find herself alone in the bed and Steffie babbling from the other room. Logan was neither visible nor audible. She felt a moment of panic when she reached Steffie's room and there was still no sign of him in the apartment. Carrying Steffie into the kitchen, she found a note on the table saying he had gone to fetch a newspaper and some milk, which by now Ronni knew meant he had gone to make a few phone calls.

There was no indication he had eaten any breakfast, so after feeding Steffie her usual oatmeal and fruit, she whipped up some pancake batter and made a fresh pot of coffee—partly because she was hungry, but mostly because she needed to keep busy. Ever since she'd awoken, her thoughts had been consumed with questions about her identity, the biggest one being why. *Why* had her mother assumed a dead woman's identity?

Until last night, she had thought her worse nightmare was Peter's defection. Now she could only wonder if she would ever be able to make the nightmares end. She tried to remember what her life had been like back in Melbourne. Her students, the other teachers at the school, even the school building itself, were out of focus in her memory. All except Billy Johnson.

Billy had been one of her second-grade students, who had spent an inordinate amount of time asking her the same question—did hospitals ever get their babies mixed up? Because their family life unit dealt with babies being born in hospitals, Ronni hadn't paid much attention to what seemed to be normal curiosity. Billy was more inquisitive than the average child and asked more questions than the rest of the second grade combined, so Ronni didn't find anything unusual in the boy's query.

It soon became apparent that Billy wasn't simply preoccupied but troubled. It was only when she had her students bring in family pictures for the bulletin board that she learned the reason why. Everyone was eager to have his or her photograph tacked to the cork board—everyone except Billy.

"Billy, didn't you bring a picture of your family?" Ronni asked.

"Yes, Mrs. Lang," he dutifully replied, but she could see he was reluctant to hand her the snapshot of five people gathered around an elderly couple. "That's me and my brother, Aaron, and my sister, Heather," he told her, pointing to the three children in the photo.

"And your grandma and grandpa, and your mom and dad," Ronni finished for him. "Although you wouldn't have had to tell me that was your dad," she said, indicating the tall man behind Billy. "You look just like him."

Eyes that had been downcast gazed up at her in joyful disbelief. "I do?" he asked with a look similar to the one he'd given her when she'd told him he'd scored the highest in the class on his math test.

Ronni studied the picture carefully. "Yes, you do. Especially in the eyes. But I think you have your mother's nose."

"My mother's nose?" he repeated, unconsciously wrinkling his nose.

"Well, actually it's your nose, but you're very lucky to have one that looks just like your mother's," Ronni told him with a grin.

By now Billy was beaming. "Do you really think I look like them?"

"Yes, but I'm surprised you haven't heard that before."

"Uh-uh," he said solemnly.

"Never" would have been more accurate, for at parent conference time, Ronni had learned that the standard line around the Johnson household was "Where did Billy come from? He doesn't look like anyone in the family. Do you suppose they got him mixed up in the hospital?" What adults had viewed as playful teasing, Billy had taken to heart. At age seven, he was suffering from an identity crisis. He didn't know who he was, despite a birth certificate and two parents who assured him he was their son.

At the time Ronni had been compassionate and had done everything she could to reassure Billy that he really was Billy Johnson. Only now, however, did she really understand the traumatic feelings the small child had had to deal with.

Billy *was* his mother and father's son. She didn't even know if she was an adopted or a natural child. She'd always assumed her mother had given birth to her, but if her mother had changed her identity when Ronni was three, could it be possible that—

"We're going to have frothy orange juice if you stir any harder."

Logan's voice brought Ronni out of her daydream. She removed the wooden spoon from the pitcher and turned her attention to the pancake griddle.

"You were up early," she commented, hoping he'd say he had some news—any news—for her.

"I went for a walk." He had a carton of milk in his hand, which he placed in the refrigerator. "Are you all right?" he asked over his shoulder as he reached for a cup of coffee.

"I'm fine," she replied, knowing perfectly well that she wasn't, but she was determined to be strong for him.

She poured two large round circles of batter on the griddle. "I still want to go back to Melbourne, though."

"Just one more day," he pleaded, holding up one finger.

Silently she wondered how she could take one more day. Aloud she said, "If you think it'll make a difference." She thought she heard a sigh of relief at her agreement.

"Why don't we take Steffie to the park? Or maybe we should go to Ocean World and see the porpoise show? Mabel told me they have dolphins and sea lions that you can feed. I think Steffie would like it. What do you say? It would do you good to take your mind off things," he coaxed.

Carefully she flipped the golden-brown pancakes, then looked at him. "All right, but I can't help but wish we were driving back to Melbourne."

Little did she know that her wish was about to come true.

CHAPTER TWELVE

RONNI HAD INVITED Mabel to accompany them to Ocean World, but she had politely declined as she had already made plans to spend the day with friends. It was a typical summer day—very hot and very humid. Ronni thought it was too hot to be strolling through a marine-life park with a fifteen-month-old child, but Logan was determined to take them. So she tied a bonnet under Steffie's chin, smeared her with suntan lotion and smiled when Logan opened the door for her.

They hadn't gone more than six blocks from the house when Ronni realized she'd left without Steffie's pacifier.

"Logan, we're going to have to go back," she said regretfully. "Steffie doesn't have her plug."

He shrugged, saying, "No problem."

They were near the entrance ramp to the highway, where cars sat bumper to bumper, barely moving in the heavy traffic. It took quite a bit of patience to turn the vehicle around under such conditions, but Logan managed to accomplish the task without losing his temper—which was what Peter would have done had he been behind the wheel. Something so trivial as forgetting Steffie's pacifier would have provoked an outburst of hollering and disparaging comments from Peter, but Logan didn't seem affected at all by the inconvenience.

"I'm really sorry, but I'm afraid if we don't go back she'll get cranky on us," Ronni apologized.

"We're in no hurry," he told her, giving her an understanding smile.

Again she found herself comparing the two men, and as usual, Logan appeared to have all the positive qualities Peter had lacked—patience, honesty, optimism and a sense of humor. It was no wonder she was attracted to him. He was everything she'd always hoped to find in a man, and just looking at him made her feel like smiling. What she had with Logan made her relationship with Peter seem empty and cold. She felt more intimate with Logan after knowing him only eight days than she had after eight years of marriage with Peter. And for the very first time in her life she wasn't lonely.

As the truck retraced its path down a street bordered by canals, Ronni could feel herself relaxing, despite the delay because of traffic and Steffie's absent pacifier. When Logan turned onto Mabel's block, she could see the palm trees lining the boulevard, their fronds gently swaying in the hot summer breeze, and she marveled at how comfortably familiar the neighborhood felt to her after such a short time. She was about to tell Logan she would run inside for the pacifier if he would wait in the car with Steffie, when he made an abrupt turn into a driveway several houses from Mabel's.

"What are you doing?" she asked as he brought the pickup to a halt beside a strange house.

"Mabel's got company," he said by way of an explanation, rolling down his window. "Two men with bodies by Schwarzenegger."

Ronni leaned forward to look around Steffie's car seat. "I can't see anything," she said, craning her neck to peer through a thick green hedge that separated two yards.

"They've slipped around to the back door. My guess is once they realize there's no one home they'll move inside." His voice was barely over a whisper.

"You think they're KGB?"

"I don't think they're selling vacuum cleaners," he returned dryly.

"But how did they find us? You said not a soul knew where we were?" There was a hint of panic in her voice.

The question was a sobering one for Logan—one he didn't want to answer right at the moment. Only one person knew of their whereabouts, and it cut like a knife to think that someone he trusted could have betrayed him. "Do you think anyone's home here?" He nodded toward the Spanish-style stucco house whose driveway they were occupying.

"There's a child's tricycle out back," she observed, "and laundry on the clothesline."

"Here's what I want you to do. Leave Steffie with me and go knock on the door. Tell whoever answers to call the police. Say you think someone is robbing your aunt's home," he instructed calmly.

"You want to call the police?" she asked, surprised.

"I don't want those two Tarzan types busting up Mabel's place." Seeing her apprehension, he added, "The local police aren't looking for you, Ronni."

"No, you're right." She unbuckled her seat belt.

"All you have to do is tell the person who answers the door to call the police, then come right back to the truck, okay?"

She nodded, exited the pickup and on wobbly legs went up to the house.

Logan watched as a young woman who looked to be about the same age as Ronni answered the knock. She appeared to be listening intently as Ronni made a sweeping gesture with her arm that had the woman looking first at Logan and Steffie, then in the direction of Mabel's place. The young woman nodded vigorously before closing the door, and Ronni came hustling back to the truck.

Logan leaned over to let her in.

"She's calling right now," Ronni said a bit breathlessly, quickly sliding back into the truck. "Now what?" she asked.

In answer, Logan shifted into reverse and backed out of the driveway. He drove to the end of the street, positioning the pickup so they could easily see Mabel's back door. "Now we wait for the police to get rid of them for us," he told her with a smug grin.

Within minutes the whine of a police siren could be heard and the two Schwarzenegger types came bounding out of the house. "Surprise, surprise," Logan mumbled as the two men were caught red-handed fleeing from the house. Logan and Ronni watched the pair get frisked and handcuffed before being escorted to a squad car. It was only after they'd been herded into the back of the police vehicle that Logan drove the truck around to the front of the house.

"Let me handle everything, all right?" he told Ronni as he parked behind a second police car, which had arrived ahead of them. She consented with a nod, too disconcerted to protest. "I want you and Steffie to wait here until I get everything straightened out. It shouldn't take long." He reached across to give her shoulder a reassuring squeeze before leaving.

Ronni watched him head straight for one of the policemen. Hands gesturing demonstratively, he spoke to the officer, occasionally glancing in her direction. At one point during the conversation, the officer took a couple of steps toward the truck, then stopped, obviously swayed by something Logan had said. But what? she wondered.

When Logan and the policeman disappeared into the house, she wanted to rush in after them, for the two Schwarzenegger types had spotted her sitting in the pickup and were staring at her with venomous expressions. She deliberately turned her back to the window, but they still managed to put an icy feeling in the pit of her stomach and it wasn't until Logan came back outside that she was able to relax.

He opened his door and with one hand on the roof of the truck leaned in to speak to her. "They didn't have time to do much damage inside, although there is a bit of a mess. Mabel's apartment wasn't touched—only ours."

"Do you think they were looking for the microchip?"

"Probably. As far as I could see, nothing's missing. According to the police, the men didn't have any stolen goods on them when they were apprehended."

"What are we going to do now?"

"We're going to pack our things and get out of here just as soon as we possibly can."

"Who were those men?" she asked, as the police car carrying the two intruders pulled away from the curb, its red lights flashing.

Logan looked up and waved a hand at the departing policemen before saying, "It doesn't matter. We'll be out of here just as soon as the police have finished and I've had a chance to talk to Mabel.''

Ronni didn't ask any more questions. She simply followed Logan's instructions, waiting until the second police car had gone before she went inside. Except for the contents of several drawers being dumped on the floor, there was little damage to the apartment. An eerie feeling washed over her at the thought that some stranger had handled her things, and if she'd had a choice, she would have left her belongings behind. Instead she found herself packing for the fourth time in a week.

As she gathered up Steffie's toys, she couldn't help but wonder where they would go next. She was tired of running, tired of living in strange places and tired of being under suspicion. She longed for her little house back in Melbourne, leaky roof and all. She wondered how much longer it would be before the missing microchip turned up and she was cleared of any wrongdoing.

When Mabel returned, Ronni realized that as anxious as she was to return to Melbourne, she was sorry she wouldn't be seeing the woman who in a short time had become very dear to her. She felt her emotions rise in her throat as she tried to say goodbye to the older woman.

"Thank you, Mabel, for everything," Ronni managed to get out with only a slight break in her voice. "I'm sorry our visit had to end this way."

"It's not your fault those hoodlums broke in," she told her.

Ronni glanced at Logan, who indicated with facial expressions that Mabel had no idea of their true situation.

"I'm happy I was able to help out," Mabel finished.

"Oh, you did help us—more than I can tell you," Ronni assured her. "This past week has been wonderful because of your hospitality. And I know Steffie is going to miss you."

"Can I give her a hug?" Mabel asked, opening her arms wide.

Ronni released Steffie with a smile, touched by the woman's obvious affection for her daughter.

"I want you to promise me you'll come back for a visit," Mabel insisted, cuddling Steffie close to her bosom. "Do you hear that, Steffie?" She turned her attention to the little face gazing into hers. "You make sure your mama brings you back so I can see how big you've grown."

Steffie gurgled a sound that seemed to agree, and they all laughed.

"You have to promise you'll come visit us, too," Ronni said, tears springing to her eyes. "We're only a couple of hours up the coast. We can take you to the space center."

"Oh, I'd like that," Mabel replied with a warm smile. "I'll bring the cribbage board." When she handed Steffie back to Ronni, she said in a low voice, "You've got a good man this time, Ronni. And if there's one thing I've always said, it's this—a good man is a treasure. I know it's going to work out for the two of you." She winked conspiratorially and grinned.

"I hope you're right," Ronni said, returning the smile. She watched as Logan hugged Mabel, noticing that he had slipped something into her hand. As soon as they'd waved goodbye and were back on the road again, she asked him about it. "What did you give Mabel back there?"

"Money for new locks. I thought she'd feel better if she changed all of them."

Ronni exhaled a long sigh. "I hope our staying with her hasn't put her in any danger."

"With us gone, there'll be no reason for anyone to bother her," Logan assured her. "And if it's any comfort to you, the police told me they'd watch the house for the next few days."

"She didn't know why we were there, did she?"

"No. I told her you were having trouble with your ex. She didn't pry any further."

Ronni smiled to herself. "She's so sweet. I'd hate to think I was responsible for anything happening to her."

They were stopped at a red light and he said, "Ronni, look at me." When she did as he requested, he stated convincingly, "Nothing's going to happen to Mabel."

"I hope you're right," she said wearily. "Logan, where are we going?"

"Back to Melbourne. I've got to find some answers."

"Me, too, Logan," Ronni replied. "Me, too."

THE DRIVE from Fort Lauderdale to Melbourne was accomplished in near silence, except for Steffie's chortling. Both Ronni and Logan were lost in their own thoughts—she wondering about her identity, he feeling betrayed by someone he'd thought he could trust.

It was dark by the time they reached Melbourne. Logan found a motel and checked them into a two-bedroom suite with a crib for Steffie. Ronni was grateful he was taking charge of everything, for she was simply too weary to deal with any other problems just now.

After seeing that Steffie was fed and bathed, she put her to bed, then took a long hot bath herself, hoping to ease the tension in muscles cramped from riding in the pickup as well as from stress. As she soaked, her thoughts returned to her mother and to what possible reasons she could have had for changing their identities. Ronni found none of the explanations comforting, as repeatedly her mind imagined the worst possibilities. Could her mother be a criminal? It seemed preposterous even to contemplate such an idea.

But, then, it seemed preposterous that she had lived practically her entire life pretending to be someone else. Right now she was a twenty-eight-year-old woman without a name. She leaned back and closed her eyes, murmuring, "The spy's wife without a name," then groaned at the painful reminder.

Legally she was still married to a spy, but it wasn't true that she didn't have a name. She had a name all right; she just didn't know what it was. Only her mother had that information, and that thought brought a rush of fresh anger. At least tomorrow she would find out who she really was, for right now that was more important than anything else.

Suddenly the bathwater felt cold. Shivering, she reached for a towel just as she heard Logan knocking on the door.

"Ronni, are you all right?" he called out, concern in his voice.

She quickly climbed out of the tub and slipped on her cotton kimono before opening the door.

"I'm fine, Logan."

She stood before him, her skin devoid of any make-up, yet having a rosy hue. She looked so fragile, yet

Logan knew there was a strength beneath that dainty exterior.

"You were in there so long, I was worried you might have fallen asleep in the tub," he said lightly, seeing the almost forlorn expression on her face.

"I was thinking," she told him as she walked past him and out into the small sitting area.

Once more he experienced a feeling of helplessness, for he knew that nothing he could say would chase away that lost little girl look. Worse yet was the knowledge that he was responsible for her troubled thoughts. All he had wanted to do was protect her, yet he'd ended up causing her pain.

"What smells so good?" she asked, wrinkling her nose.

He had shoved both his hands in his pockets. "I ordered a pizza. You didn't eat much at dinner and I thought you might be hungry."

His thoughtfulness brought a tiny rush of warmth to the coldness inside her, but her stomach rejected the idea. "It smells good, but I'm not sure I can eat anything."

Logan pulled out one of the bar stools for her, gesturing for her to be seated. "Just sit with me," he urged, easing himself onto the stool across from hers and opening the cardboard box. Again Ronni thought how nice it was to have him taking charge of everything. Even if it was wrong, it felt so good to have him look after her. It was a wonderful feeling—being cherished—which was exactly how he made her feel.

When he slid a napkin bearing a triangular piece of pepperoni pizza toward her, she smiled weakly. "You don't take no for an answer, do you?"

"Not where you're concerned." He licked a drop of tomato sauce from his finger. "Try it. It's not bad for motel pizza."

She picked off a slice of pepperoni and popped it in her mouth. "Do we have anything to drink?"

"Pick your poison. The room's equipped with a portable bar." He dug a key from his pocket and dangled it in front of her.

"What are you having?" she asked.

"A beer."

"That's fine with me, too."

"You sure?"

Seeing her nod, Logan took two beers from the portable bar and set them on the counter. After he had eaten three pieces of pizza and she was still staring at her first slice, he said, "I was hoping this would help you to relax." He covered her hand with his. "It'll be over soon, Ronni, and then you'll be able to go home."

She didn't say a word, but simply lifted her shoulders and nodded, her eyes still on the now-cold piece of pizza.

After several moments of silence, he finally said, "I'm sorry, Ronni."

She glanced at him in surprise. "Sorry? For what?"

"For telling you about Veronica and Clara Summers. I've hurt you, and it's the last thing I wanted to do."

"Oh, Logan, it's not your fault," she said on a weary sigh, taking his hand in both of hers, her fingers gently moving over his knuckles in a soothing manner. "It's my mother who's hurt me. I keep telling myself she must have had a good reason for doing what she did, but what I don't understand is why she kept it from me.

Why couldn't she have told me the truth? It seems rather ironic that Andrew's father knew, yet I didn't."

Logan took a long sip of beer and rubbed a hand over the back of his neck before answering. "There's something I haven't told you," he said soberly.

Ronni could see that that something was deeply disturbing him. "What is it?" she asked, her concern mirrored in her eyes.

"You know that I was very careful not to make any calls from Mabel's." She nodded. "And I can assure you that none of the calls I made from the public phone booths could have been traced to the Fort Lauderdale area." He toyed with the flip top of the aluminum can. "I was determined that no one would know where we were staying."

"Then how did they find us at Mabel's?" she asked, a frown knitting her brow.

"There was one person who knew where we were. I thought I could trust him, that he would be the last person on earth who would betray me. He was a man I would have given my life for because I thought he was a man of honor, loyalty."

She could see the pain it was causing him to admit his mistake, and for just a moment, she forgot about her own unhappiness. "Who was it, Logan?" she asked gently.

It seemed to take him forever to finally tell her, and then the words were barely audible. "Senator Potter."

"Oh, no, Logan. You don't mean you think Senator Potter sent those men after us?" She shook her head in disbelief.

"The only way anyone could have found us was through Doc," he said grimly.

"But what about your contacts? All those people you've been getting information from?"

"None of them knew where we were, Ronni. Only Doc had that information."

"There could be another explanation," she said optimistically.

"No, there couldn't." The look he gave her was so intense she didn't rebuke his statement. He climbed down off the bar stool and ambled over to the sofa, where in the shadows of the dimly lit room he dropped down onto the soft cushions, propping his feet up on the coffee table. He leaned back and closed his eyes. "Somehow Doc is connected to Peter," he said in an agonized drawl.

"But why would he ask you to investigate me if that was true?" She had followed him over to the sofa, and sat down beside him, placing her arm along the back of the sofa. "It doesn't make any sense."

"I haven't quite figured that out," he admitted. "You could have been a smoke screen, or maybe something backfired in his plan. He tried to discourage me from getting involved with you, but now I have to wonder if that wasn't his way of keeping me interested. This way if the KGB agents weren't successful in finding the microchip, he had me ready and waiting to return it to him."

"Are you saying you think he's the ringleader of whatever Peter was doing?"

"I've been searching all day for answers that would tell me he isn't." He shook his head disconsolately. "I wish there were something—anything—that would convince me he isn't."

Ronni found the taut muscles in Logan's neck and began to knead them. "What are you going to do?" she asked softly.

"I'll have to go to the FBI with what I know. The man's head of the Senate Intelligence Committee. I just can't do nothing and hope that I'm wrong about him."

She could see that he needed to justify his actions to himself, more than to her. "Of course you can't. It's the only thing you can do," she agreed.

"But how can I turn him in? He's been like a father to me, Ronni," he said, dropping his head into his hands. "Ever since I was knee-high I took in every word he said as though it were the gospel truth. I campaigned for him and helped him get his position on the Senate Intelligence Committee. I would have died for him. I didn't think a finer man existed. How could I have been so wrong about him?"

Ronni continued to knead the tense muscles as he talked.

"The funny thing is, I used to envy Andy because Doc was his father. Ninety percent of our squabbles were because I'd get so damn jealous that Doc was his father and not mine. I couldn't understand how Andy could talk so disparagingly of him. When Andy would tell me I didn't know the real Senator Potter, I practically laughed in his face. Now I have to question whether Andy might not be a victim in this whole mess."

"Logan, what about your father?" she asked.

"What about him?" He lifted his head to look at her.

"You always talk about Doc as though he were a father to you, yet you never mention your own father. Is he alive?"

"Oh, yes, he's alive," he said, lifting one eyebrow. "He's still running the family farm in Kansas—with the help of my brother."

"You have a brother?"

"Two of them. Lawrence, Jr. and Allen. One's a farmer, the other's a farm machinery dealer, which is why they get along better with my father than I do," he told her dryly.

"Was your father expecting you to follow in his footsteps?"

"Probably, but not necessarily farming, just something related in agriculture. He loves the land and he has a hard time understanding why anyone would not want to live that kind of life. It's all he's ever known and all he's ever wanted for his family. So you can imagine how he felt about a career like mine."

"I bet he's proud of you, Logan."

He gave her a skeptical look. "He's got a funny way of showing it if he is."

"You speak to him regularly, don't you?"

He shrugged. "As regularly as any other adult child does, I suppose. We're not estranged, Ronni. We're just not that close. For some reason, I always found it easier to talk to Doc." He steepled his fingers beneath his chin. "My dad was always a patriotic man, but Doc was more than patriotic. He represented justice and equality and all the other values that were so important to me when I was a student. Public service was his life. He's my hero, Ronni. He can't be a spy." The last few words were a plea.

She looked at him and realized he was just as disappointed in Doc as she was in her mother. "I hope you're wrong about both Andrew and his father."

He sighed heavily. "We'll soon find out. Before I contact the FBI, I'm going to go visit Andy. I want to see for myself what condition he's in. I believe he's the key to this whole mess. I only wish I didn't have to leave you and Steffie alone here."

"That's something I wanted to talk to you about," she said, facing him squarely. "My mother's plane is coming in tomorrow morning at eight. Steffie and I are supposed to be picking her up at the airport."

"You'll have to call the airlines and leave a message for her to take a cab."

It sounded like an order to her and she immediately took offense. Annoyed, she asked, "Why can't we go get her?"

"Why?" He flashed her a look of disbelief. "Have you forgotten there are several men out there who would like nothing better than to find you? That your daughter was almost kidnapped?"

"Of course I haven't," she retorted, not wanting to admit that she had. All she seemed capable of thinking about was who she could be, and it made her feel guilty to realize that she could so easily forget what had happened to Steffie.

When she didn't say anything for several seconds, he stood up and walked over to the phone. "Tell me the name of the airlines and I'll call for you."

Reluctantly she gave him the information. As soon as he had completed the call she asked, "Will you at least drop me off at my mother's apartment on your way to see Andrew?"

Logan frowned. "I like that idea even less than you going to the airport."

"Why?" She stood up and confronted him.

"Why?" he repeated, practically glaring at her. "Because I've got no way of protecting you if you go to your mother's without me."

"But I need to see her," she pleaded.

"And you will. As soon as I've had a chance to talk to Andy and after I've contacted the FBI. I'll take you to see her myself."

"But I don't want to wait. If you think you're disillusioned with Doc, imagine how I feel about my mother. She's been lying to me for over twenty-five years."

"I know how important it is to you to learn your real name," he said, his voice softening, his hands covering her shoulders. "And believe me, I do understand how you're feeling, but it's not a good idea for you to go traipsing over to your mother's. We've been through all this before, Ronni."

"It's not just learning who I am, but learning who my father is. Right now I don't know if my father is dead or alive." She turned to him with pleading eyes. "Don't you see? I've spent a lifetime wishing I had a father. It's possible that I do."

"What makes you think your mother hasn't been telling you the truth about him?"

"That's just it. She hasn't told me anything about him. All I have are a couple of photos and precious few details."

He took both her hands in his. "All I'm asking is that you be patient. It won't be much longer before the spy ring is broken and the missing microchip is found. Once that happens, you and Steffie will be safe and you'll be able to return to a normal life."

"I doubt my life will ever be normal again," she said wearily.

"It'll all work out, Ronni. Trust me."

When he wrapped his strong arms around her and whispered those words in her ear, it was impossible not to. And when he made it clear that it was her decision whether they slept together that night, she chose to share his bed, needing the comfort of him. As they made love, the exquisite pleasure of their intimacy, the oneness of body and mind, made everything else seem unimportant. All that mattered was her need to be his always.

But long after their passion was spent, Ronni found herself worrying that she was giving this man too much control in her life. She couldn't deny her feelings for him even if she had wanted to. He was her treasure, just as Mabel had said. She knew, however, that come morning, nothing he was going to say or do would prevent her from contacting her mother.

CHAPTER THIRTEEN

RONNI KEPT ONE EYE on the bathroom door and the other on Steffie as she dialed her mother's phone number. She figured she had about fifteen minutes—which was how much time it usually took Logan to shower and shave each morning. When a busy signal sounded in her ear, she replaced the receiver with a frown. She immediately tried the number again, only to get the same annoying busy tone, a pattern that kept repeating until finally, after seven of the fifteen minutes had elapsed, her mother answered. Ronni hadn't been talking to her for more than three or four minutes, when she saw the bathroom door open and Logan come out.

"I need another razor blade," he announced, the lower half of his face smothered in shaving cream.

Startled, Ronni quickly averted her head, nearly pulling the phone off the desk in an effort to turn her face away from him. "I've got to go now. I'll call you later," she told her mother in a low voice before hanging up.

"Who were you talking to?" Logan asked as soon as she had replaced the receiver. He had a towel draped over his bare shoulders, a pair of white slacks covering his legs and he was looking at her as though he already knew the answer.

As usual, the sight of his bare chest did funny things to her stomach, but she forced her eyes back to his face.

"I called my mother," she answered, standing with her arms crossed over her chest and seeming more defiant than she felt.

He appeared to be counting slowly to ten. "Why would you do that?" he inquired calmly but intensely.

"Because I knew she would be calling me as soon as she got home and I didn't want her to worry when there wasn't an answer at my place." The lie came easily to her lips. She knew it was a lie and so did he, but she wasn't about to explain again her almost desperate need to speak to her mother. "We were supposed to meet her at the airport," she reminded him. "Mothers have a tendency to worry when their daughters aren't where they're supposed to be. I wanted to make sure she knew that we were all right."

Logan didn't respond, but stood staring at her. His silence was worse than his censure, and she almost wished he'd shout at her rather than stand there coolly assessing her.

"I only talked for a couple of minutes—not long enough for a call to be traced," Ronni pointed out.

He narrowed his eyes suspiciously. "How much did you tell her?"

"Practically nothing. She asked about Vienna—I told her we didn't go. Mostly she talked about her vacation. Oh—and I also told her about Andrew's heart attack."

"Did she mention Peter?"

"Yes, but only in regard to us not going to Vienna. I'm sure she hasn't heard about his defection. She probably hasn't seen a newspaper since she's been away."

"I know you're anxious to see her, Ronni, but I want you to promise me you'll wait here until I get back from the hospital."

She moved closer to him. "I know you're only trying to protect us, Logan, but I wish you'd reconsider. I really don't want to stay here alone. If you don't want me going to see my mother, can't we at least go to the hospital with you?"

He shook his head. "It's better for you to stay put. No one knows you're here." When she would have protested, he added, "I'd never forgive myself if anything happened to either one of you." Steffie had crawled over to Logan and was pulling herself up by the leg of his slacks. He bent over and scooped her into his arms. "Will you and Steffie wait here for me?" he asked, looking at Ronni while Steffie's fingers gingerly poked at the shaving cream.

Ronni watched how tenderly he held her daughter, as he carefully wiped her soapy fingers with the towel. Seeing him with Steffie evoked such a warm feeling inside her chest it was hard not to do as he requested. "We'll wait," she finally told him.

Logan kissed both of them on the cheek, then grinned sheepishly as they each wrinkled their noses at the foamy shaving cream that accompanied his kisses. Then he set Steffie down and gave Ronni a long hard look before going back into the bathroom to finish shaving and getting dressed.

Despite Logan's optimistic frame of mind, Ronni couldn't help but feel a sense of foreboding. When he kissed her goodbye, she wanted to beg him not to go without her, but she knew her protest would be in vain.

Standing beside the plate glass window in their room, Ronni watched his lean figure cut across the motel's asphalt parking lot. With each step he moved further away from her, taking with him her sense of security. When she saw him climb into the pickup, a wave of panic swept over her. It was like an explosion of fear, and she had the horrible feeling it would be the last time she would ever see him.

Frightened by such a thought, she grabbed Steffie and went running after him. But by the time she was able to race through the lobby and out into the parking lot, the orange pickup was gone. For the first time since she and Logan had been together, she felt totally alone, and the feeling was overwhelming.

She went back to the room and waited, just as he had instructed her to do. But there was little comfort to be found in a strange motel room, and although she tried to give her undivided attention to Steffie and her toys, her eyes kept returning to the telephone. Anxiously she waited for it to ring, wanting so desperately for Logan to call and tell her the microchip had been found...that she could stop worrying about anyone trying to take Steffie from her. But it didn't ring, and the waiting became unbearable as her attention repeatedly strayed to the telephone and her wristwatch.

By midmorning, Ronni was jumping every time she heard a noise in the hallway. Convinced that something horrible had happened to Logan, she wrestled with several different plans of action until she finally came to the conclusion there was only one person who could give her any peace of mind—her mother. So, despite Logan's warning not to leave and knowing that her mother's apartment building might be under surveillance, Ronni scribbled a note for him telling him where she would be and set her plan in motion.

With her blond hair swept up beneath Logan's captain's hat and her slender curves hidden by his Hawaiian print shirt and a pair of his khakis, Ronni hoped that if she couldn't pass for a man she would at least look very different from the Veronica Lang whose picture had been splattered across the newspapers. Before calling a taxi, she scrubbed her face clean of all make-up, emptied the contents of her purse into Steffie's diaper bag, then headed for the gift shop in the lobby, where she purchased a pair of men's sunglasses and promptly perched them on the bridge of her nose.

When she climbed into the taxi, she couldn't help but cast a suspicious eye around the motel parking lot; nor could she keep from looking over her shoulder as the taxi pulled out into traffic and headed across town. Without the confines of a car seat, Steffie scrambled and wriggled about in the back of the taxi, and it took all of Ronni's energy to try to hold her still.

When they reached her mother's apartment complex, she told the driver to circle the block before stopping. Acting as though it wasn't an unusual request, the driver followed her instructions, allowing Ronni the opportunity to scrutinize the neighborhood. By the time the taxi came to a halt in front of the apartment entrance, she had seen nothing untoward, but that didn't prevent her from running the short distance between the taxi and the building. Once inside the lobby, she jostled Steffie from one hip to the other as she waited impatiently for her mother to answer the intercom.

"Come on up. Grandma's waiting for you," Ronni heard her mother say before a buzzing sound signaled that the security door was unlocked. Instead of waiting for the elevator, Ronni took the stairs to the third-floor apartment, to find her mother waiting for the two of them with a big grin on her usually taciturn face.

"Come to Grandma, pumpkin," she cooed, taking Steffie from Ronni's arms and smothering her with kisses.

"Welcome home, Mother," Ronni said dryly as she closed her mother's door and leaned against it.

"Oh, it's good to be home," Clara declared, cuddling Steffie and making her giggle. "I missed you so much. Wait until you see what I brought back. You wouldn't believe all the bargains I found in the duty-free shops—it was like paradise." She finally turned her attention to Ronni and gasped. "Veronica! What on earth are you doing in those clothes?" she asked, her face wrinkling in surprise.

"It's a long story," Ronni said wearily, removing the captain's hat and running her fingers through her hair. "Maybe we ought to sit down," she suggested, despising the weakness that had invaded her body now that she was finally in a position to learn the truth about her identity.

"Just set those packages on the floor," Clara instructed, waving an arm in the direction of the sofa, where the bargains were spread out from end to end. "Look at these darling sunsuits I found for Steffie in Saint Croix," she exclaimed, producing several colorful cotton outfits and holding them up for Ronni's inspection. "There were so many things to choose from I could have spent all my time in the shops." She started rummaging through a large shopping bag. "I wonder what I did with the swimsuit I bought for her."

There was only one subject Ronni was interested in discussing and it wasn't Steffie's new clothes. She glanced impatiently at the sunsuits, then set them aside. "Mother, I need to talk to you."

"I'm listening," Clara told her, rattling two gaily painted maracas in front of Steffie while she hummed "La Cucaracha."

Ronni grabbed the gourds before Steffie's little fingers closed around them. "She'll end up putting those in her mouth, and you don't know what kind of paint is on them," she admonished, the sharpness of her tone causing her mother's eyebrows to draw together.

Ronni's actions brought a cry of protest from Steffie. Immediately Clara began to bounce her on her knee. "Maybe I should get her the doll I bought for her in San Juan."

"If you'd set her down on the floor, she'd find her box of toys and entertain herself," Ronni remarked testily. "Then we could talk. I have something important I need to discuss with you."

Clara set Steffie down on the plush blue carpet. "Very well, but why don't I get us something cool to drink? Then you can tell me what it is that's bothering you." She started walking toward the kitchen, but Ronni stopped her.

"Mother, I don't need something cool to drink," she snapped.

Clara gave her daughter an inquisitive glare, then slowly sat back down. Two eyebrows arched. "No, I guess you don't. I think you'd better start by telling me why you're dressed like a man," she said, asserting herself with a thrust of her chin. Before Ronni could reply she added, "And why couldn't you tell me where you were when you phoned this morning? Why weren't you at home?"

"Steffie and I haven't been home since the day you left," Ronni said on a weary note, rubbing her temples with her fingertips.

"Well, for goodness' sake, why not?" Clara asked, her features softening with concern. "I thought you said you didn't go to Vienna."

"We didn't." She laughed sarcastically. "We went to Key West and to Miami and Fort Lauderdale," she said, counting off the names on her fingers.

"Whatever for? Not to avoid Peter?" Clara made a fretful sound. "He's not here in Melbourne bothering you again, is he?"

"I doubt if Peter will ever come back here again, Mother," she said bitterly. "That ought to make you happy. It's what you've wanted all along—for Peter to be out of our lives."

"I've only wanted for you and Steffie to be happy," Clara answered stiffly. "I don't know what's going on here, dear, but ever since you walked through that door you've been looking at me with that wounded expression you always toss at me whenever you're angry with me."

Ronni looked at her mother and tried to control the rush of conflicting emotions that threatened to turn her into a raging interrogator. "I need some answers," she said as calmly as she could. "And you're the only one who has them."

"Answers to what?" Clara frowned.

"Answers to the questions such as, who I am. Or maybe we should start with who you are." She looked at her mother as though she were seeing her for the first time.

"What do you mean, who am I?" Clara attempted to dismiss her question with a chuckle.

But there was no answering humor in Ronni's voice. "You know what I mean, Mother," she said soberly. "Who are we?"

"Veronica, you're not making any sense." She gave her what Ronni called her military scare-'em look, but Ronni wasn't scared. Then she pursed her lips and said,

"And I don't appreciate your tone of voice. You're angry with me. Why? What's happened?"

"What's happened is I want to know who I am. That's something you never thought you'd have to tell me, isn't it? How long were you planning on keeping it from me? Forever?" Ronni tried to keep her anger under control, but her voice rose sharply, so sharply that it startled Steffie, who looked anxiously from her mother to her grandmother, then uttered an uncertain wail.

"Keep your voice down. You're frightening Steffie," Clara rebuked her. "As well as me."

Ronni took a deep breath, hoping to slow down her hammering heart. She sat clutching her hands so tightly her knuckles were white. "I want to know who I am, Mother," she repeated, calmly yet firmly. "Twenty-five years ago Veronica and Clara Summers were killed in an automobile accident." Her gaze didn't waver from her mother's. "We're not dead, Mother."

Clara's face paled and she grabbed the wooden arms of her chair to still her trembling. For the first time in twenty-eight years, Ronni saw fear in her mother's face. "Who told you this?" she asked in a raspy voice.

"It doesn't matter who told me. What matters is who I am, and at the moment, I don't have the slightest idea who that is." She had to use every ounce of self-control not to lose the little bit of composure she was so desperately clinging to.

"You're my daughter, that's who you are," Clara said unequivocally. "We may have used someone else's names, but you are my flesh and blood, Veronica."

"So it is true," Ronni said slowly, her shoulders slumping. Until she had heard her mother's admission, there had been that slender thread of hope that Logan was wrong. Now she knew he had spoken the truth. Denial was impossible. "Why, Mother?" she gasped. "Why did you do it?"

Obviously upset by her daughter's discovery, Clara made a fretful sound, then said, "I didn't have any choice. Twenty-five years ago it was the only alternative."

"Alternative?" Ronni looked bewildered. "Alternative to what?"

"To living in continual fear."

"Fear of what?"

"Not what, but whom." After what seemed like a long silence, Clara swallowed with great difficulty before quietly saying, "Your father."

"My father?" Ronni thought the lump in her throat would constrict her breathing it was so large. "You were afraid of my father?" she whispered.

"Yes, and with good reason."

"But you said he was killed in a car crash when I was only three."

Clara looked down at her hands, which were now folded in her lap. "There was no car crash," she admitted in a low voice. "We divorced when you were two."

"Divorced? You mean, he's still alive?" The thought that her father could be alive sent a chill down her spine.

"I don't know whether he's alive or dead, nor do I want to know," Clara replied unevenly. "He made my life so miserable the short time we were married that I have no remorse about what I did."

"What did you do?" Ronni asked faintly.

"I did the only thing I could do to make sure he would never hurt either one of us again. I changed our names and moved far away from him."

"But how? Why did we end up with dead people's names?"

"I had a friend who worked in the Department of Vital Statistics. We'd been in the army together, and she was also my maid of honor at my wedding."

"You mean Marie Spenser?"

"Yes. Maybe you remember her. She visited us several times when you were just a little girl."

Vaguely Ronni recalled a matronly woman who had a tinkling laugh and smelled of lilacs.

"Well, she knew of the problems I was having with your father," Clara continued. "She had warned me against marrying him in the first place. You see, I met him while I was in the service, which was automatically one strike against him where Marie was concerned. She didn't trust soldiers."

"Then he was a military man?" Ronni asked, hungry for any information at all about her father.

"Not a career man. He had about six months of his tour of duty left when I first met him. We were both stationed in New Jersey."

"Did you get married while you were in the service?"

"Oh, no." She shook her head. "I only had four weeks left to serve when I first met him. After I was discharged, I went back to Eau Claire and got a job with the telephone company. During the next few months we corresponded by mail until he was discharged from the army. One day he turned up on my doorstep and a week later we were married."

"You must have loved him if you married him." It was more of a question than a statement.

"Oh, yes, I loved him very much in the beginning. I couldn't believe my luck when he asked me to marry him. He was so handsome, and women were after him like you wouldn't believe."

There was a dreamy look on her mother's face that Ronni had never seen before.

"He had what my mother would have called a silver tongue. He could charm the socks off a girl."

"But you had problems in your marriage?" Ronni prodded.

"He could be loving and tender, but he could also be violent. Little did I know that our life would be so troublesome—one minute tranquil, the next minute chaotic." She grimaced at the memory. "At first I excused his abusive behavior, blaming it on his upbringing. He told me that in his family a man would lose his honor if he didn't keep his woman in line. You know me, Ronni. I'm no shrinking violet. I can defend myself pretty well, but he had such a violent temper."

"You mean he struck you?" Ronni's mouth dropped open in horror and she clutched her stomach. All her life she had visualized her father as being a kind, gentle man. She didn't want to hear that he could be cruel.

"More than once. When I learned I was pregnant with you, I begged him to get some counseling with me, but he refused. Not even when I nearly had a miscarriage."

"He hit you when you were pregnant?" Ronni winced, feeling as though she were breaking out in a cold sweat as the picture became even uglier.

Clara nodded slowly. "He pushed me and I fell. When the doctor told him I could have easily lost you, it seemed to shake him up pretty badly. He didn't touch me again for the remainder of my pregnancy. I was so happy, because I thought we were finally going to be able to work things out and that he had changed."

"But he didn't change, did he?" Ronni said somberly, her eyes misting with unshed tears.

Clara shook her head sadly. "After you were born, it started all over again. The lies, the fighting, the accusations and the physical abuse. Finally I couldn't take it any longer. I was afraid that if I left him alone with you, he'd hurt you, too. So I moved out. He threatened to kill me if I left, but I took refuge at a women's shelter."

"Didn't the police do anything?"

"Oh, there were restraining orders and whatnot, but the authorities weren't overly anxious to get involved in domestic disputes—especially back then. Women didn't have the rights they have now. I wanted to run far, far away, somewhere that he'd never find us. But I had to wait for the divorce proceedings. Your father hired himself a hotshot lawyer who persuaded the judge that he should be allowed to have you every other weekend."

"Even though he was abusive?" Ronni shrieked in disbelief.

"I'm afraid so. In court, he appeared as the wronged party and had a whole parade of witnesses who testified that he was a devoted father and husband. And I had made the mistake of not reporting his abuse to the police."

Clara sighed. "I was determined not to let him take you away from me for even one hour, let alone a whole weekend. Marie offered to let me stay with her in Milwaukee, so we moved in with her. When he found out where we were, he caused trouble, and I was beginning to think we'd never be safe from him. It was then that Marie suggested I take you and move out of state. Knowing your father, I figured he'd find us no matter where we went. That's when Marie came up with the idea of assuming new identities."

"But wasn't it illegal? I mean, you just can't go take other people's names!"

"Veronica, I was desperate," her mother explained. "Because Marie worked in the Department of Public Records, she knew of a woman and her small daughter who had been killed in an automobile accident. She provided me with copies of their birth certificates and it was then that I decided to use their names so that no one would ever know where we were. Ironically the woman's name was Clara, which was similar to my given name—Clarissa."

"But what about the rest of your family? Didn't they care that you were going to disappear out of their lives?"

"I've always told you the truth about them. One of the reasons I went into the army was that I was alone. My father was killed in World War II and my mother died the summer after I graduated from high school. Except for a few cousins, I didn't have any other family, so it really wasn't hard for me to leave Wisconsin. When I moved to Florida, I closed the door on that life and began a new one."

"But using other people's names . . . it just doesn't seem right," Ronni protested. She could hardly believe that her rigid, rule-abiding mother had been able to take such measures.

"I only borrowed their names. I didn't pretend we actually were those people. All I wanted was a fresh start for the two of us. Is that so wrong? To want to give your child a new beginning?"

Ronni was too numb to make any judgments. She walked over to the bookshelf and picked up the photo of her father her mother kept in a silver frame. "That's why you never wanted to talk about him, isn't it—all those times I questioned you about him and you would always change the subject." She studied the photograph as she talked. "I always thought it was because after his death you found it too painful to talk about him." She traced the outline of his face, the strong jaw, the wide grin. It was a face she had memorized years ago—a happy face. "He was so handsome," she said wistfully. "It's hard to believe he could have been so cruel."

Clara had been watching her daughter's fingers caress the picture. "That man isn't your father, Veronica," she said quietly.

Ronni shot her mother a quizzical expression. "This isn't my father?"

Clara shook her head.

Ronni's eyes flew back to the picture, looking distastefully at the face she had loved all of her life. "If this isn't my father, who is it?"

Square shoulders lifted. "I have no idea," Clara admitted.

"Mother, you've been telling me for twenty-five years that this man is my father." She held the photograph out in front of her in an accusatory manner. "Now you're telling me that not only is he not my father, but you don't even know who the man is?" she asked incredulously.

"After your father and I were divorced, I went to work for a photographer. There was a box of unclaimed photos...that's where I found that picture and the ones you have." She watched Ronni return the silver frame to the shelf as though it burned her fingers. "You were too young to remember your father, so I took those pictures home with me to create a memory of a handsome, gentle father for you.''

Ronni closed her eyes, feeling a sense of betrayal. ''What about my real father? Do you have any pictures of him?''

''No. I destroyed all reminders of him. I wouldn't have been able to pretend he was a good and decent man if I had had to look at his picture every day.''

Ronni glanced over at Steffie, who was chomping on a rubber toy. ''Did he have red hair?''

''Oh, yes. It was like burnished copper. I used to think what a shame it was that such glorious red hair was wasted on a man.''

''What about all those pictures in the photo album—the ones of our relatives—are they phonies, too?'' she asked bitterly.

''No, they're not!'' Clara denied vehemently. ''Those are your family. Most of them still live in Wisconsin. If I have any regrets, it's that you didn't have the opportunity to know them—even if they were distant relatives.''

''What about my father's family? I must have had grandparents and aunts and uncles on his side, as well.'' She held her breath, waiting for the answer, as the thought of discovering a whole new family threatened to overwhelm her.

''Yes, and I'm sorry you weren't able to know them. But that wasn't my fault, Veronica. Your father gave me no other choice.''

''Are they still alive?''

Clara shrugged. ''I don't know. It's been twenty-five years.''

''Were they from the Wisconsin area?''

''Yes.''

"And what about your friend Marie? Does she still work in the Office of Vital Statistics?"

"Yes, she does, but surely you're not thinking of trying to find them." A look of agitation flickered in her eyes.

"I can't even begin to look for them unless I know their names."

There was a silence while Ronni waited for her mother's answer. Clara sat licking her lips as though debating whether she should tell her.

"Don't you think I have a right to know, Mother?" Ronni demanded.

Clara's eyes met hers and she said, "It's Locken. You were christened Cynthia Louise, after my mother."

"And my father's name?"

Ronni saw her mother swallow with difficulty. Her lips trembled as she said, "His name was Ronald Locken, but everyone called him 'Ronnie.'"

CHAPTER FOURTEEN

"THAT'S WHY YOU REFUSED to call me 'Ronni'—because that was his name." She spoke the sudden realization aloud, a wistful expression lingering in her eyes.

"In twenty-five years, no one has ever suspected a thing. Why now? I don't understand how you could have found out," Clara mused. "What happened while I was gone?"

Ronni gazed out the window to the street below, wondering how everything could look so peaceful outside when her life was in such a turmoil. She moved away from the window and slumped down onto the sofa. "A whole lifetime seems to have happened," she muttered. "I keep thinking I'm going to wake up and discover it's all been a bad dream." She leaned her head back and closed her eyes. "I'm not who I thought I was...the man I thought was my father isn't really my father...my husband isn't who I thought he was." A tiny moan escaped her. "If only it were a nightmare."

"Do you hate me, Veronica?"

Ronni opened her eyes and saw uncertainty in a face that had always been so stoic. She wanted to reach out and put her arm around her mother's shoulders, but something stopped her—pride, anger, confusion—she didn't know which. She had always been the one to reach out and do the touching, but at this moment her feelings were too raw, too complicated for her to respond.

"Oh, Mom, of course I don't hate you," she answered honestly. "I wish I could tell you everything is all right, but it's so hard for me to absorb it all—especially after what Peter's done." Seeing her mother's puzzled expression, she added, "I forgot. You haven't heard about Peter, have you?"

"What's he done now?" Clara asked, the worry lines at the corners of her eyes deepening.

"It's such an awful story, Mom, I don't even know where to begin," she said on a weary sigh, rubbing her fingers across her forehead. "Remember how you couldn't locate Peter for me when Steffie was in the hospital?" She didn't wait for a response from her mother, but continued. "The reason you couldn't find him was that he wasn't in Vienna. He was in the Soviet Union."

"The Soviet Union?" Clara's brow wrinkled. "What was he doing there?"

"Working for the KGB." She waved a hand impatiently. "The day you left on your cruise, Peter defected to the Soviet Union."

Clara grimaced in horror. "Are you saying he's a spy?"

"I'm afraid he is, and that's only the beginning of it." She sighed heavily. "Not only was he betraying his country with his little spy games, but he made it appear as though I was involved in the whole sordid mess," she said bitterly. "My picture was in the paper and there was even a television reporter on my doorstep, looking for a story about me."

"But that's ridiculous!" Clara protested in outrage. "Anyone who knows you would know you couldn't possibly be involved in any such thing. Didn't you go to the authorities?"

"I didn't have to. They came to me with all sorts of questions—or I should say accusations, thanks to Peter. He set me up so that the FBI suspected I was his conspirator."

"I can't believe all this! How—how could he do such a thing?" Clara sputtered indignantly.

"Quite easily, believe me, Mom. He held a press conference, during which he announced to the world that the reason I had been planning my trip to Vienna was so that I could join him when he defected."

"But that's a lie!" Clara nearly choked in anger. "I knew he was a lowlife, but I never would have thought he could be so vindictive! And probably all because you wanted to divorce him."

"The story gets worse," Ronni warned her. "If it was simply a case of my having to prove I wasn't a spy, I would have been able to defend myself." She let her glance stray to her daughter, who was busy stacking blocks on the floor. "Putting Steffie's life in danger is something I'll never forgive him for. It was a mean, despicable thing to do. He's not worthy of having her call him 'Father.'" Her voice broke with emotion.

"What do you mean, Steffie's life is in danger?" Clara shot forward in alarm.

"Peter arranged for us to come to Vienna because he was planning to take Steffie with him when he defected. After we didn't show up, he tried to kidnap her."

"How could he kidnap her? I thought you said he was in Russia?"

"He is. He sent someone else to do it. Two creepy guys. It was awful." Ronni shuddered at the memory.

"I don't know what I would have done if Logan hadn't been there."

"Logan?" Clara looked at her inquisitively.

"Logan McNeil. He's a friend of Andrew's," Ronni explained. "I met him the day Andrew had his heart attack."

Clara raised a finger in the air. "Now that you mention Andrew, that reminds me. He called earlier this morning and asked me if I knew where you were. I told him you'd be coming over later today and I would have you call him when you arrived."

"Andrew called here?" Ronni felt goose bumps travel the length of her body. Had Logan already been to see him? Was that why he'd phoned? "That must mean he's out of his coma."

"He didn't sound much like himself, but I suppose that's to be expected, considering he had a heart attack and was comatose," Clara remarked thoughtfully.

Ronni got up to use the telephone. "Do you have the number to the hospital? I think I'll try calling him."

Just as Clara reached for the phone book, the intercom buzzed. She handed the directory to Ronni before going to answer the door.

"Western Union. Telegram for a Clara Summers." The voice came smoothly over the intercom.

Clara pressed the button allowing the delivery man access to the secured apartments, then turned back to Ronni. "I hope it's not bad news. I always associate telegrams with bad news."

Ronni paused in her search for the telephone number as her mother's words registered in her consciousness. She looked across the room to where Clara stood with one hand on the doorknob, anticipating the messenger's arrival. Intuitively an alarm sounded in her brain.

"Mother, wait!" The words spilled out in a sudden panic, but her warning came too late. The door was swinging open and within seconds it had swung shut, only this time the two men who had been on the outside were now on the inside. Immediately Ronni recognized them as the men who had tried to kidnap Steffie in Miami.

"What are you doing?" Clara demanded as they muscled their way into her apartment.

With lightning swift reflexes, Ronni bolted into action, sweeping Steffie into her arms.

The smaller man pulled a gun from inside his suit jacket pocket and waved it in the air. "No one needs to get hurt if you just cooperate."

"You can't take my baby. I won't let you," Ronni cried out bravely.

Clara gasped as the armed man began to move slowly across the living room. When she would have rushed to Ronni's side, the second man stopped her, stepping in front of her with his arms folded across his chest, the sheer size and strength of him enough to intimidate any woman.

Ronni clung to Steffie, inching backward as the man advanced until she came up against the wall and could go no farther. He continued to stalk her, while she stared at him with beseeching eyes. When he was close enough that Ronni could see the pores on his face and smell the cigar smoke on his breath, he stopped.

For the first time in her life Ronni thought she knew the meaning of the expression "frightened to death." No matter how hard she tried, she couldn't seem to get any air into her lungs, so great was her fear.

"Give it to me," he demanded, looking her squarely in the eye, the gun close to his chest. He held out a hand.

Ronni squeezed Steffie so tightly the little girl squealed in protest. She tried to speak, but nothing would come out, and she was forced to answer with a toss of her blond head.

"I said give it to me," he bit out between clenched teeth, raising the gun until it was so close to her face she thought she could feel its cold metal despite the fact that it didn't touch her skin. "I want the bracelet." He enunciated each word carefully.

"Bracelet?" she finally managed to croak.

"The baby's bracelet." He waved the gun at Steffie's wrist.

Ronni's heart was pounding so hard she thought it would put a hole in her chest.

"Hand it over and no one has to get hurt."

She slowly nodded. Then, despite Steffie's wriggling and her own arms feeling like Jell-O, she managed to unclasp the Medic-Alert bracelet and drop it into the man's callused palm. He pocketed the silver chain, then motioned for the other fellow to leave. Both Ronni and Clara stood like mannequins, watching the two men swiftly cross the room and vanish out the door.

Clara was the first one to jolt into action, rushing over to bolt the chain lock in place. "Quick! Call the police!" she exclaimed. When Ronni made no move for the telephone, she repeated, "Ronni, call the police!"

"And do what? Report that someone came in here and stole my daughter's Medic-Alert bracelet?" Her voice quivered as she spoke.

There was a knock on the door and Clara jumped. "Don't answer it! Whoever it is shouldn't be here.... I didn't open the security door downstairs!"

Both women stood looking at each other like a couple of frightened rabbits, until Ronni finally said, "This is ridiculous," and walked over to peer out the peephole in the door.

As Ronni fumbled with the lock, Clara demanded in near hysteria, "What are you doing?"

"It's all right. It's Logan."

"How could he have gotten in the building?"

"I don't know, Mother," she replied a bit impatiently. "Maybe he picked the lock." Disregarding her mother's protests, Ronni opened the door, only to be lambasted by Logan.

"I should have known you wouldn't wait for me," he scolded, shaking his head in anger. "Why did you leave? Don't you realize how dangerous it is for you to be out on your own?" He looked her up and down. "And what are you doing in my clothes?"

Ronni held up her hands, trying to stop his outburst of anger. "Logan, listen to me. Those men were here— the ones who tried to kidnap Steffie. Only they didn't want her, just her bracelet."

Logan's eyes flew to Steffie's bare wrist. "And you gave it to them?"

"I didn't have any choice. They had guns." She shivered at the memory, holding Steffie close for comfort.

"How long ago did this happen?" he asked.

"Not more than a couple of minutes."

Logan rushed over to the window and looked down at the street below. "There they are." He raised his index finger to the glass. "They're getting into a blue

Buick." Before Ronni could stop him, he was tearing out of the apartment, calling over his shoulder, "Lock the door, and for God's sake stay put this time."

"Logan, wait!" she shouted after him, but he paid no attention to her plea.

"Mom, take Steffie." Ronni shoved her daughter into her mother's arms. "I have to go after him."

"But you heard what he said," Clara protested. "'Lock the door and stay put.'" she mimicked sternly.

"I can't, Mom." She frantically reached for the diaper bag, dumping its contents onto the middle of the floor. "Oh, where is it?" she moaned, combing through the bibs, bottles and baby powder splattered across the carpet. Within seconds she was clutching Steffie's old Medic-Alert bracelet.

"I hope I can catch him," she yelled as she went running out of the apartment and down the corridor to the stairwell. She raced down the three flights of steps, her hair flopping against cheeks flushed with fear. Breathless, she came flying out of the entryway, only to discover that she was too late. There was no sign of Logan or the pickup.

"Damn!" she cried out in frustration, jiggling the Medic-Alert bracelet in her hand. She was tempted to run back upstairs and get the keys to her mother's car, but she knew her chances of finding Logan were next to none. She hadn't even seen in which direction he'd gone. There was nothing she could do but wait and pray that he wouldn't catch up to the other two men.

"I was too late. He was gone," she told her mother as she dragged her weary body into the apartment. She plopped down on the sofa and absently toyed with the bracelet.

"Why did you go after him?" Clara asked, setting Steffie back on the floor.

Ronni shifted her gaze from the bracelet to her mother's face. "You saw those men. They had guns—which means Logan is putting himself in danger, and all over a worthless bracelet. But he didn't give me a chance to explain."

"I'm beginning to think you've lost your senses, girl. What are you talking about and why did you go running after the man like that?" She clicked her tongue disapprovingly.

"I went after him because I'm in love with him and I didn't want to see him get hurt," Ronni declared emotionally.

"In love with him?" her mother parroted in disbelief. "How long have you known this man?"

"Ten days, but it seems like I've known him a lifetime," Ronni told her, a bit of wonder in her voice at the realization. "And I do love him," she added defiantly.

"Love?" Clara snorted. "I can't believe any of this." She threw her arms up in the air. "First you tell me Peter's a spy, then two men with guns force their way in here. They take Steffie's Medic-Alert bracelet, although for the life of me I can't figure out why, and now you go chasing after a guy with one eye because you tell me you're in love with him."

"He has two eyes, Mother," Ronni corrected. "He wears an eye patch because he was in an accident and he's still recovering from the injury."

"Maybe you'd better tell me who this man is and why you think you're in love with him," Clara ordered in her maternal voice as she sat down opposite her.

"I am in love with him," Ronni insisted. "And I already told you—he's a friend of Andrew's. They were childhood friends in Kansas. And if you're worried about his credentials, you don't need to be. He's very close to Senator Potter and he's also worked for the government."

"He's a politician?" She arched one eyebrow, and Ronni could see how her mother would find that rather difficult to believe. From the way he dressed, not many would believe he worked for the government in any capacity.

"No, not that kind of government work. Before he was injured, he worked for the CIA."

"You mean he's a spy?" Clara looked as though that was even more difficult to believe.

"Sort of," Ronni hedged. "It doesn't really matter. The point is he did intelligence work for the government. He's a good man. Instead of looking for things wrong with Logan, Mother, you should be feeling grateful to him. He saved Steffie from being kidnapped and helped me get through the most difficult time of my life."

Her mother gave her a disapproving look. "Are you telling me you've been living with that man?"

"I didn't have anyone else to turn to." Ronni stood and walked over to the window. "I told you—after what Peter did, I didn't exactly receive an outpouring of sympathy from my friends."

"Why didn't you just go to the authorities for help?"

Ronni continued to stare out the window. "The authorities were one of the reasons I needed Logan's help. After Peter held that press conference and announced to the world that I was planning on defecting, too, the

FBI treated me like I was a spy. And after everything that had happened, I wasn't sure whom I could trust."

"Are you sure you can trust this Logan?"

"Oh, yes, Mother. I'm sure." Her response had been automatic, and she knew that if there was one thing she was certain of, it was her wholehearted trust in Logan.

"Is he the one who found out we weren't the Summerses?"

Ronni turned back to her mother and nodded. "It puzzled him for a long time. You see, it's not uncommon for Russian spies to assume dead Americans' identities when they infiltrate the country. At first he thought I might be one of them—a Russian pretending to be an American."

"Then those men who took Steffie's bracelet were Russians?"

"All I know is that they're the same ones who tried to kidnap her. But I guess Logan was right all along. They really didn't want her, only the information she had."

Clara frowned. "What information could a child possibly have?"

Ronni held Steffie's Medic-Alert bracelet up to the sunshine streaming through the window. "Whatever it is, it must be in this." She examined it carefully, but could find no evidence that it opened. "Apparently Peter must have somehow attached the missing microchip to this bracelet, although I don't see how."

"What do mean, missing microchip?" Clara demanded, getting up and walking over to stand beside Ronni.

"According to Logan, Peter had been selling American defense technology secrets to the Russians for years. When he defected, he left behind a microchip that supposedly contained information necessary to break some sort of intelligence code. Until those men burst in here, I had no idea where he could have put that information. Now it's obvious he must have slipped it into Steffie's bracelet somehow.''

Again she studied the bracelet, turning it over and over. "Logan told me a microchip is so small it would be difficult for the naked eye to discern. Maybe that's why I don't see it, although it does look as though there's a flaw on the underside. What do you think?'' She handed the bracelet to her mother.

Clara peered at the metal, scratching it with her fingernail. "It's hard to tell. There are all sorts of marks on this, but they could be from Steffie banging it.'' She gave it back to Ronni and said, "You think those men wanted her bracelet because it contained defense secrets?''

Ronni nodded. "Peter must have somehow attached the microchip when he was home at Christmas, believing that when we traveled to Vienna to see him, we'd be bringing it with us.'' She dangled the silver chain from her fingers. "What he didn't expect was that Steffie would get a rash from the bracelet, and I would replace it with a sterling silver one.''

"So those men took the sterling silver bracelet, when all along it was her old metal bracelet that had the information.'' Clara glanced nervously at her daughter. "What's going to happen when those men discover they've got the wrong bracelet?''

Ronni pressed her hands to her temples and shook her head. "I don't know.''

"I think you'd better call the authorities—now,'' Clara advised.

"I think we should wait until Logan gets back before we do anything."

"Wait?" Clara repeated in disbelief. "You don't even know if he's coming back. Those men had guns, Veronica."

The cold fingers of fate seemed to reach out and wrap themselves around Ronni. "Mother, for Pete's sake. Of course he'll be back. He's an ex-CIA agent," she said with more conviction than she was feeling. It worried her that he had gone after them—especially when it hadn't been necessary. She felt a spurt of anger that he hadn't given her the opportunity to tell him she had the missing microchip.

"I still think you should call the FBI," Clara said, bending over to pick up Steffie, who was beginning to fuss. "Steffie's probably hungry. Why don't I make her some lunch while you make that phone call?"

Ronni was not about to be railroaded by her mother. "We'll all have lunch," she announced firmly. "Then, if I haven't heard from Logan by the time we've finished, I'll call."

Clara didn't look pleased, but she acquiesced. The three of them ate lunch, although Ronni spent more time pushing food around on her plate than putting it in her mouth. As soon as they'd finished, Clara offered to read Steffie a story, and got her ready for her nap while Ronni cleaned up the kitchen. Ronni was staring out the window, hoping for some sign of Logan when her mother reappeared.

"Well? Did you make that phone call?" Clara asked.

Ronni glanced at her watch. "No, I didn't. Can't we give him another half hour?"

"All right," Clara reluctantly conceded. "But come away from that window. You know what they say—a watched pot never boils.'' She pulled a deck of cards from the desk drawer. "Why don't we play some gin?"

Ronni wanted to decline, but her mother was already sitting down at the dining-room table, shuffling the cards. Reluctantly Ronni pulled out a chair and sat down across from her. "I tried calling the hospital, but they wouldn't let me speak to Andrew. They said he isn't able to use the phone," she commented, picking up the playing cards her mother was dealing her.

"That's odd...considering he called here this morning." Dark eyebrows peppered with gray drew together. "Do you suppose he's taken a turn for the worse?"

"I don't think so. When I spoke to his nurse I was told he probably would be moved out of the cardiac care unit today. What's strange, though, is that she was under the impression he hasn't been able to use the telephone since he was admitted."

"Of course he has," Clara said, rearranging her cards. "He called me."

Ronni chewed on her lower lip. "I was thinking about that. What if it wasn't Andrew who called this morning, but someone pretending to be him? Maybe it was someone connected with those men who took Steffie's bracelet." She drummed her fingers on the table. "I wonder if there's a tap on your phone."

"For heaven's sake, Veronica, this is worse than a James Bond film." Clara slapped her cards down and placed both palms on the table. "If you're not going to call someone, then I will." She started to stand, but Ronni put out her hand to stop her.

"Please wait just a little longer," she begged. "Logan is convinced that Peter's contact here in the States is working within the government. If he's right, it wouldn't be wise for us to call.''

Clara eyed her skeptically, then sat back down. "Do you realize how long he's been gone?"

Again Ronni looked at her watch, and frowned. "Too long. If he would just call so I could tell him about the bracelet.'' Ronni tossed her cards into the center of the table and got to her feet.

"If you're going to go look out that window again, I'm going to go make us a fresh pot of coffee,'' Clara said.

Ronni did cross the room and peeked out the window at the street below. Then she began to pace, until finally Clara shoved a magazine in her hand and ordered her to sit down and read. Ronni had little interest in the weekly news magazine, but flipped through the pages to appease her mother.

As she was glancing at the magazine, however, one photo managed to catch her attention. It was of Senator Potter and several other congressmen. Upon closer inspection, Ronni noticed a familiar face in the background, although the caption beneath the photo didn't identify the man.

"What are you looking at?'' Clara asked, when Ronni muttered an unintelligible comment under her breath.

"This picture of Andrew's father. It just made me realize something,'' she said thoughtfully. Suddenly the intercom buzzed, causing Ronni to practically leap off the sofa and rush for the door. Her heart turned over at the sound of Logan's voice.

She was waiting at the elevator when the doors slid open and he stepped out. She launched herself against his chest, wrapping her arms around him possessively.

"You're all right," she cried, tears of joy streaming down her face as she looked up at him.

"I'm fine," he assured her, appreciating her exuberant welcome. "You weren't worried, were you?" he asked, covering her tears with his thumbs.

"Of course I was. Those men had guns," she told him wide-eyed. "Come inside," she urged, steering him toward her mother's apartment, where Clara stood guarding the door with a posture that made Ronni want to salute her as she ushered Logan past her.

With an arm wrapped around his waist, Ronni led Logan into the living room, where she pulled him down beside her on the sofa.

"Tell me what happened," she said.

"I lost them. I thought I had them and..." He snapped his fingers. "Like that they were gone." He raked a hand through his hair. "Some hero, eh?" He laughed sardonically.

"Thank God you didn't catch them," Ronni exclaimed.

He looked at her quizzically. "Ronni, this means they've got the microchip. It was in Steffie's bracelet."

"I know it was in Steffie's bracelet. I figured that out for myself," she gently chided him. "But, Logan, they don't have Steffie's bracelet."

Confused, he said, "You're not making any sense. You told me you gave them Steffie's bracelet."

"I did," she admitted. "But you came exploding in here, then went tearing out before I could explain to you that Steffie has *two* Medic-Alert bracelets." Her eyes lit up in excitement as she pulled Steffie's original bracelet from her pocket and held it out in front of Logan. "If Peter put the microchip on a bracelet, it's got to be on this one."

Logan took the bracelet and examined it carefully. "What makes you think it's on this one?"

"This is the bracelet Steffie's had ever since she was diagnosed as being allergic to penicillin. She's worn it for months, and I wouldn't have bought a different one except that she developed a rash on her wrist. Thinking it was the metal in the bracelet, I ordered her a sterling silver bracelet that was hypoallergenic."

"And Peter didn't know she had the extra bracelet?"

"No. It only arrived the day we left for Key West. I put it on Steffie's wrist when we stopped for dinner at Cooter's place. I almost threw the old bracelet away, but decided to stick it in the diaper bag in case something happened to the new one." She smiled in relief. "Little did I know how important it was."

Logan looked bewildered and Ronni playfully punched him on the shoulder. "Look happy. The microchip is in your hands. Trust me."

CHAPTER FIFTEEN

"IF ONLY WE'D KNOWN that this little thing was what they were looking for," Logan remarked, jiggling the bracelet in his cupped hand. His expression changed from one of relief to uncertainty. "The problem is, now that we've found it, what do we do with it?"

"Does that mean you still suspect Senator Potter?" Ronni asked.

Before he could reply, Clara stepped forward and said with a slight edge of annoyance in her tone, "Since Veronica's not going to introduce us... I'm Clara Summers." She offered Logan her hand. "Are those two men going to come back here when they realize they don't have the right bracelet?"

Logan stood up and acknowledged her introduction. "I'm Logan McNeil, and I'm afraid I don't have the answer to your question, Mrs. Summers."

Ronni could sense her mother's readiness to cross-examine Logan, for there was disapproval in her narrowed eyes and her pointed chin. Before Clara could pounce on his reply, Ronni gave her a warning glance and said, "Mother, why don't you get us some coffee?"

Ronni half expected her mother to tell her to go get the coffee, but Clara excused herself and disappeared into the kitchen. As soon as she was gone, Ronni slipped her arm through Logan's and asked, "Are those two men likely to come back?"

"If they think you still have the microchip, yes," he answered truthfully.

"Can't we give it back to the government? Surely you can trust the FBI."

"So far the FBI's been unable to find the key man behind the conspiracy. He's covered his tracks pretty well." Logan arched both his eyebrows. "The microchip might be the only way we can identify who was working with Peter."

"Have you told them you suspect the senator?"

Regretfully he said, "I can't—not until I'm certain he's the one."

"What did Andrew say when you talked to him?"

He shook his head. "Nothing that would incriminate his father."

"Mom said he called here earlier this morning asking for me."

"He did call . . . right after I spoke to you this morning," Clara confirmed, returning with a silver tray laden with cups and saucers, which she set down on the glass-topped coffee table.

"Are you sure it was him?" Logan asked, accepting a china cup from Clara. "He didn't look to me as though he'd be strong enough to use the phone. I was only allowed to talk to him for ten minutes."

"But why would somebody call and pretend to be Andrew?" Ronni asked suspiciously.

Logan took a sip of the coffee. "I don't know, unless it was simply a way of finding out if you and Steffie were here."

"Could it have been the senator?" Ronni asked over the rim of her cup.

Logan shrugged and looked as though he didn't want to even consider the possibility. "He was supposed to meet me at the hospital this morning, but he never showed up."

"Why would Senator Potter pretend to be his son?" Clara asked with a puzzled frown.

Ronni ignored her mother's question and said to her, "Logan uses sugar in his coffee." Clara, who had been hovering beside the two of them with her arms folded across her chest, reluctantly went back to the kitchen.

Ronni waited until her mother was out of sight before saying, "Logan, are you sure the senator doesn't know Andrew is gay?"

"Yes. Why do you ask?"

She reached for the newsmagazine on the coffee table and began flipping through the pages. "While you were gone I happened to be glancing through this and I noticed something." She found the page she was looking for, then held the magazine out in front of him. "See this picture?"

"What about it?" he asked, glancing at the photo of Doc and several congressmen on the Capitol steps.

"See that man in the background—the one with the mustache?" She cocked her head as she peered over his shoulder.

"Yeah, that's Smithson. He works for Senator Potter," he stated simply. "He's been his personal aide for at least five or six years." He held her gaze, waiting for her to continue.

"Then I don't see how the senator could not know that Andrew's gay. That man—" she tapped her fingernail on Smithson's face "—was Andrew's lover."

"Smithson?" Logan was obviously caught off guard by her announcement. She could see the disbelief in his face, and something else—maybe anger?

"Andrew never called him by that name, but I'm positive that's the man," Ronni said confidently. "I only saw him once or twice, and that was by accident. You see, Andrew got very upset that I'd seen him at all. Although he himself had told me about his homosexuality, he became rather embarrassed that I'd actually discovered who his lover was."

"Andrew's a homosexual?" Clara muttered under her breath, nearly dropping the sugar bowl in reaction to Ronni's statement. "How come you never told me?" she admonished her daughter as she slowly lowered her ample figure onto the chair.

"It's not something one broadcasts, Mother," Ronni replied. "Andrew's private life was none of my business. I knew he had men friends, but with the exception of this guy, I never saw any of them."

"Are you sure it was him?" Logan looked again at the man in the picture.

"Yes, that's him. Although I think their affair ended shortly after I found out about it." Ronni glanced at her mother, whose mouth was gaping. "Don't you have some cookies or brownies to go with the coffee?"

"In the freezer, but . . ." Clara's voice trailed off.

"Pop them in the microwave and they'll be fine," Ronni said pointedly, causing Clara to excuse herself and disappear once more into the kitchen.

"She doesn't look like a dragon to me," Logan commented softly after she'd retreated again, remembering how Ronni had told him her mother was so tough she could puff smoke without a cigarette.

"You haven't seen her in her command mode yet," Ronni said dryly. "And don't you dare say I look like her," she warned.

"You do look like her, especially when you point your chin at me," he teased. He brushed a quick kiss over her pursed lips, then quickly slipped back into a serious mood. "Tell me about Andy and Smithson."

"At first I thought I was responsible for breaking them up, especially because I had to move in with Andrew after Peter and I separated. But Andrew assured me that my staying with him wasn't a problem, since this guy lived out of town and theirs was a long distance affair."

"And he never mentioned that this guy worked for his father?" Logan asked.

"No. All I knew was that because of both of their reputations, secrecy was important. I promised Andrew I'd never mention it to anyone, and I never did. In fact, I had forgotten all about it until I saw that picture."

Logan regarded the photo pensively. "He could be the honey trap."

"What do you mean?" Ronni asked.

"Do you remember when I asked you if you knew what a honey trap was?"

"Yes, when we were in Key West," she replied. "Does it have something to do with spying?"

"A honey trap is a sexual seduction—a common recruitment device spies often use," Logan explained.

"Usually it's a female who seduces a male, then threatens to reveal that she's been sleeping with him unless he gets the information she wants. It's a type of blackmail."

"And you think that's what might have happened to Andrew, only in his case the person doing the seducing wasn't a woman but a man?" Ronni suggested.

"It would explain a lot of things—including why those men were able to find us in Fort Lauderdale. Smithson knows every move the senator makes, and even though I asked Doc not to tell anyone where we were, it wouldn't surprise me if Smithson was able to get the information out of him. Doc trusts him implicitly."

"Does this mean that Senator Potter is innocent?" she asked encouragingly.

He exhaled a long sigh of relief. "This is the first time in the past two days that I thought there's a good possibility he is innocent," Logan replied, a look of hope on his face. "You know how difficult it was for me to believe he could be guilty. The problem is, how do I go about proving he's innocent?" He contemplated the question, staring absently into space.

"Can't you just contact the FBI and let them handle it?"

He let his face slip into a grin. "That would be Plan B."

Ronni could see that he was scheming, and a flutter of apprehension had her cautiously asking, "What's Plan A? You're not going to do anything dangerous, are you?"

"Plan A is a little meeting with Mr. Smithson and the senator," he said smugly.

"Did I hear someone say 'dangerous'?" Clara asked, returning this time with a plateful of cookies. "What are you two up to?"

"Logan has a plan that will trap the man responsible for all the horrible things that have been happening to me and Steffie," Ronni explained in a tone more befitting a mother speaking to a child than a child speaking to a mother.

"I hope his plan doesn't involve you," Clara said anxiously.

"You can relax, Mrs. Summers," Logan reassured her. "I wouldn't let Ronni anywhere near this guy."

"What do you mean you won't *let* me?" Ronni asked indignantly, hands on her hips. "I'm the one who recognized Smithson from the photo, and if I want to come with you, I'm going to come with you."

"You're not coming with me," Logan said firmly. "Catching spies is my business, Ronni, not yours."

"Veronica, listen to the man," Clara advised. "He knows what he's talking about. My goodness, we've just had two men with guns break in here and steal Steffie's bracelet!"

"There must be something I can do," Ronni lamented.

"You can give me the keys to your house," Logan said. "And Steffie's bracelet. And I'm going to need to use the telephone."

An hour later, Ronni accompanied Logan to the lobby of her mother's apartment building, where they waited for a man called Nat. Six-foot-tall and an ex-marine, Nat was the bodyguard Logan had arranged to stay with Ronni and her mother while he was gone. Although Logan felt comfortable with the arrangement,

Ronni wasn't—not because she resented having a bodyguard, but because she didn't want Logan going alone to her house.

"You're worrying over nothing, Ronni," Logan told her when she expressed such sentiments. "I've been in intelligence work for over ten years. I'm not going to get hurt."

"You were the one who said desperate men are dangerous," Ronni reminded him, trying to control the shivers of apprehension that made her want to fling herself against the door and not let him leave.

"If our suspicions are correct and Doc is innocent, it'll be two against one." He laid his hand on her cheek. "Trust me."

Ronni reached up and covered his hand with hers. "I wish you'd let me come along. I promise I won't get in the way. I could hide in one of the bedrooms. You wouldn't even know I was there." She looked up at him beseechingly.

"I wish I could say I want you to come with me, Ronni, but the truth is it's better if you wait here."

"But I want to be there, Logan. Do you realize what this guy has done to me? He's blackmailed Andrew into committing treason, he's helped convince the FBI that I was involved with Peter, and worst of all, he's put Steffie's life in danger."

"He's one of their best," he acknowledged with a sigh. "For five years he's managed to fool one of the sharpest men I know."

"Logan, what are you going to do if Senator Potter was in on all of this?"

"He wasn't." The words were swift and positive. "I'd bet my life on it."

"You sound awfully confident."

"Didn't I tell you? I've got a sixth sense when it comes to detecting spies. When I see someone I know is legit, I get a flutter right here." He nudged his rib cage with his fist.

"Is that what happened when you met me? You got a flutter right there?" She touched the same spot.

"With you, the flutter was in an entirely different place," he said huskily. "Actually it was more of a throb."

"And when did you first notice this...ah...throb?" she asked, his nearness causing her body to respond in a natural way.

"When Doc showed me a picture of you. You were wearing the most delicious green swimsuit." He smiled dangerously. "I took one look at you and I told Doc you weren't a spy."

"Do I have this...ah...throb to thank for your helping me and Steffie?" She inched her fingers teasingly between the buttons on his shirt.

"I suppose it played a part in my decision to come after you," he confessed with a seductive grin.

"You did have a few doubts along the way," she reminded him.

"When you've been an agent as long as I have, it's hard not to be suspicious of your own mother." He reached out and caressed her cheeks with his fingertips. "I want you to know something, Ronni. When it comes to what's happened with us, there are no doubts."

"For me, neither," she told him, turning her head so that her lips met his palm.

He leaned over and kissed her long and hard. "I'm not going to let anything happen, I promise," he murmured.

"It'll all work out." They both knew she wasn't talking just about Smithson being apprehended. "If I'm frightened at all, it's only because I'm worried that when it's all over you're going to walk out of my life." She looked at him with pleading eyes.

Logan reluctantly released her. "This isn't the time or the place to be talking about that." He glanced over his shoulder and out the glass doors. "Nat's coming across the street."

Ronni reached up and wiped the smeared lipstick from his mouth. "I love you, Logan," she told him just seconds before the bodyguard entered the lobby. Logan looked as though he was going to say something to her, but Nat greeted him with a big grin and a raised hand.

"Hey, Mick!" He slapped Logan's hand in a high-five manner. "It's good to see you, buddy."

Logan slapped the outstretched hand back and smiled warmly. "Nat, this is Ronni. She and her mother are going to wait upstairs until I get back."

Ronni shook Nat's big burly hand and returned his grin. "Hi, Nat. It's nice to meet you. I'm going to walk Logan to his car, then I'll take you upstairs."

Nat looked to Logan for confirmation.

Logan nodded, then tapped Nat on the arm. "I appreciate your coming over," he said gratefully, then opened the door for Ronni.

As soon as they were outdoors, she said, "You weren't kidding when you said he was big." She glanced back over her shoulder and saw the blond giant standing in the doorway. "I think his arm is bigger than my leg."

"What frightens me more than confronting Smithson is the thought of leaving you alone," Logan said with more emotion than she was expecting to hear in his voice. "If I can't be there to protect you, I want to make certain the guy who is can handle the job."

"But if Smithson is Peter's contact and he knows you're bringing the microchip with you, there isn't much chance that he'd send anybody here, is there?"

"It's a chance I'm not going to take." They had arrived at the pickup, and the apprehension she was feeling about him leaving was written all over her face. Logan hooked a finger beneath her chin and said, "Hey, don't look at me as though I'm walking into a firing squad."

She lowered her eyes. "I'm sorry. I'm just a little nervous."

He quickly pressed one last kiss on her mouth, only it wasn't a quick kiss, but a slow, lingering caress that left both of them breathing a little harder. Logan leaned his forehead against hers and said, "Relax, it's a piece of cake."

She pressed her hands against his chest, unwittingly finding the shoulder holster, and she stiffened. "I thought you said agents seldom carried guns?"

"This is seldom," he said, looking away in the distance.

She bit on her lower lip. "Please don't go, Logan. Let the FBI handle this," she pleaded.

He returned his gaze to her, searching for understanding. "Ronni, I can't. If Doc is guilty, I have to be the first one to know."

Unsteadily she nodded.

"Look, I've got to go." He grabbed her one last time and planted one more long, hard kiss on her mouth. "I love you, too, Ronni," he murmured, then signaled to Nat that he was leaving.

"Be careful," she called out as he climbed into the orange pickup.

He rolled down the window. "It'll all work out. Trust me."

Ronni could only nod and wave goodbye. Long after his truck had disappeared out of sight, she stood staring at the street, until finally Nat called out to her to come inside. Slowly she walked back to the apartment building, her mind racing ahead to what would happen when Logan confronted Smithson and Doc in her home. She tried not to think about that meeting, forcing her thoughts to images of what it would be like when it was over. She would be cleared of any involvement with Peter, she could go home again and she and Steffie would be out of danger.

What would happen to Andrew she could only speculate on. Even if his involvement was the result of being blackmailed, she assumed he would be tried and sent to prison. Not only was Steffie going to lose her father, but her godfather, as well.

And she herself would still be married to Peter, but in love with another man. Logan had said he loved her. Those three words had unleashed a torrent of hopes and dreams, which she'd been secretly harboring ever since she'd discovered how much she loved him. She knew, however, that just because he'd said he loved her didn't mean he wanted to make a commitment.

It was a lot to ask of a man—accepting the responsibility of parenting a child. She wasn't just a married woman; she was a married woman with child. And they hadn't had time to talk about what the future held. They had been too busy discovering each other.

ALL THE WAY to Ronni's house, Logan's thoughts were filled with images of her tear-stained face, how appealing she had looked begging him not to go. He was just as apprehensive as she was—not about trapping Smithson, but about what was going to happen to the two of them. In a very short time Ronni and her daughter had managed to become a part of his life—a part he didn't want to lose. Yet when all this craziness was over and he was no longer needed to protect them, would she still want him in her life? As much as he wanted to believe that she loved him, he knew that circumstances had played a big part in their relationship. Maybe she was simply in love with the dangerous secret agent image he represented.

As he parked the pickup beside her house, memories of the last time he'd been there rushed to greet him. Automatically his gaze flickered to the large, overgrown bougainvillea on the corner, and as he expected, there sat a television repair van. So far so good.

He climbed out of the truck and followed the cement walk to the front door. As soon as he was inside, he found the telephone in the living room, pulled a small metal disk from his pocket and placed it on the underside of the cradle. Then he went to the refrigerator, extracted a bottle of spring water and looked curiously around Ronni's house while he waited for his visitors.

He didn't have to wait long. Smithson pulled into the narrow driveway, carefully maneuvering the large town car. Logan watched him open the door for the senator and help him out in his usual attentive manner. Doc looked even more haggard than the last time Logan had seen him. His suit was slightly wrinkled, his gray hair less than immaculately groomed. He appeared troubled and tired, and Logan's heart balked at what he knew he had to do to the old man. He wanted to console him, not interrogate him. But he couldn't—not until he was absolutely certain that Doc wasn't involved in the spy ring.

Smithson on the other hand looked impeccable. Despite the heat, he wore a three-piece pin-striped suit without a wrinkle in it—not even a crease in the pants. Logan had often wondered how anyone could sit down and not wrinkle his pants, but Smithson had always managed it. His hair was cut shorter now, and his mustache was gone. He looked as honest as a judge, and Logan had to remind himself that beneath that gentlemanly facade lurked a deceptive mind.

"You made good time," Logan said by way of a greeting, as he opened the door for them to enter.

"The hospital gave me your message as soon as I arrived," Doc explained, following Logan into the living room. He had withdrawn a handkerchief from his pocket and was blotting his forehead.

"Are you all right, Doc?" Logan asked, gesturing for the two men to be seated.

Doc dismissed Logan's concern with a wave of his hand. "I'm fine. I'm just a little warm." He accepted Logan's offer of a chair, but Smithson expressed a desire to remain standing.

Logan searched for some signs of anxiety in the younger man, but there was none. He figured it could mean one of two things: either Smithson didn't suspect that Logan knew he was Peter's conspirator, or else he was confident that no matter what happened, he would get the microchip. Logan hoped that it was the former. He also wished that he had Smithson's confidence, for right now his insides were churning. He wasn't sure he could play charades with Doc, yet he knew he had no choice but to give it his best shot.

"Warm, eh, Doc?" Logan shoved his hands in his pockets and stood looking down at the older man. "You wouldn't be nervous about seeing me, would you?"

Doc gave him a puzzled look. "This whole business of the microchip has me nervous. Do you realize how important that tiny piece of information is?"

"Maybe you ought to tell me why it's so important to you," Logan suggested, an edge to his voice. He raised a hand to his forehead and gently massaged his temple.

Doc caught the gesture and asked, "What's wrong with you? Is your eye bothering you?"

Logan gave a couple of quick shakes of his head. "It's nothing."

"Where's the microchip?" Doc asked.

"It's right here." Logan reached inside his pocket and withdrew the bracelet, dangling it in midair.

"A bracelet?" Doc looked quizzically at him.

"Surprised?" Logan asked.

"You mean to tell me the microchip is in that bracelet?" The senator appeared skeptical.

"Very good, Doc," Logan said sarcastically, and just as Doc was about to reach for the chain, Logan stepped back and snatched it out of his reach. "But you can cut the ignorant number. You know damn well the microchip is in the bracelet. That's why you sent those two goons to steal it off Steffie Lang's wrist." With the accusation came the appearance of the gun, as Logan smoothly pulled it from under his arm.

Doc gasped and fell back against the sofa cushions. "What the hell are you talking about?" he demanded.

"I'm talking about treason. You know, selling secrets to foreign governments," Logan said, pointing the gun at his mentor.

"Logan, you can't possibly think that *I'm* involved in the Lang affair," Doc challenged.

Coolly Smithson spoke up in defense of his boss. "Come on, Logan, you're out of line on this."

"I think not," Logan went on. "I knew there had to be someone on the inside—a top brass. You fooled the feds— you even fooled me—well, almost. Why did you do it, Doc? How could you have set me up like that?" he asked painfully.

"I didn't set you up!" Doc emphatically denied. "Logan, you've got to be sick if you think I'd do such a thing. Sit down and put that gun away."

The senator attempted to rise, but Logan pointed the gun directly at his face.

"You're right about one thing, Doc. I am sick," Logan rasped. "I'm sick at heart to think that someone I loved like a father could have done this to me."

"I can't believe you would think such a thing of me," Doc said, again protesting his innocence.

Smithson finally spoke up. "Logan, are you certain about this?"

"Of course he's not certain," Doc interjected. "He's confused. I don't know why or how he came to such a conclusion."

"It's over, Doc. You can save your defense." Logan turned to Smithson. "Take this and keep him covered while I call the FBI." He handed the gun to Smithson, then walked over to the desk and started to dial.

"Smithson, quit waving that gun around," Doc ordered. "Let him call the feds. They'll tell him how wrong he is." He made a move to get up again, but Smithson pushed him back with the point of his gun.

"Nobody's calling anybody," Smithson declared in a threatening tone of voice.

Logan glanced over his shoulder and saw that Smithson didn't just have the senator covered, but was aiming the gun at him, as well. "Hey, be careful where you're pointing that thing," he said uneasily.

Smithson chuckled nastily. "Sure, Logan. Just as soon as you've put down that telephone and given me that little silver chain. After all, we want to make sure it reaches the proper authorities, don't we?" he said with a smirk, his palm outstretched.

Logan stood staring at Smithson for several seconds before he finally uttered, "You?" He gave him a look of disbelief that could have won him an Academy Award.

"I'm waiting for it, Logan," Smithson reminded him.

Slowly Logan replaced the telephone on its cradle, then walked over to Smithson and dropped the bracelet in his hand. Smithson's fingers quickly snapped shut around it.

"Now move over there next to Doc and keep your hands up over your head where I can see them," Smithson directed, gesturing with the gun.

Logan did as he was told, eyeing Smithson suspiciously as he sat down beside the senator. "You're not going to get away with this," he warned.

"Who's going to stop me? You?" He chuckled sarcastically. "It's no wonder the Agency retired you. Admit it, Logan. You've lost it. Or maybe I should say you met someone smarter than you, Mr. Spy Catcher."

Doc was sputtering and shaking his head in disbelief. "You were the mastermind behind Peter Lang?"

"Have been for five years, Doc," Smithson confessed proudly. "Since the day you hired me." With one hand, he examined the bracelet, scratching a small metal piece on the underside. "Bingo! There it is. Right where it's supposed to be." An evil grin spread across his face. "Thanks, fellas." He slipped the bracelet into his pocket. "This little piece of jewelry is going to set me up for life. I'll finally be able to return home."

"Home?" Doc queried.

"Leningrad." Again Smithson smirked. "There's no place like home, is there?"

"You're a Russian? But what about your credentials? I had you thoroughly investigated before I ever hired you," Doc insisted.

"Kenneth Smithson was created to be the perfect congressional aide...and he was," he said smugly. "I don't think I've ever seen a more impressive résumé. Amazing what contacts in the right places can do, isn't it?" He gave a little laugh. "We worked well together, Senator, and I enjoyed our partnership...especially now that it's given me the opportunity to return home a hero."

"You disgust me!"

When the senator would have lunged at the man, Logan grabbed him.

"Stop it, Doc. He's not worth getting shot over."

"You really are washed up, aren't you?" Smithson directed his loathing at Logan. "First you hand me the gun, then you expect me to walk out of here with the two of you still breathing." He shook his head disbelievingly. "When I leave, I leave two dead fools behind."

"Tell me how Andrew is involved in this," Doc demanded.

"Ah, yes, Andrew."

Smithson appeared to be considering how much he should tell the older man, and Logan knew it was time he intervened with some questioning. "As long as we're dead meat, why don't you tell these two fools just how many people were involved in this Peter Lang affair?"

"Does it bother you that you weren't able to crack it?" Smithson chided.

"All right, so you fooled me," Logan admitted. "But how do I know it was you who masterminded this whole scheme? Maybe Andrew was the brains behind it."

Smithson laughed. "Andrew followed orders I issued." He looked at the senator. "Your son is bright, Doc, but he's spineless."

"How did you trap him? Was it the Lang woman?" Doc asked, and Logan held his breath waiting for the answer.

"What makes you think he had to be trapped? Andrew is just as greedy as any other man," Smithson replied.

"He did it for money?" Doc asked, and Logan could see the agony on the lined face.

"What's wrong, Senator? Does it bother you to think that your son could sell his idealism for material things? It shouldn't surprise you. You've known all along that Andy doesn't share your patriotic sentiment. He's not righteous and strong like Logan here. He's weak, Doc. But you've known that all along, too, haven't you?"

"Isn't that what attracted you to him in the first place?" Logan asked, hating to have to bring up the subject, but knowing he had no choice. "You got a thing about weak men, Smithson?" There was no way either man could have missed the double meaning.

"Logan, are you saying that Andrew and Smithson were..." Doc's voice trailed off, his face paling.

"Lovers," Logan finished for him, hating to have to be the one to say the word.

A small bead of perspiration lined Smithson's thin lips. "How did you find out?"

"I'm glad you're not going to deny it," Logan said soberly. "You know, you were good, Smithson. You fooled Doc. You fooled me. Luckily Mrs. Lang saw your picture in a magazine. Apparently Andy didn't keep your affair as secret as you had hoped. Tell me, did you blackmail him into spying for you, or was he already mixed up with Peter Lang?"

He pressed his lips together so tightly they almost disappeared. "Andy's more like his father than he wants him to believe he is. Fortunately his feelings for his father were strong enough to want to keep his sexual preferences private.''

"So you threatened to expose him if he didn't cooperate," Logan inserted. "So what happened to this wonderful arrangement?"

"Andrew began having an attack of conscience, especially when Peter told him the microchip was going to be delivered on the wrist of his daughter. He did as he was told—saw to it that it was affixed to the baby's bracelet, but he threatened to expose all of us if anything happened to either the child or its mother," Smithson explained.

"So you countered his threat with one of your own. You made sure that Andrew had a change of heart— literally—injecting him with a drug that nearly stopped his heart permanently," Logan accused.

"I can't believe you'd do such a thing!" Doc exclaimed, gaping at the man who'd been his trusted aide for the past five years.

"Oh, it's true, Doc," Logan assured him. "That day you visited me, Smithson here flew to Melbourne."

"You told me you had to visit your mother," Doc said to Smithson.

"All those visits he supposedly made to his mother— convincing you he was a dutiful son—they were actually visits to Andy," Logan continued.

"Well, well, well," Smithson said. "The old one-eyed agent isn't as foolish as I thought." His eyes flew to the gun in his hand, and in an almost panicky move, he squeezed the trigger.

"Sorry, Smithson," Logan said when the only sound heard was the click of an empty barrel. "I don't like to carry a loaded gun." He shot him a wicked grin.

Immediately Smithson dropped the gun, but when he would have reached inside his coat pocket for his own weapon, a voice called over Smithson's shoulder, "Freeze!"

Smithson had no choice, for a heavy-duty Magnum was aimed directly at him.

Logan looked up to see Wicklund and Mahoney searching Smithson for any other weapons. "It's about time you two showed up," he said, a hint of relief in his voice. "I was beginning to worry."

"You're the one who said you wanted time to get the whole story," Stan Wicklund reminded him with a crooked grin.

CHAPTER SIXTEEN

LOGAN WANTED NOTHING more than to rush right over to Clara Summers's apartment to see Ronni, but the senator was slumped wearily on the sofa. Even though his face reflected no emotion, he looked like a broken man, and Logan wondered if there was anything he could say that would ease the heartache the man was suffering.

As soon as the others had gone, Logan sat down beside him and put a hand on his sagging shoulder. "I'm sorry, Doc. I didn't mean to be so hard on you, but it was the only way I knew how to get Smithson to confess."

Doc seemed to be lost in a world of his own and didn't respond.

Worried, Logan asked, "Are you okay, Doc?"

"How could I have been so blind?" he asked quietly, closing his eyes as he shook his head regretfully. "Smithson is right—I am an old fool."

"You've never been a fool in my eyes," Logan said sincerely.

Doc stared at his hands. "How long have you known about all this?"

"I only put the final pieces together this afternoon. I went to the hospital looking for you this morning, but you and Smithson hadn't arrived yet. You see, you were the only person who knew we were staying in Fort Lauderdale. When the KGB agents showed up there, I figured it had to be someone in your office."

"Or me?" Doc looked him in the eye. "You did think it was me, didn't you?"

Logan wanted to lie and tell him he'd never lost his faith in him, but he'd never pulled any punches with Doc, so he told him the truth. "I wouldn't be a good agent if I hadn't suspected you. But deep down in my heart I knew that you were innocent. Although I must confess it's not easy being objective when people you care about are involved."

Dejectedly Doc said, "I've lost everything, Logan. My son...my job—I'm going to have to resign from the Senate."

Logan didn't try to pretend otherwise. "You're the one who's been telling me for quite some time now that this was going to be your last term, that you wanted to go back to the farm."

"Yes, well, I didn't want to leave with my tail tucked between my legs." He smoothed a hand across the thin spot on the back of his head. "There'll be a formal investigation. I haven't anything to hide," he said proudly.

"I didn't think you did," Logan assured him. "Tell me, Doc, how much did you know about Andy's part in all this?"

"The first indication I had that he could be involved with Lang was when I came to you. Like you said, sometimes you lose your objectivity with people you care about. As I look back now, I can see the signs were all there, but I chose to ignore them." There was self-recrimination in his voice, then he chuckled and shook his head in amazement. "I thought that all those weekends Smithson spent in Cocoa Beach he was visiting his mother."

"He fooled me, too, Doc," Logan admitted. "You're the one who told me that a good agent isn't fooled but betrayed."

"I was betrayed by my right-hand man and my own son. That kind of betrayal makes a man feel foolish."

"Smithson was a pro—and a damn good one. He knew exactly what he was doing and for what reasons. Andy, on the other hand, was a victim—maybe not an innocent victim, but still a victim. Tell me something, Doc. If Veronica Lang had been the honey trap, would that have made it any easier for you to accept Andy's treason?"

Doc considered the question carefully. "No, I guess it wouldn't have," he finally said. "I only wish Andrew had come to me and told me what was happening. Did he think I wouldn't understand about his homosexuality?"

"Knowing Andy, he probably figured it would be one more reason for you to be disappointed in him. Or maybe he hasn't truly accepted his homosexuality himself. And you have to remember, he didn't want to blemish your reputation with ugly gossip. It was that vulnerability that allowed Smithson to use him. The threat of exposure was all he needed to keep Andy in line."

"Andrew is going to end up in prison," Doc said sadly.

"More than likely, although at this point we don't know to what extent he was involved. It's possible he could get a reduced sentence depending on his testimony. Andy must have been ready to go to the authorities, otherwise the Russians wouldn't have tried to kill him.''

Doc sighed. ''I hope you're right.'' He heaved his large frame up off the sofa. ''I guess I'd better get over to the hospital. I told Wicklund and Mahoney I'd meet them there.''

''Do you want me to come with you?'' Logan offered.

''I guess I'll need a ride,'' the senator said, patting his pockets. ''Smithson took the keys to the town car.''

Logan threw his arm around the rounded shoulders and said, ''Come on. I'll show you what it's like to ride in an ultra orange machine. I can drop you off on my way to get Ronni.''

As it turned out, it was quite late by the time Logan got back to Clara Summers's apartment. The meeting with Wicklund and Mahoney had been a painful one for Doc, as Andrew, with the doctor's permission, had talked with the FBI and openly admitted his involvement with Smithson. Logan had hung around to the bitter end, hoping his presence could in some small way compensate for the misery he knew Doc was suffering. As eager as he was to get over to see Ronni, he couldn't leave the senator to face such adversity alone.

He had called Ronni from the hospital and learned that she had decided to spend the night with her mother, since Steffie had fallen asleep shortly after dinner. When Clara admitted him to the apartment, Logan saw Nat sitting in front of the television with a bowl of popcorn on his lap, while Ronni was curled up on the couch, asleep.

Logan wanted to run over and kiss her awake, but he forced himself to settle up with Nat, exchanging a few words and a handshake while Clara turned off the television, then gently nudged Ronni's shoulder. Startled, Ronni awoke, stretching like a cat before noticing that Logan was ushering Nat out the door. Clara discreetly announced that she was going to bed, and as the dead bolt clicked shut behind Nat, Ronni joyously rushed into Logan's arms.

"I'm so glad it's finally over," she said when he had finished telling her about Smithson's arrest. "It is over, isn't it, Logan?"

"I can't guarantee that the FBI won't want to speak with you again, but at least they know you were simply an innocent bystander caught up in circumstances beyond your control."

"Andrew wasn't innocent, though, was he?" she asked solemnly.

Logan shook his head. "It's true that Smithson was blackmailing him, but he was involved, more so than we first thought. Andy was the one who put the microchip on Steffie's wrist."

"It wasn't Peter?"

"No. Apparently Andy went out and bought a Medic-Alert bracelet identical to Steffie's, had the microchip affixed to the metal—sort of a false front so you couldn't tell it was there. Then, before you were supposed to leave for Vienna, he made the switch."

Ronni's brow wrinkled. "It must have been when he invited us over for dinner. He said it was a bon voyage supper."

"Peter was supposed to make another switch, substituting an identical bracelet for the one with the microchip once you got to Vienna."

"Only we never made it to Vienna," Ronni said solemnly. "That must be why Andrew told us to come directly to his house the morning of his heart attack. He wanted to get the microchip off of Steffie's wrist." She shook her head in disappointment. "When the paramedics were wheeling him out to the ambulance, he pulled off his oxygen mask and asked about Steffie. I thought he was worried about her health, when all along he was only worried about getting the microchip back."

"He does care about her," Logan said in Andrew's defense, which only drew a skeptical look from Ronni. "Apparently Smithson had promised Andy that the transfer of the microchip would be the last assignment he would have to complete. At first Andy refused to be a part of anything involving you and Steffie, but Smithson warned him that if someone else was assigned to the task, he couldn't promise you wouldn't get hurt. So Andy did the job, thinking he would at least be able to protect the two of you."

"Did he know that Peter was going to defect?"

"Not until it was too late to stop you from going to Vienna—or at least he thought it was too late. That's when he started making his own threats about exposing the spy ring if anything happened to either you or Steffie. When Smithson got word that you never made it to Vienna, he had two problems on his hands. One was to retrieve the microchip, the other was to silence Andy, who by now was close to telling his father everything."

"Are you saying that Smithson tried to kill Andrew?" Her eyes widened in disbelief.

"You were right about Andy being in good health. As it turned out, his heart attack was drug induced. Smithson paid him a visit shortly before you and I arrived at his house."

"I don't know whether to be angry with him or to pity him," she said sadly.

"I'd say you're entitled to do both." He studied the tumble of blond hair framing her face and tucked a strand behind her ear.

"I think I'm too numb to know what I'm feeling," Ronni said flatly as tears blurred her vision. "All I know is it hurts."

Logan pulled her into his arms and gently rocked her. "I did everything I could to protect you, Ronni, but there simply wasn't any way I could protect you from the emotional pain of all this," he said regretfully.

"I'm just happy you're here for me," she whispered, taking comfort in both his strength and his gentleness. "Steffie fell asleep before you called, otherwise we would have gone home."

"I think it's a good idea that you're staying the night here. You look tired."

"I am, but what about you? Where are you going to stay? You can use my place if you like," she offered, a smile creeping across her face.

Logan knew the inevitable moment had come. He had to tell her he was leaving. "I'm not staying in Melbourne tonight. I'm going back to Washington with the senator."

"Tonight?"

She looked at him in alarm, and his resolve nearly crumpled. "The sooner all this gets cleared up, the better. Unofficially I'm involved in the investigation. Plus there are a few matters I need to attend to in Virginia."

"Virginia?"

"That's where the pickle factory is." He grinned, then added, "CIA headquarters."

"How long will you be gone?"

He shrugged. "I'm hoping it won't take more than a few days...maybe a week. I figured you probably wanted to spend some time with your mother—after everything that's happened."

She wanted to say she needed to spend some time with him, but she didn't. Suddenly she felt unsure about his feelings. Had she read too much into his declaration of love?

"Did your mother have the answers you were looking for?" he asked, concern in his voice.

But Ronni didn't want his concern. She wanted him to stay with her—to tell her everything was going to be all right, that he still loved her. Nervously she answered, "She told me what happened and why we're using other people's names."

"Do you want to tell me about it?"

She shrugged. "There's not much to tell really. She's not a criminal," she was quick to point out.

"I didn't think she was."

No, he wouldn't have, Ronni thought. If Logan was anything, he was just. She'd turned away from him and was absently fingering a clay pot her mother kept on the bookshelf. It was an art project Ronni had made in the fourth grade, and despite its childlike design, it still held a treasured spot in her mother's home. "She did it to protect me."

"That sounds like a pretty normal reaction to me—wanting to protect the ones you love," Logan remarked.

Ronni rubbed her hands across the lumpy clay pot. "Yes, I guess it is." She gave him an abbreviated version of the story her mother had told her. By the time she'd finished her eyes reflected no emotion, yet Logan knew better.

"You still feel betrayed by her, don't you?"

His voice was gentle and understanding. But, then, she knew it would be. He understood her the way no one else ever had.

She nodded. "Maybe if Peter and Andrew hadn't done what they did, I'd be in a better frame of mind to try to understand my mother's behavior. What's funny is that in my head I do understand, but my heart still aches, Logan. Maybe my father was a real jerk—just like Steffie's—but I feel cheated out of the chance to find that out for myself." She pushed her hands into her pockets and shrugged. "I know this probably doesn't make sense to you...it doesn't make much sense to me."

"I think you're going to need to give it some time," Logan advised.

At the mention of the word "time," Ronni felt a flutter of panic. They needed time with each other, time that wasn't filled with fear and danger, time to talk about their future together. But he had just told her he was going to be spending time away from her. She wanted to scream at him, *Don't go to Washington, Logan, please*. She didn't need to shout it out aloud, for her expressive face said it all.

Logan felt torn. Here was a woman he loved, a woman who needed him, yet the senator needed him, too. There was also his professional obligation to complete the investigation. And in his heart he knew that he and Ronni needed the time apart to examine feelings, to make sure their romance wasn't simply a result of two people being thrown together in the excitement of intrigue and danger.

"I hate leaving. If I could stay with you, I would," he told her, moving closer to her. "But there's one thing I've learned about you. You're a strong woman, Ronni. You're going to get through all this."

"It's 'Cynthia,'" she corrected. "My real name is Cynthia Locken."

He hooked a finger under her chin and turned her face up to his. "You'll always be 'Ronni' to me."

"Is there an always for us, Logan?" she asked, raising her eyes to his.

He couldn't immediately assure her there was, for he wasn't sure himself, and if there was one thing he always wanted to be with her, it was honest.

When he didn't reply right away but stood studying her face, she said, "You don't think there is, do you?"

"It's been a wonderful ten days, Ronni...ten days I'll never forget..." he began, but she cut him off before he could tell her everything it had meant to him.

"But that's all it was, right? Ten days out of your life." She bit down on her lower lip—so hard she was surprised she didn't draw blood. At the same time the phone rang, and on wobbly legs she went to answer it. "It's for you," she said flatly, handing him the receiver.

Feeling awkward, she escaped into the kitchen, opening the refrigerator and appraising its contents, despite not being the least bit hungry. She pulled out a pitcher of orange juice and poured herself a glass, only to jump when she heard Logan's footsteps behind her.

"Do you want some juice?" she blurted out.

He simply shook his head. "That was Doc. He managed to get a private plane to take us to Washington. They're waiting for me at the airport."

She nodded in understanding, although she wasn't understanding anything. Why was Logan leaving her when they had so much unfinished business? She moved her gaze from his face back to the glass of orange juice. "You'd better get going, then." Her voice was stilted, her movements jerky. "I want to thank you, Logan, for everything. I'll always be grateful for what you did for me and Steffie."

"Look at me, Ronni," he commanded, turning her around to face him. "I'm not going to be gone forever," he told her, hoping his words would erase the worry on her face. "I wouldn't be honest with you if I said I knew what the future holds for us. But I want you to remember this while I'm gone. It's not over between us." Then he kissed her, a deep, possessive kiss that left her with no doubts that indeed it wasn't over between them. It couldn't be.

REPEATEDLY DURING the following weeks, Ronni relived that kiss, as well as all the other intimate moments they had shared during their brief interlude together. For that's what their experience seemed like with him gone—simply a brief interlude of fantasy in which she had met the man of her dreams, only to have reality intrude.

Logan's business took longer than he expected, and the longer he was gone, the less hope she had that their relationship would ever be anything other than a fantasy. He seemed to be in her thoughts day and night, and she was powerless to resist the images that haunted her.

In the morning, she'd imagine how wonderful it would be to have him wake her with a caress, his head beside hers on the pillow. While she made breakfast for Steffie, she'd remember how Logan had stood at the stove, taking great pride in what he called his "farmboy skills," cooking up breakfast for the three of them. As she cleaned house, she'd wonder if he would want to move into her little house or if they'd look for a bigger place. Would they even live in Melbourne, or would he want to go back to Key West? At the grocery store she'd pass the frozen food section and want to load several of the microwavable entrées into her cart, knowing he thought of them as staples. And as she folded the freshly laundered linens, she'd think about the night they had argued over the wet towels, chiding herself for getting upset over something so trivial.

Several times he had phoned, but the phone calls were brief and never contained the news she wanted to hear— when he would be coming home. As insecure as she was feeling about their relationship, Ronni was beginning to believe Logan didn't want to return. She wondered if he was having second thoughts about severing all ties with the CIA, especially when she went to see Andrew and he implied that Logan would be encouraged to return to intelligence work. The longer he stayed away, the more she worried that she and Steffie weren't going to be included in his future.

Once the press broke the news of the congressional aide and the senator's son, Ronni's story appeared to be of little interest to the media. She was amazed at how easily her life did return to normal. So much had happened, so many things had changed, yet life seemed to go on as though nothing had happened, nothing had changed.

After several conversations with her mother, Ronni was able to piece together enough details about her father and his family that she felt she had sufficient information to search for them. Clara gave her the addresses she had, even though it was unlikely that after twenty-five years they were correct. Ronni wrote them all down and tucked them away in the top drawer of her jewelry chest, uncertain about what she was going to do with them. There were still five weeks left before school started again—plenty of time to journey to Wisconsin. She told herself she was waiting until emotionally she felt rested, when the truth was she was afraid to leave in case Logan returned and found her gone.

Little did she know that Logan was conducting an investigation of his own. Tracing the background of one Ronald Locken, he discovered that Ronni's father was indeed alive and well in Wisconsin, working as a plumber for Ronni's uncle, a general contractor. Although he had remarried since his divorce from Clara, he was single again, but the father of a second daughter, twenty-four-year-old Kelly Locken. From the pictures Logan had seen, Kelly resembled Ronni, but had red hair and lots of freckles. Besides several cousins and distant relatives, there were also paternal grandparents, who were retired and now living in Naples, Florida.

It was with this information that Logan packed his bags and prepared to leave for Melbourne. Between testifying before the Senate Intelligence Committee and following up on his medical treatment, he had been forced to stay away from Ronni far too long. He had thought that a little distance between them would enable him to better understand their relationship. But the only thing distance had done was frustrate him with longing for her.

It had also prevented him from being the one to tell her about Peter Lang's death. When word had arrived that the defector had been killed in an automobile crash in the Soviet Union, Logan had nearly told the Senate Intelligence Committee they could stick their investigation—he was leaving. However, as usual, his strong sense of duty had prevailed and he had stayed, and Ronni was notified of Peter's death by someone from the government. He doubted whether the official report included any details of the accident. Few people outside the Agency knew that unimportant defectors often succumbed to "accidental deaths" in the Soviet Union.

Now Logan no longer needed to worry about such matters. His work was completed and there was no reason for him not to return to Melbourne. The question that had his stomach tied up in knots as the big jet landed in Florida was, did Ronni want him to return?

It had been three weeks since he'd been gone. Except for brief telephone conversations sandwiched between important meetings, they'd hardly spoken to each other.

And those conversations had done little to ease his anxiety about whether she still felt the same for him as he did for her. There was only one way to find out her true feelings, he told himself as he stood up to retrieve his carryon bag from the overhead compartment of the plane. Face-to-face. With a deep breath, he followed the rest of the passengers out the exit, a smile on his face at the thought that she was waiting for him.

A half hour later the smile was gone, as was a good share of his optimism. She hadn't been waiting for him at the terminal. There weren't any messages for him at the information desk, and there was no answer when he telephoned her house. He was on the verge of letting insecurity overrule his logic and doing something drastic—like taking the car he'd just rented and driving all the way back to Kansas. Then he berated himself for acting like some kind of fool in love. Ronni wasn't the kind of person to convey messages with her absence.

A quick phone call to Clara Summers revealed that Ronni had left Steffie with her grandmother so that she would be free to pick him up at the airport. However, Clara was under the impression that Logan's plane wasn't due in until later that evening, which would account for Ronni's absence. Clara also mentioned that Ronni had planned to spend the afternoon shopping, which would explain why there was no answer at her house. Clara suggested that he stop by and pick up a key to Ronni's house, then go wait for her there.

Logan took Clara's advice, and after stopping off for a brief visit with her and Steffie, he drove to Ronni's home. When he arrived, he could see that her car was parked under the carport, but she was nowhere in sight. After several minutes of knocking on the front door and ringing the doorbell, he inserted the key in the lock and stepped inside.

The first thing he noticed was a small mound of shopping bags dumped in the middle of the carpet. A pair of red espadrilles looked as though they'd been kicked off in a hurry, and as the air conditioner switched off, he realized there was another sound in the house—running water. She was in the shower.

Trying—unsuccessfully—to keep from smiling, he tiptoed across the carpet toward the bathroom. The door was wide open, and for a moment, he simply lingered in the doorway, listening to the sounds of her splashing in the shower. Then, almost without any conscious effort, he began prying loose the knot in his tie. He couldn't see her through the dark blue plastic curtain, but he could hear her moving around, and the thought of what she looked like nearly drove him wild. He'd taken off his trousers, but was wearing his shirt, his tie undone but still dangling around his neck, when she opened the shower curtain and let out a bloodcurdling scream.

Then she threw a wet washrag at him, cursing, "Damn you, Logan McNeil! You nearly scared me to death. What are you doing here?"

Her outburst startled him, stopping his hands in the middle of what they were doing—removing his underwear—so that now he stood before her with his briefs down around his knees.

"What does it look like I'm doing?" he retaliated dryly as he realized what a comic sight he must be. She slowly looked him over from head to foot, then met his gaze, noticing for the first time that he wasn't wearing the eye patch.

"Your eye...is it all right?" she asked hopefully.

"As right as rain," he replied with a grin. "Well, not exactly as right, but almost." He reached over into his suit jacket pocket and pulled out a pair of eyeglasses. "I'm supposed to wear these," he said, placing them on the bridge of his nose. "What do you think?"

"I think for a guy who has his underwear down around his knees they look pretty good."

They both laughed and he stepped out of his briefs.

Then the humor disappeared from his face, replaced by another emotion, one Ronni had longed to see for three weeks. "And I think you're even more beautiful than ever," he said as his eyes seemed to be savoring every inch of her.

"Oh, Logan, I've missed you so," she cried as she reached for him. Her fingers were trembling as she helped him undo the buttons on his shirt.

"I love you, Ronni, and I want to marry you," he whispered as he carelessly tossed aside the silk tie.

Ronni stopped and looked up at him. "What?"

He took both his hands in hers and kissed her fingertips. "I had planned on taking you out to dinner and proposing over champagne, but I have to know right now what your answer's going to be. Will you marry me, Ronni?" he asked again.

"Of course," she answered without hesitation, a grin lighting up her face.

"Of course," he repeated, lifting her off the floor. Then he carried her into her bedroom, where he deposited her in the middle of the bed. He sat down on the edge to remove the last of his clothing—his shoes and socks. Then he was lying beside her, holding her close as he said, "I need you...now and forever."

"And I need you," she returned softly, loving the feel of him as his weight pressed down on her. "I feel as though I always have and I always will."

He smiled at her, kissing her, caressing her, letting his hardness insinuate itself between them so that she could feel his desire for her. "I never thought I'd find what I've found in your arms," he murmured as his tongue tasted her hot flesh in its most sensitive places.

Then he was lying on top of her, covering her body with his strength, his warmth and his love. As exquisite pleasure drove all thought from her head, Ronni cried out, "Promise me this will never end."

"I'll love you forever, Ronni," he said on a ragged breath, his body emphasizing his words with its intimate rhythm.

Afterward they lay together, side by side, content with the silence, wanting to absorb being together after a long absence from each other, touching, comforting, appreciating.

"I've missed you, too," Logan said, pulling a sheet up around them when their bodies had finally cooled down. "I wanted to come when I heard about Peter, but it didn't work out."

"It's all right, Logan. I know how important your testimony was." She rested her head on his chest. "It's probably better that you didn't see me. I couldn't cry for him or feel any sort of loss. Somehow that doesn't seem right. Despite everything he did, he was still Steffie's father, yet I felt as though someone had told me a stranger had died."

"Did anyone ever tell you his story? I know you've heard how Andy and Smithson were involved, but what about Peter?" He gently played with her fingers. "I want you to know that I'll never lie to you, Ronni. If you ever want to know anything, all you have to do is ask."

"To be honest with you, Logan, I don't think I want to know. If he did it for money or for revenge—what does it matter now?"

"It doesn't. It's all over, and as I told you a long time ago, I never thought he was a subject worth talking about."

"Then let's not." She hugged him tightly. "I'm moving forward with my life. Steffie and I are making a new beginning."

"Does that new beginning include an overprotective, bossy beach bum?"

"Beach bum? Does this mean you're not going back to work for the CIA?" She looked up at him.

"What makes you think I'd want to?"

"Andrew hinted you might, and I talked to the senator."

"You called the senator?"

"No, he called me. He wanted to apologize for sicking you on me," she teased, planting a tiny kiss on his chin. "Actually he did apologize, He told me how he had suspected that I was Andrew's honey trap, and despite your protests in my defense, he continued to believe that right up until the time Smithson confessed."

"What he didn't expect was that we would get caught in a honey trap of our own." He cupped her face with his hands and kissed her.

"But this is more than a sexual seduction," she said throatily.

"Yes, it is," he agreed, nuzzling her neck. "Much, much more, which is why Doc called you. He knows how I feel about you."

"He also wanted to tell me a few things about you."

"Such as?"

She lay back against the pillow in an indolent pose. "Let's see," she drawled. "He said you have too keen of a sense of duty and responsibility and that you're a Soviet expert and that you help out with the Special Olympics every year."

"Sounds like you two had some conversation," Logan said dryly, not sure whether he appreciated Doc's words.

"He was very nice. I know why you're so fond of him, Logan. He's a fine man, and I can't help but feel sorry for him."

"It's been rough on him these past few weeks, but he's a tough old guy. Did he actually tell you I was going back into intelligence work?"

"I think he was hoping I could influence you."

"Is that what you want? For me to return to the Agency?" He leaned back and looked at her expectantly.

"Only if it's what you want. I could be happy passing out life jackets on the glass-bottom boat."

"What about raising corn in Kansas?"

"You want to return to the farm?"

He shook his head. "Despite my father's wildest dreams, I'll never be a farmer...or a tractor salesman. I have had a few job offers, but none of them in Florida, I'm afraid."

"I thought you knew by now that we're portable," she teased.

"You wouldn't mind leaving your job?" he asked, surprised by her easy acquiescence.

"After everything that's happened, it's probably simpler if I do. Melbourne is a relatively small community, and I'm not sure how people are going to respond when school resumes. There have to be other teaching positions—even in Kansas. Wherever you are is where I want to be," she said, then punctuated her declaration with a kiss.

"Why is it that whenever you're beside me I feel as though all I need is the air that I breathe and to be with you?" he whispered huskily.

"Because that's all that really does matter. Whether we're on a beach in Florida, a farm in Kansas or wherever. We're going to be happy, Logan," she said with a smile, then added softly, "trust me."

Harlequin Superromance®

COMING NEXT MONTH

#382 THE CLOSER WE GET • Ruth Glick
A mining accident had left Stephen Gallagher
confined to a wheelchair. He couldn't marry Elena
Castille under such circumstances . . . no matter how
much he loved her. But he'd underestimated Elena's
ability to overcome any obstacle thrown in her path.

#383 BLUE MOON • Dawn Stewardson
In 1862, a gold miner lugged a beautiful, strangely
dressed woman into Dr. Henry Lockhart's office.
The woman—Erica James—was unconscious, but
Hank reckoned there wasn't much wrong with her.
Then she came to and started muttering nonsense
about being from the future. From 1989, to
be exact. . . .

#384 TO WEAVE TOMORROW • Debbi Bedford
Jamie Forrester had come to the Texas-Mexican
border to teach immigrant children about life in the
land of opportunity. Unfortunately, even her
classroom wasn't a refuge from *"La Migra"*—
border guard Daniel Salinas. Despite their
conflicting loyalties, Jamie fell in love. But love
knows no boundaries and there was a wall wider than
the Rio Grande around Daniel's heart. . . .

#385 CROSS TIDES • Elaine K. Stirling
Talia Gibrian was fiery, dark, exotic—a striking
contrast to Matt Lehtonen's blond good looks and
gentle disposition. And while Matt had been busy
farming and raising his two kids, Talia had been
overthrowing a government. Matt was convinced
that *he* was about to be her next coup!

HARLEQUIN Temptation

Montana Man
BARBARA DELINSKY

When you think of Harlequin Temptation, it's hard not to think of Barbara Delinsky. She was there from the start to help establish Temptation as a fresh, exciting line featuring extremely talented storytellers. The title of her very first Temptation—*A Special Something*—describes what Barbara has continued to bring to you over the years.

We thought it was high time to officially recognize Barbara Delinsky's contribution to Harlequin. And by happy coincidence, she gave us *Montana Man* for publication in December. We couldn't have hoped for a better book to carry Harlequin's Award of Excellence or a better gift to give *you* during the holiday season.

It's tempting to say that, of Barbara's eighteen Temptations, *Montana Man* is the most moving, most satisfying, most wonderful story she's ever written. But each of her books evokes that response. We'll let you be the judge in December. . . .

AE-MM-1

Especially for you,
Christmas from
HARLEQUIN HISTORICALS

An enchanting collection of three Christmas
stories by some of your favorite authors captures
the spirit of the season in the 1800s

TUMBLEWEED CHRISTMAS by Kristin James

A "Bah, humbug" Texas rancher meets his match in his
new housekeeper, a woman determined to bring the spirit
of a Tumbleweed Christmas into his life—and love into
his heart.

A CINDERELLA CHRISTMAS by Lucy Elliot

The perfect granddaughter, sister and aunt, Mary Hillyer
seemed destined for spinsterhood until Jack Gates arrived
to discover a woman with dreams and passions that were
meant to be shared during a Cinderella Christmas.

HOME FOR CHRISTMAS
by Heather Graham Pozzessere

The magic of the season brings peace Home For
Christmas when a Yankee captain and a Southern heiress
fall in love during the Civil War.

Look for HARLEQUIN HISTORICALS CHRISTMAS
STORIES in November wherever Harlequin books are sold.

HIST-XMAS-1

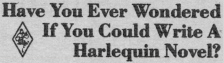

Have You Ever Wondered If You Could Write A Harlequin Novel?

Here's great news—Harlequin is offering a series of cassette tapes to help you do just that. Written by Harlequin editors, these tapes give practical advice on how to make your characters—and your story— come alive. There's a tape for each contemporary romance series Harlequin publishes.

Mail order only

All sales final

HARLEQUIN'S "BIG WIN"
SWEEPSTAKES RULES & REGULATIONS
NO PURCHASE NECESSARY TO ENTER OR RECEIVE A PRIZE

Wonderful, luxurious gifts can be yours with proofs-of-purchase from any specially marked "Indulge A Little" Harlequin or Silhouette book with the Offer Certificate properly completed, plus a check or money order (do not send cash) to cover postage and handling payable to Harlequin/Silhouette "Indulge A Little, Give A Lot" Offer. We will send you the specified gift.

Mail-in-Offer

OFFER CERTIFICATE

Item	A. Collector's Doll	B. Soaps in a Basket	C. Potpourri Sachet	D Scented Hangers
# of Proofs-of-Purchase	18	12	6	4
Postage & Handling	$3.25	$2.75	$2.25	$2.00
Check One				

Name _____

Address _____ Apt # _____

City _____ State _____ Zip _____

ONE PROOF OF PURCHASE

To collect your free gift by mail you must include the necessary number of proofs-of-purchase plus postage and handling with offer certificate.

HS-2

Harlequin®/Silhouette®

Mail this certificate, designated number of proofs-of-purchase and check or money order for postage and handling to:

INDULGE A LITTLE
P.O. Box 9055
Buffalo, N.Y. 14269-9055